"Unique,"

—Agence France Presse

"It is unconceivable that *Anguille sous Roche* won't make a splash."

—Marine Landrot, *Télérama*

"Impressive"

—*Grazia*

"Ali Zamir's writing reads like a breath or a heartbeat"

—LCI

"This book will keep, nothing will put it out of fashion"

—Julien Delmaire, author

This edition first published in Great Britain 2019 by
Jacaranda Books Art Music Ltd
27 Old Gloucester Street
London WC1N 3AX
www.jacarandabooksartmusic.co.uk

Originally published in France by Le Tripode in 2016
under the title *Anguille sous roche*

A CIP catalogue record for this book is available from the
British Library

ISBN: 9781909762817
eISBN: 9781909762824

Jacket Design: Rodney Dive
Typesetting: Kamillah Brandes
Printed and bound in the UK

This book has been selected to receive financial assistance from English PEN's "PEN Translates" programme, supported by Arts Council England. English PEN exists to promote literature and our understanding of it, to uphold writers' freedoms around the world, to campaign against the persecution and imprisonment of writers for stating their views, and to promote the friendly co-operation of writers and the free exchange of ideas. www.englishpen.org

This book is supported by the Institut Français (Royaume-Uni) as part of the Burgess programme.

A Girl Called Eel has been produced with the support of the Centre National du Livre.

A Girl
Called
Eel

ALI ZAMIR

TRANSLATED BY

ANEESA ABBAS HIGGINS

JACARANDA

My father, All-Knowing, thinks he really knows it all

Oh, the earth spat me out, the seas are devouring me, I'm expected in heaven but here I am coming to my senses again and I can't see, can't hear, can't feel anything but so what, I'm just a nobody, why should I care if this is where it all ends, as my father, the wise and wonderful All-Knowing used to say *"once you're dead and buried you won't care if you rot,"* it was my father, All-Knowing, who decided to call me Eel, little did he know that everyone lives in an eel pond of their own, that under every rock there lurks an eel, in every silence, a surprise, the deeper the silence the bigger the surprise,

I say my father, All-Knowing, because I have another father somewhere, or so I'm told, some guy roaming around out there, it shouldn't really surprise you whoever you are, some people have one father, some have several, and right now I have two, but that's a whole other story,

it's completely deserted here, nothing seems real, I feel as if I'm in a dark, bottomless pit, it's a tomb, it must be, is this my final resting place, what's happened to the others, the rest of the miserable rabble I was with, the terror consuming everyone but me, the heartrending cries, good grief, those outbursts of agonised sobbing, all gone, vanished without a trace, not a living thing in sight, what is this place, answer me, I know you can hear me, there's nothing remotely alive here, nothing but wreckage, is there anyone here can tell me if I'm alive or dead, someone answer me, for the love of an eel, can someone set my mind at rest, I must be hallucinating, there's no other explanation, it all seems so empty, so futile, even the hollow, crushing blackness has gone, now it's just dark, nothing but watery darkness, and that terrible cacophony filling my head, the roar of the waves, oh God, those nightmarish waves crashing down on us like raging monsters, all mixed up with the shrieks of terrified women and children, men calling for help, their voices gradually dying out in despair, as if they knew they had no choice but to accept their tragic fate, like outcasts fallen in battle, dying a silent death in the midst of hideous carnage, but the weirdest thing is that while I'm talking to myself here, I can't feel anything at all, I feel completely detached, nothing makes any sense, for goodness sake, what's happened to me, am I in some kind of limbo, I can't even feel the water surging around me, doing its best to finish me off for good, the gigantic breakers crashing down on my flesh, taking swipes at me, the searing cold,

but there is one thing I can be sure of, even here in this labyrinthine void, I realise that in spite of the darkness, the eerie silence and absence of feeling, I can see everything again now, although not with my eyes, mark you, I have no idea how I can see all this, I'm just parroting words I've learned to use in this theatre we call the world, I can see images spinning around in my head, streaming by, a crowd of them, pushing and shoving, crashing up against each other, I don't know where to begin, how to choose from this swarm of fleeting visions,

I see my home town first, Mutsamudu, with its inner sanctum, the medina, my rock where I was moulded, and now here I am in this place of death, clinging on to life, more vulnerable than that so-called hero Achilles with his heel and all because I was forced to leave my rock and the silence that lay at its heart, that silence was my last refuge and now I'm breaking it, kicking and screaming, I'm opening my eel's mouth to speak, which is something you've probably never seen before but what else can I do, when you lose your rock you lose its silence too, your true self, with all its secrets, but you don't need me to tell you this, I'm not here to lecture you, I'm just a miserable outcast paying the price for making a royal mess of things, so bear with me while I get it all off my chest before I'm sucked into the vortex of eternal sleep,

there, I've managed to pin down my first vision as it hurtled by like a wild beast in flight, no question about where I come from at least, God, that wasn't easy, there it is again and I can see our neighbourhood, Mjihari, the oldest part of Mutsamudu, oh, such wonderful memories, what a joy it is to look back amidst all this wreckage, to look back without bitterness, for I regret none of it, just to be myself again as I breathe my last is balm to my spirit, so for the time

13

being, I'm happy with the two images I've managed to seize, after all, a bird in the hand is worth two in the bush and I wouldn't want to end up with nothing to show but an empty belly,

it's hungry work all this remembering, it takes everything out of you but I've got two creatures within my grasp, no, I don't know exactly what animals they are, please don't ask me any questions, the main thing is that I've pinned them down, there they are, Mutsamudu and Mjihari, names that conjure so much for me, youthful delights, delicious adventures, a life bubbling with excitement, their names alone are enough to bring it all back to me, and other names are popping into my head too, of their own accord, thank God for that, you have to try and remember, even if you're groping in the dark, poking around blindly in the past, much better to give it a go than just wait here at death's door getting pissed off, teeth chattering, bemoaning your fate, like a wretch who's lost the plot,

this time the neighbourhood is close enough to touch, I can see it and feel it, so light and airy, like a smiling child, there it is, throbbing with life, I can see the beach with the pirogues lined up, nose to tail, side by side, left to right, right to left, at the water's edge, on the promontory, like the cars I used to see parked on the sidewalks whenever there was a wedding under the badamier tree, and there are the fishermen, those heroes of the sea, how they loved to brag about their boats, like rich men with their cars, always envying each other, squabbling, arguing, coming to blows

14

even like little kids fighting over a toy in the playground, same as it's always been since the world began,

what am I saying, as if the world wasn't always there, I've hardly started and I'm already going off the rails and spouting shit, I know what my father All-Knowing would say *"empty vessels make the loudest noise,"*

enough of this, let's get back to our flock as they say, now, see that's the kind of thing that comes out of my stupid mouth, what flock for God's sake, I'm not a shepherd that was Mussa Muda's job, and who's Mussa Muda, you may well ask, we'll come back to him later, he's not really important in my story, in fact he's probably best left to the historians, it's just that if you want to make sense of my life you need to know something about an eel's life at sea, a subject that remains a mystery even to the so-called experts, take fishermen for a start, so although it's true that I started on land, there's a world of difference between my life and a shepherd's and as they say, you have to separate the sheep from the goats, oh that's enough, I'm tired of all this stuff about sheep and goats, all these hackneyed phrases, I'd rather tell my story in my own words, so we'll stick with Eel and leave it at that, let's get back to Mjihari and work out how I ended up in this bind,

so, I was talking about the fishermen, those men who came from all over Mutsamudu to gather in Mjihari, where life really is life, with a capital L, because as you know, some places are more dead than alive, like here for example,

although this as good a place as any for an eel to die, floun-
dering and thrashing about as if I were trying to hit someone,
although of course there's no one here to hit, it's just what
an eel does when it's in its death throes, so as I was saying,
the fishermen were always arguing, either because they had
a bumper catch and couldn't agree on how to divvy up the
customers, or because the catch was meagre and wouldn't
measure up to the tide of customer demand, and then they'd
all do their best to stay out of the firing line in an effort to
avoid the evil eye, and you could be sure that if the fish were
scarce there'd be no shortage of those, it didn't take much for
things to flare up, the smallest thing could become a bone
of contention,

they'd squabble among themselves but underneath they
knew they were all in it together, like kith and kin, if a
customer happened to pick a fight with one of them, it
was an attack on all the fishermen, every one of them, they
were always ready to stand up for each other, to fight tooth
and nail against any outsider that threatened the family,
customers would do their best to get the better of them by
demanding a lower price when there was a bumper catch but
that only worked if one of the fishermen stabbed his mates
in the back and quietly accepted the customer's price, most
of the time they were as thick as thieves and they weren't
about to be hoodwinked, if one of them had a beef with
a customer they'd all join in, the hapless customer had no
choice but to buy at the price decided by the group, and the
fishermen would let the punter know in no uncertain terms
that they'd rather eat the fish themselves, thank you very

much, even if was off, for it was a rare fisherman who could boast of owning a fridge, although to tell the truth that was because they didn't want to cough up for the electricity bills, I knew they were just trying to lead the customer up the garden path, get him to take the bait, like the fish in the sea, they'd claim they'd rather dine on rotten fish than be taken for a ride by a stingy customer, but I ask you, where's the fisherman who can say no to a handful of coins and go home to rotting fish for dinner, eh, it was all just an act, and of course I'd have a good laugh, it was great fun watching these hilarious scenes from the terrace of our house, it was classic theatre, just like the comedies we studied at school, yes, my mind would turn to those plays as I watched the fishermen down on the shore, grabbing hold of a fish, reaching for the scales or maybe even an oar when they couldn't come to a harmonious agreement on some point or other,

I'd sit there for ages feasting my eyes on the show, I couldn't hear their repartee most of the time so I'd try and imagine what they were saying while I waited for my father All-Knowing to come home and fill in the details, I didn't have to ask him, he'd rattle away of his own accord, all the time, he loved the sound of his own voice, wind him up and off he'd go, one day I was watching a fisherman laying into a customer, it was hard to hear what they were saying because of the wind whipping round my ears, and the sun was so bright I had to shield my eyes with my hand, but I could see All-Knowing laughing along with the others while one of the men ripped into an elderly customer with *"you try going out to sea day after day, you'll soon see, you think we're impressed with your paltry offer, well let me tell you, we're not a running a charity here, you could never pay us enough for everything we have to put up with, what have we got to lose anyway,"* and that was when another fisherman there coined the slogan that became a favourite with All-Knowing, he'd always say it when he came in from a day at sea *"what's a sailor got to lose,"* and if a customer happened to annoy him, All-Knowing would get all hot under the collar and come home so worked up he'd start in on his tirades, I don't really know if that's the right word, his outpourings weren't really addressed to anyone in particular, they were just words spilling out of his mouth, I think it calmed him down to keep talking, especially when he came out with *"what's a sailor got to lose,"* or *"they can say what they like , but every man is lord of his own manor,"* All-Knowing used to say that a customer who insists on bargaining is like a hunter who doesn't respect the forest, no, if you crossed the fishermen's path you'd better watch your step, they'd always find a reason to fight like tigers to hold their ground,

I used to think I was the only one watching these displays, except for the handful of onlookers passing the time of day on the low wall along the beach, but I realised the cows too were enjoying having a ringside seat at these delightful spectacles, for people kept their cattle at the beach and these cows roamed freely, they had more than their share of freedom, far more than I did, I was kept under lock and key to make sure I behaved like a good eel, why am I bringing this up, oh for heaven's sake, put yourself in my position for once, I'm telling you those cows were free as birds, they could wander back into town at nightfall and stroll about like young lovers on their honeymoon in the promised land, they knew the medina with all its ins and outs much better than I did, and they never missed a chance to make an appearance when people were least expecting them, they liked nothing better than to take the faithful by surprise as they were on their way to morning prayer, they even killed an old lady once, without touching her of course, they were quite oblivious to it all, she didn't even know they were there until she turned a corner and walked straight into them, and there she stayed, standing bolt upright *ad vitam aeternam,* eyes and mouth wide open, they didn't find the body until the next morning and no one realised it was a corpse, it looked more like a marble statue straight out of a museum, someone touched the body very lightly to see if it was real and it toppled over like an uprooted tree, as for the cows, they weren't bothered at all, they had their walk to complete, they just carried on calmly plodding along without a care in the world, swinging their tails from left to right as if to say it was time for them to rule the town, but that's another story, we were talking about the cows and the shows put on by the fishermen on the beach, you talk too much Eel, damn it, you haven't got all day, stop beating about the bush you nitwit and get on with the job,

the cows would watch the arguments too, you could see they loved it, they'd crap all the time and moo to calm the situation if things started to get out of hand, but if one of them happened to come too close, the fishermen would pelt the unfortunate beast with rocks, it didn't occur to them that the cow might want to make a name for itself by keeping the peace, who knows, it could be a contender for one of those Nobel prizes or whatever they're called, anyway, being smarter than you'd take them to be the cows would keep their distance, to avoid the taint of blood as they say around here, they'd just carry on mooing and munching on the kitchen waste dumped on the beach, chewing their cud and winking to show they weren't happy or to demonstrate their outrage at something or other,

one day my father All-Knowing came back from the beach and said a cow had peed on his right foot while he was having a lively discussion with his best friend Guarantee, All-Knowing had laid into the cow declaring he wanted to slit its throat there and then, but Guarantee had jumped on him and stopped him doing something really stupid that could have cost him dearly, something the owner would never have let him forget, All-Knowing had made a furious grab for a huge knife he used for gutting fish, they all gutted their fish before weighing them, and Guarantee grabbed the hand he was holding the knife with and said *"you don't seriously intend to slaughter a cow just because it pissed on you, that's not a good idea, it's crazy, surely you can see that, do you really think you'd sleep easy in your bed after that,"* and All-Knowing retorted *"the long arm of the law doesn't scare me, they can throw me in jail for all I care, a sailor's got nothing to lose I tell you, that damn cow thinks it can spray its fucking urine on me, huh, what does it take itself for, God's gift to the world,"* and then he attacked the cow from behind, he gave it a violent kick and announced to the cows and innocent bystanders alike *"and you needn't think I'm like that poor old woman you killed in the medina, you think you're so tough, I'll show you what tough means,"* the cow was long gone by this time, but All-Knowing went on ranting and raving like a madman, looking down at his foot and muttering *"filthy beast, I should have just slit your throat, what gives you the right to swan around like that,"* he was still holding forth on the subject when he came home from the beach, you'd think he'd been drinking from the toilet bowl as we say around here, the cow had given him a haughty look while it was pissing on him he said, which was proof the beast thought it was better than him *"if I hadn't kicked it, the damn thing would have gone on taking the piss out of me, bloody vermin,"* I'd had enough of listening to his demented raving, all that fuss over a bit of cow piss, *basta*, so to shut him up I told him I'd made his favourite dish for dinner, he peered at me for a moment, realising what I was trying to do and gave me a look that said *"I'd keep my mouth shut if I were you,"*

I'd cooked breadfruit with fish, a dish we called *mtsongolo* that All-Knowing always enjoyed, you make it by boiling the breadfruit first and then mixing it with a fish or meat sauce, and I'd made it the way All-Knowing liked his *mtsongolo*, hot and spicy,

as usual, before he said anything directly to me, he'd ask me the same question without even looking at me, as if he was talking to the walls *"and what about Rattler, I suppose she's still not home, what on earth does she do at school at this hour,"* and he'd start talking about my sister Rattler, using me as a sounding board for his threats, he was like a little kid, asking the same question over and over again, he always wanted to know what Rattler was doing, he never tired of castigating her, whenever she wasn't home he'd say *"I don't like it, your sister's trying to pull one over on me, she doesn't realise she's playing with fire, she'll find out soon enough though, I'll show her what stubborn means, we'll see who's the first to crack,"* sometimes he'd suddenly clam up and I'd make the mistake of thinking he'd finished his diatribe, he was probably waiting for me to say something, hoping I'd back him up, that I'd agree with whatever punishment he might come up with for Rattler, but he never got so much as a word out of me, and he'd start up again all of a sudden *"how many times have I told her not to waste her time hanging around with those louts, eh, useless layabouts, she'll soon find out what I'm made of, it's not enough just to tell a child that chillies are hot,"* at some point, he'd change his tone and set about explaining his views on life in general, at great length, almost as if he was trying to justify all the demands he made on us and then he'd declare *"oh, why upset myself like this, I do everything I can to make sure you do well in life, it wasn't for nothing I gave you those names,"* and after that he was off on our names and why he chose them, it was always the same, whenever he railed against Rattler he'd bring up our names, especially Rattler's *"I called you Rattler to protect you, can't you understand that, you're a rattlesnake, you're supposed to use that rattle of yours to scare off those louts, not to stretch my nerves to the limit and pile disappointments on me, after all the trouble I've gone to, why don't you listen to me, Rattler, when are you going to wake up and stop dragging your boyfriends with you wherever you*

22

go, it's high time you stopped roaming the streets with that pack of stray dogs, you'll end up fair game for anyone, you mark my words," he'd pause for a moment as if he was thinking of a solution, I could see him getting worked up until it was all too much for him, and then he'd start up again, chiding her with *"why don't you act more like your sister, Eel, try and follow her example, I've never seen her with any of those layabouts, she comes home on time, I'm sure if one of those good-for-nothings were to approach her she'd say what I've told you to say to them 'if you're a man worthy of the name you can go and speak to my father before you say anything at all to me',"*

to be honest I thought it was all a load of nonsense, I'd never have said that to anyone, my personality was abrasive enough, people were wary of me anyway, yes, it's true I was very different from Rattler, but I was far from being the Eel All-Knowing believed me to be, he thought the moon was made of cheese and ended up learning the hard way, he had no idea what he was doing advising Rattler to follow in my footsteps, I trod stealthily, my footprints were dangerously invisible to the naked eyed, and I need hardly tell you that it's a rare eye can see through a silence that masks a cry for help, no, for something like that you need brainpower, or shit power perhaps, just to spice things up a bit,

All-Knowing would always come back to our names when he wanted to explain the mysteries of life to us, to lecture us with the teachings of a second-rate philosopher marooned on an island in the Indian Ocean, but I couldn't stand it when he made comparisons between me and Rattler, for the simple reason that he didn't know me at all, he was making a grave error using me as his yardstick, God damn it, when will people realise that this world is a vast ocean, full of all kinds of creatures, and no two of them are exactly alike,

so where were we, oh yes, All-Knowing, the great moraliser, and his reasons for naming us as he did, so after a brief pause he'd carry on holding forth against Rattler *"a rattlesnake is supposed to repel people, what kind of rattlesnake makes itself attractive, eh, a rattlesnake that plays dumb and then rolls over to be stroked and petted like a kitten,"* my father All-Knowing imagined all kinds of things about Rattler, he had much more faith in me, he'd give her a dressing-down at least three times a week, but she never budged an inch, she refused to give up her friends or change her ways, she carried on living it up with her gang, I knew she often cut class, I'd see her sometimes in the school grounds, under a tree with a group of girls, all with their boyfriends, reclining on the grass like cats sunning themselves, I'd make myself scarce and pretend I hadn't seen anything, and whenever my father asked me, I'd always give the same reply *"she's still in class,"* Rattler knew I'd never say anything to our father, but other people filled him in, the very same people you'd see sitting under the giant badamier tree not far from our house, the scene of so many goings-on, but let's not get dragged into all that, fuck it, I want to work out how I got into this mess before I slip into my final slumber, so give it a rest Eel, you dope, let's get on with it, you don't want to look like a fool when you're on your last legs, so let's get back to where we were when we left off, the day the cow peed on All-Knowing's foot, and unleashed a flood of talk about Rattler from the old windbag, he'd gone red in the face and got himself all wound up, grumbling on and on, I realised it wasn't just the cow he was angry about, it was all mixed up with Rattler not being there, it scared me to see him like that, all fired up with anger like a lion, so I avoided speaking to him at all, apart from what I'd said to him about the meal I'd cooked, but he'd just about managed to pull himself together when all of a sudden we heard the creaking of the old metal door, an ancient thing that'd been there since it was made fifty years ago by my father himself when he was young, and he'd never replaced it,

Rattler came in the door and All-Knowing gave her an inquisitorial look, staring at her without batting an eyelid, but Rattler pretended not to notice, she came out with her customary "*hi everyone*," and carried on as usual, going straight to our room, double quick, just as she always did, and staying there for quite a while before emerging to help me in the kitchen, the bedroom we shared was pretty small, it was our parents' living-room before we were born, our house had the two bedrooms, a tiny kitchen and a miniscule bathroom, we did all our homework in our bedroom, but when I got fed up with Rattler reading out loud I'd go up to the terrace, I loved doing my homework up there, I'd savour the peace and quiet, that was what I liked best about it, and don't forget, silence was my rock, it's important to remember that, on days like this, when Rattler came home with that attitude of haughty indifference, All-Knowing wouldn't say a word, he'd wait until evening to talk to her calmly, as if she left him no choice, and that's when he'd give her the lecture about why he'd named her Rattler, but I knew that by waiting, he was giving himself a chance to practice a few of his catch-phrases from the repertoire he reeled out to us endlessly *"you don't tuck in to a steak the minute you take it off the stove, you let it cool down first, any more than you go chasing after a farmyard chicken that's wandered off, you wait, and when it's good and ready it comes back of its own accord,"*

actually, since last year when Rattler had been held back a year at school, my father was trying not to be so tough on her, but it hadn't helped, Rattler hadn't changed her ways at all, she still came home late, she was like a cat, she always appeared at the same time, two hours or so after school finished, and school wasn't that far, it was barely fifteen minutes' walk away even at snail's pace, All-Knowing knew she was hanging around with her gang for hours on end after school, and since, as he always said, he wasn't the kind of parent to show no interest in what his children got up to, the kind who didn't care if his daughters went off the rails, he'd show up at school on the first day of term and come with us to meet the principal and the teachers, he'd make sure he was up to speed on the timetable too, and he made a point of knowing all our teachers by name, some of them would even end up being pally with him, I knew it was only because they were hoping to get special treatment at the fish market, they thought they were so smart, all clustered around All-Knowing as if he were some kind of venerable sage, and when they saw him at school they'd give him the full courteous treatment and let it be known that his position as provider of nourishment to the people entitled him to a certain amount of respect, and that would make our resident moraliser really believe he was a Great Man, it was no laughing matter, when he realised he was in their good graces the great All-Knowing of Mutsamudu would think nothing of comparing himself to Nelson Mandela, didn't he have to fight against adversity too, going out to fish every day, it was a constant struggle to provide food for himself and others and what's more he had to battle against juvenile delinquency, he'd try and curry favour with the teachers with his pronouncements, saying things like *"we have our responsibilities, you and me, our kind have our responsibilities to face up to,"* and they'd all agree with him, and before you knew it there was friendship and bonhomie all round,

All-Knowing committed everything on our timetables to memory, from the names of our teachers to the class times and room numbers, something we never managed to get our heads round all term, I did wonder how he managed to memorise all those names and numbers, although he didn't seem so interested in the classes themselves, I suggested to Rattler one day that the reason our father All-Knowing avoided learning the names of the subjects was because it was difficult for him, maybe it was beyond him, maybe he had no idea what philosophy, history and geography were, or even maths, although to be honest I knew perfectly well that wasn't true at all, he knew exactly what they were, it wasn't for nothing he was called All-Knowing, as he was always reminding people, he knew every bit as much as people who'd been to high school, or even to university, he'd always refused to be ignorant about anything whatsoever, which is exactly why the name of All-Knowing was well known to all the residents of Mutsamudu, and especially people from Mjihari,

All-Knowing never had the opportunity to go to high school, his parents were too poor, his father was a fisherman like him but he struggled to feed his family, so the young All-Knowing had left school at the age of twelve while he was in the middle school in Hombo, he'd learned to read and write but his handwriting was terrible, an indecipherable scrawl that looked like mumbo-jumbo, but as he always said, the important thing was being able to read and not so much to write, I'd crack up inside whenever I heard that, I'd think about what he was always saying to us about losers harbouring secret regrets *"Satan hankered after paradise too, and when he didn't get there he claimed he didn't care, but that was just sour grapes,"* as far as All-Knowing was concerned, it was being able to read that mattered, he'd say it quite openly and add smugly that this was why he read everything he could lay his hands on, everything he could glean from ads and posters along the roads, he'd read them slowly, so people could see he knew how to read, he was simply showing-off, that's all, he'd stand with his hands in his pockets, perusing the department store ads, the ones you find in public places, in the medina, even ads for pharmacies, like the ad for the Frenchman's pharmacy, the most well-known drugstore in Mutsamudu, Pharmacie Patrick I think it was, but you know, he never dared set foot in there, he claimed it was too expensive, that the pharmacist was over-charging, that his medicines cost too much, that traditional reme-dies were more effective, but the truth is that All-Knowing was nothing but an old skinflint who preferred to treat his family with cheap herbal remedies, he singled out the owner of this particular pharmacy to rant about at home "*what does he think, this Frenchman, eh, that I'm going to hand over my money just because his drugs come from Paris, huh, are his drugs going to banish death on Earth for ever, will they guarantee you go straight to heaven once you're dead or what, that pharmacist has some explaining to do,*" he'd declare, all pumped up and full of himself, to hear him talk you'd think he actually knew what the drugs cost, whereas in fact he didn't have a clue, he was simply repeating what he heard from people who were even more penny-pinching than he was, other fishermen most likely, they're all cut from the same cloth,

All-Knowing followed the news every day, he'd read scraps of newspapers left lying around and when he came up against a word he didn't know, he'd carry on regardless, without stopping, but he'd bring the bit of newspaper back home with him and get out the dictionary, the *Petit Robert* he'd bought for us, and he'd pore over it until he'd satisfied his curiosity, it was a habit he'd had all his life, and that's the way he'd learned the meanings of a whole host of words, our names included,

what happened was that All-Knowing had stumbled on

half a magazine lying in the road in Mjihari, a special edition featuring animals apparently, he'd found all sorts of passages with information about the birth and development of various marine and land animals such as turtles, frogs, eels, crabs, snakes, scorpions, all of which really piqued his curiosity, he read all sorts of things into those animals' characters, he was fascinated by their defence mechanisms and their lifestyles, take eels for example, he'd learned not just that they are to be found all over the world but that they are by nature calm, patient and cautious and what's more, they use their extremely slippery skin as a means of defence, they can slither out of dangerous, potentially lethal situations, they can even escape the clutches of seriously nasty creatures, like sharks for example, All-Knowing was big on the strategies various animals used for feeding and self-defence, which explains why he decided to give his children names that were completely unheard of in our part of the world, it was a way of making his mark, he was a man who always tried to stand out from the crowd, he liked to shake things up, to be noticed, he'd often call out to the people sitting under the badamier tree *"my friends,"* he'd say *"you'd do well to pay attention to me when I tell you what's going on in the world, I read the newspapers, there's no fisherman better informed than I am, so listen up, this is a funny old world I tell you, if you want people to respect you, all you have to do is turn things upside-down, and you'll get a fancy funeral with your ashes placed in a pantheon, like the one in Paris, and you can be sure that none of those ashes in the Pantheon in Paris were ever sent to a psychiatric lab to see what kind of worm was eating away at the deceased person's brain, so those worms are still at large, they're still giving people parasites, and just as well too, I'd do the same myself,"* nothing could stop him if he had an audience when he was off on one of these riffs, but they'd get tired of listening and one by one they'd drift away, and there he'd be, all on his own, with a few stragglers who'd fallen asleep on the benches snoring at full belt and then All-Knowing would grind to a halt in frustration and come back home all hot under the collar,

when our deceased mother fell pregnant, All-Knowing had already decided on my name, he hadn't yet picked Rattler as he didn't know my mother was expecting twins, it was just the name Eel that had lodged in his brain *"the eel is a ubiquitous species,"* he'd inform us *"eels are smart, very much in demand, the envy of all other fish,"* and he'd tell us that the day he conceived the idea, he'd dashed home quick as a flash and announced to Mum that the baby would be called Eel *"boy or girl, Eel is what it'll be,"* and because my mother obviously hadn't understood what he was on about, he'd expanded on this and said *"I intend to make a difference, I want my child to be an example for the next generation, a child who can stand up for themself, make their mark on the world, a child whose every pronouncement will enlighten the ignorant,"*

God he was full of himself, he really did think he could change the world, Mum would be all ears as he described the child he fantasised about, and on this particular occasion he'd started up again *"if it's a girl, she'll need to be able to escape the hunters' traps, and there's no shortage of those around, you have to be able to negotiate all sorts of traps in this life if*

*you want to emerge unscathed, blink and you lose it all, as our
ancestors used to say, no room in this world for dreamers,"*

he never tired of criticising parents who let their fifteen-year
old daughters run wild, he blamed it all on the parents, girls
like that were losers, he said, the saddest cases of all, he had
much the same to say about the boys who hung around on
the streets of Mutsamudu *"I'll stop at nothing to make sure
my offspring don't go down the wrong path,"* he'd say to my
mother over and over again, and as always she'd keep her
thoughts to herself, but when he started on about the name
Eel she couldn't believe her ears, All-Knowing hadn't given
her a chance to get a word in edgeways, but when the cock
starts to crow it's usually best to keep your own counsel, to
stay quiet as a mouse and listen, All-Knowing was never
one to change his mind, my mother did try to impress on
him that it was an outlandish name to give a child, that
the whole idea was beyond the pale but he'd responded
by holding forth at great length *"everything about this life
is outlandish, why shouldn't a child have an outlandish name,
he has to learn, even before he comes into this world, he has to
know what to expect in this life, the world being what it is, it's
no laughing matter, these days a name can mean whatever you
want it to mean, people give human names to animals, why not
give an animal name to a human being, I'm serious, haven't you
ever heard the name of the neighbour's cat, you know what it's
called, Bacari, a bit outlandish don't you think, eh, or another
thing, when the Soviets sent their dog into space on the third of
November nineteen fifty-seven, what was the dog called, Laïka,
a lovely name, worthy of a beautiful woman like yourself,"*

on and on he'd go, interminably, any excuse to give full rein to his gift of the gab, he'd stop at nothing to win over the person he was talking to, fact or fiction it was all the same to him "*I was telling you just the other day about this writer who'd made his name with a story about an animal that makes fun of human beings, doesn't that just say it all, it shows you what kind of world we live in, eh, how do I know all these things, from the bits of newspapers I read every day, people think I'm crazy but I don't care what they think, sooner or later they'll understand that there's more to a chicken's arse than meets the eye, it's not there just for pooping and pissing, it's for shagging too, and laying eggs,*"

he was incapable of saying anything without falling back on stock phrases of one sort or another, and they didn't always make much sense, I often wondered if his thoughts didn't run on batteries like a mechanical instrument of some sort, he was convinced he was the smartest person around, he'd say to Mum, all puffed up with pride "*while others are wasting their time dreaming, I'm busy reading the newspapers I pick up from the trash on the beach, I swear to you even the people who throw them away have no idea what's in the papers, I'm sure of it, they only buy them to make it look like they're educated, they think all they have to do is stick a pair of spectacles on the end of their nose and hold up a newspaper for a few seconds, and everyone will think they're an intellectual, to hell with that, I'm a sucker for a newspaper, even one that's been ripped to shreds, I'm a compulsive reader, I read when I'm out fishing, I forget what I'm doing sometimes, I forget all about my line and let it drift, I start reading something and those sly fish cash in on their luck and gorge themselves on my bait, strip it bare, hook, line and sinker, it happens all the time, it doesn't bother me though, bloody fish, I curse them but it doesn't stop me, when I set out at dawn for a day at sea, I'm always looking for a few scraps of newspaper on the beach to take with me, and that's how I've learned about all the stupid things men have done, worse than anything you can imagine, I'd never want to be like that, I have a goal in life, I intend to protect my offspring, you see, that's what this life is all about, you have to come up with the opposite of what other people do to survive, if we call our child Eel it'll be all smooth sailing, I'll have less to worry about because people will probably keep her at arm's length, everyone that is except a man who's worthy of that title, a man who's worth his mettle never balks at approaching a fearsome beast, no it's the creature itself that backs away, what animal hasn't learnt something from all those traps set for them by hunters,"* my mother had no choice in the end but to resign herself to this scheme of his, she simply didn't know what to say, she just sat there, dumbfounded and defeated,

on the day we were born, a torrential rainstorm fell on the town, and with my mother in the throes of agonising labour pains, our father All-Knowing decided to take himself off to the market to buy some medicinal herbs, leaving our mother with her sister Tranquil to attend to the birth, the downpour didn't let up at all and our father was held up and didn't come back for a couple of hours, by the time he eventually arrived he was soaked to the skin, he opened the front door and stood there on the threshold, shaking from the cold, dumbstruck by the sight that greeted him, for most of the neighbours were there, old men and women, teenagers, and even children, poking their noses in, curious to see what their parents and grandparents were doing in our house, All-Knowing was rendered speechless when he saw this gathering of people all dressed in their *boubous*, with their skullcaps and headscarves, clutching their worry-beads, and when they glimpsed All-Knowing standing there, they immediately moved aside for him, eyes cast down as if they were ashamed of themselves, like school children caught in the act by their teacher, trying not to look guilty in an effort to avoid being punished, and when they suddenly fell silent, All-Knowing wondered why and stepped over the threshold still trying to work out what was going on, the silence weighed on him as he walked across the courtyard and gazed at those bowed heads, the figures standing still as statues, when suddenly he heard the cry of a newborn ringing out from the room at the back, he approached it cautiously and stepped into the tiny room that was later to become our bedroom, and beheld Aunt Tranquil, sitting there in silence, her head bowed, holding two babies in her arms, and still All-Knowing didn't understand, he was simply happy to learn that he was the father of two, but he was troubled by the attitude of that strange crowd, and most of all by Tranquil, why wasn't she happy, why didn't she look up to see who'd walked in the room, and then All-Knowing couldn't stop himself, he burst into tears, even though he still didn't understand what had happened, he'd walked nonplussed into that room where he'd left my mother before he went out, but then he saw Mum's body on the bed, wrapped in a white shroud and he uttered one long cry, in that split second he was ripped from his moorings and saw his whole life crumbling around him, and as the tears streamed down his face, Tranquil sat there stock still, not uttering a word, not even moving her arms to rock the infants cradled in them, their innocent cries the only signs of life in that house, and as he gazed at his sister-in-law, All-Knowing sobbed his heart out, for death can strike like a sword, shattering one rock to build another from the pieces and this was one of those times, the game of life goes on, the baton is always there, waiting to be passed, you won't understand what I mean by this unless you follow me to the end of this tale, if there is indeed an end, death is an enigma and when it strikes it can rob a living being of the power of speech, it weighs like a heavy burden on that person, even on the most happy-go-lucky of souls, it makes no sense at all,

Tranquil was reduced to silence by her sister's death, she said nothing at all for the next month and people began to wonder if she would ever open her mouth to speak again, my mother was buried at sundown and all of Mjihari was there, politicians, businessmen, students, workers, and fishermen who came not just from Mjihari, but from all over Mutsamudu to show their solidarity with their friend All-Knowing, it made him realise that he was a man of some standing in the city, but his wife's death taught him something else too, he learned how illusory life's journey can be, yes, life is like a road that's both long and short, a road that leads us through a shared landscape of dreams, we don't realise we're dreaming, and if we do try and wake up and break free it's bound to end in disaster, for the end of the dream is inevitable, and there's no escaping it,

All-Knowing took comfort from being the father of twin girls, he told himself he'd lost his wife but gained two precious jewels, Tranquil had suggested after my mother's funeral that she raise us herself, but All-Knowing wouldn't be parted from us, so they agreed that Tranquil would take us with her to Hombo and look after us there, but only until we turned five, she bottle-fed us at first, for about six months, which was no mean feat since Rattler and I were apparently very much alike and Tranquil often wondered whether she wasn't feeding the same baby twice, in the end she made marks on our foreheads to avoid confusion and when the five years were up, All-Knowing took charge of us and enrolled us in the primary school in Missiri,

life carried on for him much the same as before, apart from the fact that he came home early from work to look after us, and as we grew, it became easier to tell us apart, time began to make its mark on us as it does on everything that crosses its path, that's the way life is, things are constantly made and remade, but it all happens in silence, you go to sleep young and smartly dressed and wake up a broken-down stranger clad in threadbare rags, another unsolved mystery, it's all part of the show,

I loved it when All-Knowing told us bedtime stories, my favourite was the one about the three girls who were once the greatest of friends but now are sworn enemies, they're still alive, those three girls, their names are Hand, Ear and

Fly, oh, it's so wonderful reminiscing like this, here I am, Eel, with a capital E, daughter of two fathers, with all this devastation around me, and I'm remembering this story, I don't even have to struggle to summon up the details, no, it all comes back to me so easily, flowing like a river, babbling pleasantly in my head,

these three girls never thought for one moment that their friendship would be blown apart, they were alike in every respect and had complete trust in one another, until the day when one of them betrayed that trust, you'll see who it was in due course, it all started when these three friends decided to have a picnic one day in Mpouzini, it was a perfect spot for nature-loving girls, a place of idyllic beauty, surrounded by fields of crops with a delightful river and a magnificent beach further downstream,

the three friends had all pitched in some money to buy a goat, and after they bought it they all agreed that Hand, Ear's sister, would look after it until the day of the picnic, so the goat was left at Miss Hand's house, and then, out of the blue, on the eve of the picnic, Hand came to see her sister Ear, who lived next door, with a tale of woe, she told her that the goat had been stolen and that she was at a loss for what to do, and Ear, who was the most tender-hearted of the three, listened sympathetically to her sister's sorry tale and promised her she'd tell Fly what had happened, so Ear summoned Fly to her house, and Fly, who was the most headstrong of this strange threesome, went to Ear's house and listened to her friend telling her what Hand had said,

Ear begged Fly to forget about the goat, what mattered was
their friendship, she said, they could always buy another
goat,

Fly listened without saying anything at first, but then she
said it all seemed rather odd to her, she didn't give much
credence to this scenario, and she was convinced it was just
that, a scenario, since nothing had ever been stolen from
their friend Hand's house in all the time they'd known each
other, and why should it happen now, just as they'd bought
this goat together, she declared that she intended to get to
the truth of the matter and off she went to see for herself
what was going on at their friend Hand's house, and when
she got there, what did she find but a goatskin, stretched
out in the courtyard, with signs of blood all around and a
smell of cooking, her first thought was to dash back and tell
Ear what she'd seen, but it was too late, Hand had already
spotted her and went running after her, lickety-split, ready
to show her the back of her hand, for she was the strongest
of the three and was expert at delivering a good thrashing,

well, you can imagine Ear's surprise when she saw the two
of them, but Fly was scared of Hand and ran off as fast
as her legs could carry her and managed to slip away, so
Hand gave up chasing her and went straight to Ear's house,
where she made up a pack of lies on the spot, making out
that Fly was planning to do something nasty to Hand and
Ear because she suspected them of eating the goat, so now,
ever since that day, whenever Ear hears Fly, or any member
of her family, coming towards her, she calls on Hand to

come and protect her and chase off the insect in question, or even sometimes to squash it, and all because Ear was too bone-idle to take care of herself, she just lazed around all day long, rooted to the spot, like a great lump of poo stuck to the ground, and in the end, as a result of being despised by her former friends, Fly started to believe that Hand and her sister, Ear, had plotted to eat the goat together, and so Fly and all of her relations swore on their lives that they would get back at Ear and Hand and all of their family by sucking their blood and giving them diseases whenever they had a chance, unless they made amends, and since amends were never made, the three old friends and their families were condemned to be enemies for ever more, and that's how these three friends were torn apart and have stayed that way to this very day,

Hand would obviously have a heavy price to pay if Ear were to find out that her sister had betrayed them, and that's why every time an insect comes near us, our hand doesn't think twice and starts screaming blue murder, when in fact it's the hand that caused all the trouble in the first place and as All-Knowing loved to say whenever he came to the end of this story, our ancestors knew what they were talking about when they said "*beware of cutting off the hand that leads you astray,*" for we all have one hand that's liable to lead us astray, it's up to us to learn how to manage it carefully if we don't want to end up lost in a sea of mistakes that blow up in our face, yes, it's true, but nor should we forget that we are each mistress of our own body, we can do what we want with it and I happen to have chosen to throw mine into a

40

savagely roiling volcano, which is as good a choice as any, don't you think,

whenever All-Knowing came to the end of this story, I'd ask him innocently *"and when is Fly going to tell Ear, so the misunderstanding can be cleared up and she can finally stop being angry,"* All-Knowing would laugh and say *"listen, Miss Clever Clogs, the hand will never allow any kind of insect to come near any of its family, would you let a mosquito get close enough to you to take a bite out of you, eh, for the sake of some story about a goat, well, would you,"* I for one still couldn't make sense of this tale, but I was even more stubborn than the fly and I wasn't going to let some cock-and-bull story get the better of me, so one day I confronted All-Knowing with the question I'd been dying to ask *"what if I let a mosquito land on my ear and tell me the secret, that would be the end of it, right,"* and All-Knowing shot straight back with *"don't even think about it, never let a mosquito land on your ear, unless you want it causing you all kinds of grief, you hear me, little Miss Know-it-All,"* I nodded in agreement, but inside I wasn't satisfied, I didn't like people being dishonest or unfair, I wanted a better explanation, All-Knowing hadn't really been able to convince me, and even though I was only five, I was already as pig-headed as they come, he kept telling me to leave well alone, he said it was best if the ear knew nothing about the whole business, from now until the end of time, as if time could ever to come to an end, people just don't seem to understand that they're the ones who are going to come to an end, not time, or the world, we're all going to die, every single one of us, we'll leave the stage, and it'll be empty because at the end of the show the actors have to bow out and head for the wings, some with a bitter taste and some with a sweet taste in their mouth, depending on how they've played their part,

in telling me this story of the three friends, All-Knowing had given me to understand that in this life there is always a victim, someone had to pay the price so the others could get off scot-free, which wasn't what I wanted to hear, even if it was the truth, I can see that when some dope dies a vulture gets to live, it's quite obvious, but it's a bleak message, and All-Knowing would tell us this story at bedtime *"hurry up and go to sleep now, before the bogeyman gets you,"* he'd murmur in our ears as he was standing up to leave the room, it was another of his tall tales that he expected us to swallow, like the bogeyman story he made up, it wasn't until much later, when I was older, that I realised he'd told us a bunch of lies about that particular character, but I dwelt on the one about the three friends and pondered it for days on end, wondering about that grasping hand, I'd lie there in bed, staring at my own hand, as if it was something alien, not really part of my body, until I eventually dropped off and fell abruptly into the arms of Morpheus,

one day, I decided as I was lying in my bed that I'd let a mosquito land on my ear and let me tell you, with all the mosquitoes buzzing around our house I was spoiled for choice, but then this happened, the damn thing sang me a song I couldn't make head or tail of, even though I forced myself to listen to it until my head started to spin and then all of sudden it went quiet, I couldn't hear a thing, I felt a sharp prick, as if someone was sticking a needle in my ear, it hurt like hell, but I didn't give in, I carried on trying to listen, not hearing anything in particular, but I did feel a throbbing pain that got worse and worse and I said to myself then that if that was the secret I was better off not hearing it, to hell with the creature and I swiped furiously at my ear to strike the mosquito and squash it but all I did was hit myself several times without even touching the thing,

it was too late, that vampire had murmured "*my little Eel*" in my ear and left me with a stabbing pain that seemed as if it would go on for ever, I scratched and scratched and rubbed it so hard that I began to feel a burning sensation on my left temple, and by now there were two places that hurt, the mosquito bite was mixed up with the damage I'd inflicted on myself trying to hit it, I'll never forget it to my dying day, even though I can't say when that will be, I have no idea what will become of me, even now as I drift towards my final slumber, will I be a spirit I wonder, a fleck of dust, of maybe a fish, after all I am at sea and I was named for a fish, or maybe I'll be a cow, like the ones on the beach in Mjihari, oh, if I were to come back as a cow, I'd see all sorts of things on the strand there, I'd be the happiest beast in the world, the only problem is that I'd end up with my throat slit, and all those wretched fishermen would be only too happy, they don't like those cows watching their antics at all, so let's just say that I'll be nothing at all, it's probably best left at that,

you're wasting time, Eel, and you only have a few minutes

left, maybe even a few seconds, who knows, oh I'm getting all wound up about some stupid thing, what's come over me, where were we, oh for the love of an eel, can't you tell me, damn it, there, I've got it, I was talking about the pesky little mosquito that bit me, that's it, right, well this is what happened next,

I came down with a bad case of malaria the very next day, I was flat out in my bed, if I tried to sit up for more than a few seconds my head would start to spin, I had the shakes all the time and I couldn't eat a thing, every time I tried to put something in my mouth I'd gag on it, All-Knowing smeared aloe resin on my head and in my hair and made me drink infusions of cinchona bark, nutmeg, bitter aloes and all kinds of plants with names that meant nothing to me, I remember putting up quite a fight when he tried to make me drink these herbal remedies, he'd bend my head backwards and pour them down my throat, yes, that's exactly what he did, he was quite casual about it, and I'd fight tooth and nail, especially when it came to aloes with that bitter, acrid taste I hated more than anything else, I'd look at that green viscous concoction on the spoon, with its nauseating smell, my body shaking constantly, and All-Knowing would take hold of me like a little goat whose throat he was about to slit, pinning my head and hands with his arms, and I'd wail like a kitten screaming for its mother, just like the ones you hear on the roof at night, I'd spit on the ground, batting my hands and stamping my feet on the hard floor like a kid having a tantrum and then All-Knowing would try and appease me, bribing me with wooden dolls he'd made

himself, it didn't fool me though, I knew he was resorting
to a strategy parents often use to try and win over their
children, parents are no different from politicians, they try
and outsmart their kids and when that doesn't work, they
promise the moon, just as politicians do,

how I loathed those dolls All-Knowing gave me, he'd try
and use them as bait and I'd hurl them as far as I could , then
he'd sigh despairingly and leave me to sob my heart out and
in the end I'd wear myself out and stop crying of my own
accord and drift off to sleep, which I think you'll agree was
exactly what I needed, crying is a way of banishing pain and
injury, of freeing the heart of the sorrows it struggles to bear
in silence, we cry to ease our burdens, to sweeten the bitter
after-taste of experiences we'd rather not have had, so yes, I
did need to rest and let the well of my tears run dry, I was
too young to know that silence could be my refuge, tears
were my only defence against the clamour of life,

after we went to live with our father All-Knowing we hardly
ever saw Aunt Tranquil, she'd stop by sometimes and stay
for half an hour, and bring us things to eat, like the manioc
and bananas from her garden in Hombo and then she'd be
off home again like a shot, claiming she had lots to do and
insisting she wasn't one to waste her time, as if that were
remotely possible, I mean has such a person ever existed,
someone who didn't fritter away their time every single
day, what claptrap people come up with, you'd have to be
some sort of infernal machine to spend all your time doing
something useful, you'd be firing on all pistons every second,

every minute, every hour, like a donkey farting, you'd rip your arse to shreds in no time at all, no way, this old world is full of things that make no sense at all, but it pays to play along with the whole show, so let's keep going,

but seriously, Tranquil really did amaze me, I wondered if she wasn't actually a machine after all, with someone pressing her buttons to keep her going, and what's more she'd always show up when our father All-Knowing was out at sea, she'd go on and on at us about giving him her best wishes and then she'd leave, whenever Rattler tried to get her to stay and have something to eat she'd come out with ever more bizarre turns of phrase, things like *"you eat, that's food enough for me,"* as if people could eat together by telepathy or something, then she'd come back a month later and, still in the same vein, she'd ask weirdly basic questions like *"you're not bored, I hope,"* or *"do you need anything, if there's anything you want, just tell me, whatever it is, OK,"* and then she'd pause for a few moments, as if she was searching for exactly the right words *"you know I'm like a mother to you, I've always been your mother, right from the start, I raised you as my own daughters, and if truth be told, I'd rather have kept you with me for ever but there we are, I feel a great sense of responsibility towards you, that's the main thing, yes, I feel responsible for you,"* I did my best to reassure Tranquil, without realising there was something I didn't understand, it wasn't easy to make sense of what she said, people thought that Tranquil had clammed up and become a woman of few words as a result of her sister's death, but they had it all wrong, and I did too, it was one of those mix-ups that add spice to life and make it so astounding, life can either be a pain in the arse or it can take your breath away, it all depends on how you play your part and on the nature of the misunderstanding too, but I think it's fair to say that you do need a few crossed wires in this play of life with its multiple acts, to give it some spark, so there we all were, living under this misapprehension and I would say to Tranquil in all sinnocence *"don't worry Aunt Tranquil, we love you so much, you'd be the first to know if we had any problems,"* she'd sit there tight-lipped for a few seconds, and then she'd get up to leave, a worried look on her face, and in response to our invitation to stay and eat, she'd say, as she slammed the door behind her *"you eat, that's food enough for me,"* always the same, every time,

truth to tell, Tranquil worked night and day, she wasn't one of those idlers who never get off their backside, those lard-arse madams who won't stoop to do the cooking, those ladies who only get up from the table to go to the bathroom or drag themselves into their beds, food, shit and sex, that's all there is to their lives, no, Tranquil was no shirker, she moved her arse so much it ran on automatic pilot, if you've ever seen such a thing as an arse on automatic pilot, she was the ultimate busy little bee, that woman, especially since her husband was the owner of a plot of land where he grew cloves, vanilla, bananas, coconuts and manioc and very productive land it was,

that valiant couple worked those fields tirelessly and turned their smallholding into a flourishing business with bountiful harvests, Aunt Tranquil's husband did business with a whole string of vendors who came every day to put in their orders, and with their takings Tranquil and her husband bought cows and goats to provide them with milk and there in that verdant spot they'd built themselves a splendid new house, surrounded by the twittering of birds, the bleating of goats, the river babbling alongside the fields, and all melodiously combining to give the place its bucolic feeling,

that soundtrack was the only aspect of rural life that appealed to me, I loved to feel those sweet sounds caressing my soul and stirring it to mystical ecstasy, yes, nature whispers her secrets not to our ears but to our souls, it's only when you close your eyes and ears that you can really sense what she's tracing in the depths of your soul in those moments of deafening silence, it's not just a matter of blocking your ears and eyes, as some fools might think, although that's really not my concern, I'll just keep going, besides, I don't have much time, I need to wrap things up, I can't keep getting all worked up over a particular image, I need to focus on working out how I got myself into this fix,

so, I was enchanted by nature's bewitching music, by those mellifluous, highly-charged notes that drowned out the ills of this world, it was a song that carried more force than any atomic bomb, it made its way into my soul and set my whole body throbbing in time with the blood coursing through my veins, and Tranquil and her husband lived in the country, in Hombo, they were skilled farmers and they prospered financially, but Tranquil wanted children, she'd have been happy with one but in spite of all their efforts they still had none, it was very distressing for them, neither of them could accept the unpleasant reality of their situation, they argued incessantly about their infertility, each one believing the other to be the cause, Tranquil's husband took her to the best healers on the island of Anjouan and they spent a great deal of money, for they were generous souls and couldn't resist the temptation to try and please the people offering their services to them, but sad to say they were constantly disappointed, needlessly consuming plants from all three corners of the island, I say the three corners since in fact the island is triangular in shape, as our teacher told us one day in a geography lesson, one of our primary school teachers, another of those lying so-and-sos, who knows where he got his information from,

it was a race against time, nothing had worked in their battle against infertility, all it gave them was an endless stream of arguments and reproaches, the poor couple didn't know which way to turn, in the end they had no choice but to accept their fate, bitter as it was, but a tree that gives no fruit does have its part to play, it can shade the destitute from the noonday sun, its role is as life-giving as any other, and they realised they had to find something else in life if they weren't to let this unwanted sterility make a barren field of their nice comfortable lives, they couldn't just let everything turn to shit, they'd understood that it wasn't enough just to lead the good life, you need a measure of courage and gratitude for what you have in this world if you're to have any hope of letting in a glimmer of light from God knows where, okay, let's call a spade a spade, we're talking about happiness here, that thing you feel in your heart, your body, your soul, or your arse, it all depends on who you are, oh God, I don't really understand this kind of talk, what does that word happiness actually mean, does it even mean anything at all, people get caught up in the trap of that one little word, All-Knowing would hear Rattler and me having philosophical chats and he'd say to us *"happiness is accepting who you are, it's pie in the sky to think that anyone else can make you happy,"* and then he'd start telling us that Aunt Tranquil had changed, that she was actually much tougher than she seemed, in her own way, she was happy,

All-Knowing had told us that when Mum was alive, Tranquil and her husband would often visit him and Mum, they'd arrive while he was still out fishing and when he came home, the four of them would all eat together and tell funny stories like the one about the thief that Tranquil's husband surprised one day at the crack of dawn in a coconut palm in their field, the thief had climbed a tall tree laden with coconuts and was helping himself as if they were his to take, Tranquil and her husband had just woken up and were getting ready to go to work when they heard the sound of coconuts falling, the husband guessed what was going on, he knew that people sometimes stole his crops, he was always finding thieves' footprints in the field in the morning, so he ran stealthily up to the tree to catch the thief in the act and saw this character knocking the coconuts from the tree one after another and when he asked him who he was the thief turned the question back on him and said *"and*

who are you exactly," now around here, we're always asking
questions, it happens all the time, when you ask a question
you'll usually get another one in response, you never get a
straightforward answer, just another question, if you want
to see how a question can trip you up, look no further than
this island, I'm told a white man came here once, looking
for proof of this tradition of answering a question with
another question, he'd heard about it in Europe but he didn't
believe it, white people always want proof, they're always
poking around, I'm telling you, it's God's honest truth, when
will they ever learn, so this gentleman had set out to find
examples of this tradition and chosen the island of Anjouan
as his destination, and after he landed at the airport in Ouani,
he took a taxi into Mutsamudu and in the taxi this European
gentleman said to the driver taking him to the capital "*excuse
me, Monsieur, I understand that when you ask a question here,
you get another question for an answer, is this true,*" and that
blasted driver, what did he do, oh when I think about it now,
damn it, instead of just answering the goddamn question
and staying away from pointless philosophising, what did he
say but "*and who told you this, Monsieur,*" and the white man
could see that he'd already accomplished what he came here
to do and told the driver to turn round and take him back
to the airport, the driver was embarrassed and completely
baffled, he just didn't get it, the poor sap, he was an
unwitting guinea pig, the living proof of a proud tradition,
and the white man simply said "*I've got what I came here for,
I don't see any point in going any further since you yourself have
asked me a question in response to mine,*" and off he went back
to Europe that very same day, okay, I know, I talk too much

but I wanted to show you that people here can never pass up a chance to indulge in a bit of philosophising, you see a boat in front of you and you know perfectly well what it is and what do you but turn to the person next to you and ask them *"is that a boat,"* I mean what's that all about, are we supposed to hoot with laughter, toot, more likely,

okay, so back to Mjihari, no, the thief, I was talking about the thief in the coconut tree, the cheeky sod who turned Tranquil's husband's question back on him, quite pushily too, because at first he didn't believe Tranquil's husband really was the owner of the field, he thought he was another thief, which did often happen, one thief could trick another into thinking he was the owner and scare him off and then he'd have the whole field to himself, so the thief up in the coconut palm was trying to make like he was the owner too and Tranquil's husband started in with a curt *"what a cheek,"* and then in a louder voice he said *"we'll see who's the owner of this field, you go ahead and carry on with your work there but you'd better have wings to fly away with because if you think you're going to use your hands and feet once you're down here on the ground, you've got another think coming, you'll have no arms or legs left when I've finished with you, you'll be dragging your- self along the ground like some miserable cripple, I won't even let you get as far as the ground, I'll cut you up into a thousand pieces with my machete here,"* Tranquil's husband had barely finished his speech when he heard this character landing on the ground like a sack of rice thrown from the top of the coconut palm, and the funniest thing was that the thief jumped straight up and went limping off, bumping into the tree trunks like a stumbling drunk who was completely stewed, even a little kid could have caught him without any trouble, but Tranquil's husband knew what he was doing, he let him go on purpose, he knew this fellow would be suffering the next day, who knows, he might even die, he'd only shouted at him as a joke, to add a bit of drama to the situation *"there he is, let's get him, the crook, we'll finish him off in no time,"* and the thief tried to up his wretched pace, which just made it all worse, he kept falling down and having to get up again on the double, and my parents would laugh their heads off as they heard Tranquil telling this story *"Tranquil was different in those days"* All-Knowing would say over and over again,

after our mother died Tranquil stopped coming to our house with her husband, she'd come by herself and not stay very long, it was almost as if she'd been trying to avoid All-Knowing for the last twelve years, ever since he'd wrenched us away from her, it was twelve years ago wasn't it, yes, that's right, I'm seventeen now,

it wasn't until my final year at the lycée that I started neglecting my studies and hiding away under a rock like a proper eel, Rattler had already had to repeat the previous year, by this time Tranquil and her husband had given up flogging themselves to death trying desperately to have a child, especially since Tranquil was weary of mothering after five years of rearing us as her own children,

All-Knowing couldn't go on telling me what to do

ad infinitum, who did he think he was, this lowly fisherman, the man who'd left school at the age of eleven, fool that he was, he was in no position to harangue us for something he'd failed to do himself when he had the chance, and we'd stuck with it for longer than he did,

we're all free to live as we please, under our own rock, without being told what to do by some lowlife moraliser who doesn't know his arse from a hole in the ground, there were lots of things he did know though, I'll give him that, things he'd gleaned from scraps of newspapers, but it's not enough, okay you can learn things at school or from the papers but what really matters are the things you learn in the street, things that astound and scare you and teach you much more than school or newspapers can, that's right, things people do every day, real life is a completely different matter, school is nothing but a place to joke around, to be bored, it's not real, it's a fiction, a world away from reality, people study law and political science but they still use brute force to govern and people follow along like sheep, but we eels watch from under our rocks and see it all,

as for the newspapers, they're nothing but soap operas, entertainment for people who can't get their hands on the latest best-seller, morality is the last thing on anyone's mind,

All-Knowing started fishing to help his parents at a very young age, he was well known among the fishermen, with his bits of information gleaned from newspapers that no other fisherman knew anything about, they knew he was on

54

good terms with lots of other people from all walks of life, businessmen, politicians, officials, workers, dockers, farmers, fishermen, everyone knew him but what the fishermen all found surprising was the fact that he didn't have a wife, they'd been speculating about it for seventeen years under the badamier tree and in other places where people gathered all over Mjihari, they all wondered how a man could go for seventeen years without a woman by his side, you see, life is like marriage, like the woman you marry for better or for worse, a man by himself is nothing but an empty shell, he doesn't budge an inch until a woman gets him moving, so whether you like it or not, the truth is there's a woman at the heart of everything in life, that's just the way it is,

All-Knowing decided not to marry again, we were saved from the fate of a certain fairy-tale heroine by the name of Cinderella because he was wary of subjecting us to the whims of a fearsome stepmother, he let it be known that Rattler and I were his number one concern and did everything in his power to make sure our lives were comfortable and care-free, and whenever he was accosted under the badamier tree by someone telling him he should get married, he would fly into a rage and snap *"all you ever think about is women, you don't know the first thing about how to make them happy, it's pathetic, all you do is sit around mooning about where you're going to stick your goddamn cock, you need to get off your arse and start acting like a real man,"*

this kind of thing went on all the time under the badamier tree and in squares all over the town, people were maligned, mocked, threatened and worse, but we won't go into all that now, we'll come back to it later,

All-Knowing used to warn us about the demon that could all too easily take hold of the hearts of young girls of our age, he'd tell us that we shouldn't see everything through rose-coloured spectacles *"life isn't always a sweet-tasting fruit,"* he'd say *"most of the time it's bitter-sweet, it's acidic, salty and sugary all at once, tasting this mish-mash is what living is all about,"* I don't know about this demon business, after all, what does it really mean, as far as I'm concerned we're all responsible for our own bit of rock, and playing dirty is just not on, but maybe All-Knowing wasn't entirely wrong about life in general, I can grant him that, so yes, in life, you do have to taste this strange fruit with its fatal combination of flavours and it so happens that I have tasted it, I've glimpsed that unearthly ray of light known as happiness, yes, I've savoured it in my own way, in secret under my rock, hidden from view, oh God, I'm starting to get tired now, I'm running low on energy, my hands are losing their grip on this fuel tank, I can't go on holding on to it for ever, this is the end of the line for me I know but before I bow out once and for all, I want to get through all these pictures, and there are still a lot of them left, I want to see how my memories turn out, but am I really remembering all these things, or am I just imagining them, it's so wonderful to see your life being relived, like a dream, especially if you were an odd sort of creature, a fish who walked on two legs, or a slippery girl who coiled along the ground, slithering from wall to wall, unseen and unheard, hidden under her rock, a creature unto herself, but we're not out of the woods yet, because, as I've been saying from the very beginning, these images are pushing and shoving each other around in my head, like sightless monsters, but maybe I will be able to keep going after all, for I have my first two images, Mutsamudu and Mjihari, to guide me through this long, exhausting, exhilarating adventure,

Mutsamudu owes its existence to the pastor I was talking about at the beginning, Mussa Mudu, which means literally *Black Mussa,* or as some would say, *Black Moses,* yes, he was a pastor in the royal palace, according to All-Knowing, the story goes that he was looking for a stray goat, although some say he'd gone in search of new pastures, whatever, it's not important, let's plough on, he'd been searching high and low and found this corner of the island that was soon to bear his name and apparently, while he was making his way through the woods, wandering this way and that, this pastor had ended up in a spot with a clear view of the sea, and that spot was none other than Mjihari, so the name Mutsamuda is really just derived from the pastor's name, Mussa Mudu, as for why this area is known as Mjihari, well, we'll get to that in good time, this is all taking far too long though, I don't put much faith in all these old tales, I'm not here to give you a history lesson, God forbid that people should think me one of that band of liars, no, I'm interested in stories with a twist, eel-shaped like me, stories that are really true, weirdly weird, and if you're one of those people who reads the newspapers all the time, or best-sellers for that matter, you know nothing of what really goes on, I'm telling you, if you're writing or reading stories that are anything other than eel-shaped, you're living in cloud-cuckoo land,

All-Knowing would head out to sea at the crack of dawn and not come back until sunset, or sometimes even after dark, especially when the weather was good, so I was free to do exactly as I pleased, the life I was living was much fuller and more exciting than the existence our dear All-Knowing wanted for me, he'd kept me under lock and key, he'd shaped me but I found a taste for things he'd forbidden to us, he'd done everything in his power keep us well away from them but there was a basic truth that eluded him, something everyone should know, he didn't realise that although you can overpower the body and keep it immobilised and lifeless, you can't pin down the soul, it won't be forced to the ground with broken wings, All-Knowing was convinced he knew me really well but you can't know everything about another person, I don't care how old and wise you are, or what they teach you on whatever planet you come from, for a person's life is a vast cavernous palace with bedrooms, antechambers and cellars and some of those rooms are well lit while others are dark and wrapped in secrecy, our lives are like oceans in a way, oceans in an infinity of oceans, each one harbouring an inexhaustible array of creatures in its depths, and the secrets hidden there can't be picked up from poring over scraps of newspapers day after day as our resident philosopher liked to believe and you won't find them in the most magnificent of libraries either, there's no book, no librarian, and no scholar that's even come close to revealing all the mysteries of the oceans, and in the midst of all those secrets you'll find my life, a tiny drop of water barely rippling the surface of that vast ocean in whose black depths every glimmer of light is extinguished,

at home, I was quietly following All-Knowing's every move, Rattler had no idea what he got up to and I think that may be partly why he wasn't very loving towards her, he wanted people to be involved in his fantasies, All-Knowing was the star of his own show and everything revolved around him, yes, he was the master of his own house and he was absolutely convinced he knew what was best but truth to tell he was the biggest sap I ever met, I'd watch him in silence, usually on the sly, so that I could go my dizzyingly twisted way in secret, I knew he'd put a stop to things if he were to learn where I was headed but I was certain he'd never find out, I kept an eagle eye on him, the better to know my enemy and stop him from blocking my way along what he would have considered the road to perdition,

I would watch All-Knowing gazing up at the stars at night, he'd raise his eyes to heaven then look down and say "*oh, it's going to be a beautiful day tomorrow, thank God, I'll be able to go out in the boat, it'll be nice and calm, I might even head for the open seas,*" and I'd be thinking to myself that while he was out at sea I'd be able to take care of some important business, each to his own, his passion was for the sea and mine was for love, so if during his star-gazing All-Knowing came out with something like "*son of a gun, looks like it's going to be rough tomorrow,*" I knew he'd be sure to come back as early as he could, in other words the cat would be home early and any mouse liable to be surprised playing had better watch out, and then he'd add something like *"yeah, I'm afraid the sea's getting very rough, I'll have to stay close to the shore so I can get out of there double quick if I have to, yup, you never know,"* I had him all worked out but I sat there looking like butter wouldn't melt in my mouth, not that he ever suspected me of anything at all, he didn't pay much attention to me, he never stopped to think about the fact that sometimes, when he came back from the beach, he'd have to call up to me on the terrace, yelling loud enough to wake the dead, he never asked what I was doing up there, but the terrace was where it all started, I was up there when I first set eyes on the man of my dreams, the man who could make me tremble from head to foot the minute I sensed his shadow approaching, the man whose touch would make my heart melt like butter in a hot pan, a fisherman, a friend of my father's, the best-looking fisherman in town, Voracious, that's right, his name was Voracious,

every day I'd plant myself on the terrace, and stay there rooted to the spot, gazing out at the sea, I'd watch the fishermen squabbling and fighting, I'd see who was leaving and who was returning, the winners and the losers, yes, some of them always came back with their boat loaded up with fish, while others returned empty-handed, I could see who was happy with their catch and who wasn't, some of them came back so exhausted they could barely haul their boat up on the beach, gather up their belongings and head home, without uttering a single word, like survivors of a shipwreck rescued by a passing ship, you could see their efforts had been in vain, the shame of their failure was written all over them, like a streak of shit on their forehead, I could see it all, everything that happened on that beach, our house was situated right across from it, the perfect spot for someone like me, who was intent less on listening to the song of the sea than on dancing with the waves, and as you're probably aware, you people frittering away your time following my ravings, the sea can certainly lead us a merry dance,

from my vantage point on our terrace, I could see the distinctive outline of Mutsamudu's medina, a part of town that was an ocean unto itself, and behind me, when I turned to gaze at the sea, was the famous citadel that rises above the medina, a great fortress that I felt added a touch of artistic splendour to Mutsamudu, all eyes were drawn to this imposing structure, and those of a discerning nature took comfort from its harmonious form,

good heavens, there'd be tourists from all over world feasting their eyes on Mutsumudu's citadel, endlessly aiming their cameras at it and bombarding it with flashes, as if that would make it yield the secrets promised by its lined face and white hair, All-Knowing said it was built from 1783 to 1790 by Sultan Abdullah Almaceli I, to protect the city from foreign invaders, that is, of course, after the island's capital was moved from Domodi to Mutsamudu, it occupied a majestic position, with a clear view over the city and out to sea, standing watch over the medina and all its goings-on, cannons pointed towards the sea, the port of Mutsamudu and the hillsides all around, and the fortress walls were adorned with plants and flowers that grew within the citadel and made it look from certain angles like a bearded sage, for just like a patriarch's bristles and wrinkles, the plants and moss that grow on fortress walls can speak volumes, and from afar, you could see the birds swooping, diving and soaring overhead, adding further to the beauty of this witness to history,

I could see the long stairway leading up to the foot of the citadel and I'd sit there on the terrace watching the figures climbing the stairs trying to work out who they were, oh come on Eel, get to the point, shit you're in your death throes here, it's time to get serious, okay, I know but please just bear with me, I'm doing the best I can,

so, I spent most of my time facing the other way, towards the sea, not paying much attention to the citadel behind me, I'd gaze for hours at the great watery expanse ebbing and flowing, weaving like a snake in front of me, so much closer than the citadel that I'd occasionally turn round to look at and strain my eyes from trying to make out the details, I'd let my gaze linger on the waves as they rose and fell, and as I watched the succession of peaks and troughs on the surface of that moving desert I'd fall into a reverie and let my imagination flow in concert with the movement of the water and without realising it, I'd be out there on those ripples, my mind stirred up by the lapping of the waves, I'd try and work out where each one came from, but no sooner had I begun than my field of vision would be blurred by the arrival of another one, and as the waves jostled together I'd forget where I was and a strange feeling would come over me, I yearned to be carried away on those waves, to roam the oceans and taste all the delights of this earth before I died, for we are not so different from those waves, each one born from another, yes, that's exactly what it is, human beings are tangled up together like waves, we merge into each other, we love and admire one another, we kiss and bring each other to life but we despise one another too, we tear each other apart and in the end we die and newborns take our place, it's exactly the same as a play in the theatre and that's the truth of it,

I would turn and face the beach and see the boats all lined up and the cows mooing and chewing their cud all day long and of course I'd watch the fantastic spectacle of the fishermen heading out to sea and returning with their plunder, always spoiling for a fight, with their jealous rivalries those fishermen were like a bunch of women, the ones who owned a motorboat would brag about it in front of those who didn't, and the ones who had their own nets would look down on those who fished with hook and line, mocking them openly and even pulling faces at them, they only felt good about themselves when they found someone worse off than they were, even if that person didn't give a fig about where they were in the pecking order, always the same competitive spirit, day in and day out, and as for All-Knowing, he owned a net but he had a hook and line too, bought from an Indian shopkeeper, they were the businessmen of Mutsamudu, the ones with the monopoly on all foreign trade, among the motorboat-owning fisherman was a young man by the name of Voracious, he was tall and well-built, a real Adonis, his muscles visible through the fabric of his nylon shirt, I had no idea at first that I was going to end up falling for him, I started by looking at him just for the sake of looking and before long it turned into an obsession, I had to see him, not a day passed when I didn't try and catch a glimpse of him, I couldn't get enough of gazing dreamily at him, I couldn't resist it, how was I to know I'd fallen prey to a lethal bait, I didn't realise that young fisherman was a master of his trade, he certainly managed to snare me, a land-dwelling eel, I can't deny that, he wasn't the talkative sort, he didn't blather on about the weather all the time like the other fishermen, he was strong as an ox and they were wary of him, although he was never anything but courteous towards his fellow fishermen,

out at sea, the fisherman behaved as if they were all in some big race, they'd even argue about claiming certain areas as their own so they could maximise their catch, as if the sea was something they could divide up among themselves, they acted like they could see to the bottom of the ocean and knew where the fish were going to congregate, they'd look askance at the last person to arrive in any one area and eye each other suspiciously all the time, as for Voracious, he'd go fish further out and come back with bigger specimens, completely different from what the other lazy good-for-nothings brought in, All-Knowing would catch nothing but tiny little fish, never the shark or tuna that Voracious would bring in, I had a perfect view of them from our terrace, he'd have at least five big sharks and about thirty cod and tuna, I'd stare at them for long enough to be able to count them as he unloaded them from his boat with his friends, his closest friend was Voilà, he was the one I was most familiar with, a drunkard of the first order who I'll tell you more about later, it was Voracious's friends who sold his fish, Voracious was good at his work, he didn't give a toss for the idiots who thought they were better than the others just because they had a motorboat, who thought they were the bee's knees because they could go further out to sea where the fish were plentiful,

I loved to watch Voracious when he was washing his hands, sometimes he'd carefully remove his shirt and stand there bare-chested for a long time while he cooled off, those were the sweetest moments of my daily vigil, seeing him stripped to the waist liked that, his skin glistening like a sea snake's, I imagined how soft it would be, with its luminous reflections slipping and slithering over its surface, it sent shivers through me like shots of a substance injected to awaken an insatiable hunger, I'd stare at his muscles bulging like big fat mangoes stuffed carefully into a plastic bag, I assumed he couldn't see me from that distance and anyway his attention was usually directed towards the crowd of people on the beach, or the ones passing the time of day in the street or under the badamier tree, so I'd gaze at Voracious with gay abandon, day after day, until one day he stopped to help All-Knowing with his fish and his gear, All-Knowing had made a good catch that day, but he had a lot to carry as he hadn't been able to sell all his fish and his friend Guarantee hadn't arrived yet, Guarantee was the tough old soul who sold All-Knowing's fish in town, and that day he was very late and All-Knowing was tired and wanted to go home, he hadn't landed on the beach until after all the other fishermen had finished selling their fish so there were hardly any customers left for All-Knowing, every day when the boats came in customers would be waiting on the beach for them, they'd go down to the beach and plant themselves there like trees and stand there, watching, with arms folded, you'd hardly know they were there at times, especially if it was dark, the first one to approach a boat as it came in would always be served first, which meant that as soon as a boat pulled up on shore the customers would rush head-long towards the fisherman, pretending they wanted to help him unload his tackle, well, what do you expect, *c'est la vie*, you have to know how to put on an act, pull the wool over people's eyes, play the sucker when the occasion demands, it adds spice to the show, that's all it is,

when it was really blowing up a storm, the fishermen who took the risk of going to sea knew they'd be able to crank up their prices, they knew that once they landed, prices would rise rapidly and they'd be the heroes of the day, yes, the stars of the show, women would be all over them, grabbing at them like jewels, they'd be the envy of shopkeepers and even of office workers, who suddenly became their best friends, but if the weather was calm and there were plenty of them going out to sea, the fishermen would be begging the customers to buy their wares, they'd squabble among themselves and spend their time fighting over customers while their fish lay rotting in the sun, stinking to high heaven with flies crawling all over them, all those fish, forgotten and slowly decomposing, but any fisherman who had a refrigerator would come back the next day to sell their fish while the others were forced to sell their catch at disastrous prices *"better to take a small loss than end up losing everything"* as All-Knowing used to say, he'd sell what he could or else he'd leave Guarantee to do the selling and come back home with two kilos of fish, and it was a day when Guarantee wasn't there that Voracious helped him carry his things,

I'm wasting time again aren't I, I should be telling you about Voracious, I must be going soft in the head, come on Eel, get your act together, stop wittering on about trifles, let's get back to Mjihari

so Voracious had offered to give All-Knowing a hand that day, where I come from young people were expected to show respect for their elders, if an older person needed help, it was your duty to offer it, that was the way it was, although there were some young people whose behaviour was openly disrespectful, like the ones who had the nerve to smoke in front of their parents, and even blow smoke in their faces, punishing them, I suppose, for bringing them into the world, so the point is that All-Knowing accepted the offer of help, Voracious had a reputation for being courteous and if he was also known to drink, well that was none of All-Knowing's business, so he accepted the offer and Voracious came back to our house with him, I could see them coming from the terrace, I felt my heart pounding in my chest, resonating in my head like a shout echoing in a closed space, as they drew near the house my legs started shaking, Voracious was behind All-Knowing, carrying two oars and a nylon bag filled with about ten kilos of fish, sardines, herrings and mackerel, All-Knowing had a bag over his right shoulder with his net, his line and his box of hooks, and in his left hand he was carrying a bag with another ten kilos or so of fish, and as soon as I saw them approach the door, I rushed down the stairs into the court-yard so as not to arouse any suspicions and end up getting into trouble, All-Knowing didn't like us sitting up on the terrace watching what was going on outside, woe betide us if we went up there even to play with the cat, and I was just about at the bottom of the stairs I when I heard the long drawn-out creaking of the door before it slammed shut, you couldn't touch that old door without everyone in the house hearing, it was filled with the secrets it had been absorbing since before we saw the light of day and it was still collecting them in spite of the dreadful howling noises it made, that long scraping sound that drove me mad and threatened to give me away and strip me of all my secrets, but I managed to escape by the skin of my teeth, how, you ask, well, it'll all be explained eventually, when an eel's on its last legs it wiggles around crapping all over the place until it gets to its final destination, and that's what I'm doing here, so take a deep breath and get your mind around what happened next,

All-Knowing and Voracious had gone inside, All-Knowing first, shouting and going on as if he was talking to a deaf person, he always managed to find something to pontificate about, he was ranting on, jumping from one thing to another, Voracious couldn't possibly have kept up with him, first it was the weather and then suddenly he was turning the conversation around to himself and his seafaring experience, he prided himself on knowing the sea like the back of his hand and boasted about his prowess as a fisherman, Voracious could barely conceal a smile when the old braggart said to him *"you listen to me sonny, I'm an old hand, believe me, I've seen it all,"* a claim made by all the old fishermen, Voracious laughed, they'd stopped in the court-yard, right by the door and Voracious seemed to be concentrating, staring intently at All-Knowing who'd kept up his spiel with *"yes, some people seem to think going out on the open seas is a piece of cake, I'd like to see them try it, just for once, then we'd see who really has the balls, correct me if I'm wrong, eh my lad, you tell me, sixty-five years of experience, you get my drift, sonny, sixty-five years, when I head out from here I know exactly what I want and I know precisely where I'm going,"* he stopped abruptly to put the things he was carrying down on the ground, it was probably quite a weight and it might have got in the way of him talking, I suppose, so he put his hands on his hips like a teacher preparing to deliver a difficult lesson and he ploughed on, calling Voracious sonny over and over again *"you see, sonny, when I set out to sea I don't think about going all the way to Peru, no, I just think I'm going to catch whatever I can and come away happy,"* he took his hands off his hips and stopped to mull things over in his head before launching himself again at full pelt, he couldn't get enough of talking about the sea, it was a subject that never failed to enchant him, he'd pepper his tales with his favourite sayings to underline his points and end up with his catchphrase *"what's a sailor got to lose,"* I was standing completely still and I could see Voracious sneaking a look at me, I wanted to smile or laugh at what All-Knowing was saying but I couldn't manage it, the looks I'd been getting had set my head in a spin, I was trying to act like I hadn't noticed anything, I sat down on the bottom stair and twiddled my fingers as if I wasn't paying attention to any of it, but Voracious had cast a spell on me, I was utterly, completely bewitched, I didn't know what to do with myself, I suddenly remembered that I was supposed to help All-Knowing put away his tackle as I usually did, I was worried the old man might have noticed that I wasn't listening and make some remark, so I quickly stood up and All-Knowing stopped in full flow and pointed at the oars Voracious was carrying and said to me *"you'd best take the oars first, let my friend Voracious here catch his breath, eh, sonny,"* Voracious was still looking at me as if I was a creature from another planet, his eyes pierced right through me, I was paralysed, how was I to walk towards that gaze of such deadly allure, it was worse than having a sword brandished in my direction, and when I managed to take a few steps towards him, he carried on staring at me, not blinking at all, isn't that amazing, I was expecting at least a flutter of the eyelids, but no, not at all, he stood there like a perfectly sculpted statue, a mummy more like, I'd never seen anything like it before, in all my sad little life, I had no choice but to avert my eyes from the glare of that gaze, and yet I wanted to look him in the eye, stupid of me, wasn't it, I wanted to show him I wasn't afraid, I'm not talking about being ashamed, that's a different thing altogether, you know, and I wasn't scared, I didn't behave like a coward in front of him, I looked up to meet his gaze and we stared into each others' eyes, just like in a love story, I felt a weight lift from my heart, I was saved, I'd made direct contact with him and for those few exquisite, blissful seconds we communicated in silence, yes, I tried to work out what his eyes were saying to me, what that look actually meant, but did I really make any sense of it,

that was the day I understood that eyes have their own way of stripping the heart bare, they speak directly and show you exactly what lies hidden behind the clouds, how do I know, because I let myself be swept along by the hunger in that gaze, I was conquered unawares, when Voracious flashed me a smile full of God knows what, I was thrown into turmoil, I didn't know what I was doing, I flailed around and instead of taking the oars he was holding out to me, I held his wrists for the longest time and gave him a demented look, really, like a mad woman, I couldn't stop myself, I wanted to feel the coolness of his skin, I touched it with my fingers but I felt its warmth in my heart, its freshness in my eyes, and then there was his dazzling, seductive smile, with those fine teeth, shining like pearls, I swear I couldn't move a muscle, and then all of a sudden he seemed concerned about my demeanour, he waved his hands a bit as if to wake me up, and it's true, at that moment I was asleep, I wrenched myself from my stupor with a start and hastily seized the oars with both hands but before I turned back towards All-Knowing, who was busy with his fish, I returned his smile, I went to put the oars away in the kitchen, turning round from time to

71

time to see if Voracious was still there and of course he was and he was watching me all the time,

All-Knowing finished putting away his bags of fish to save until his friend Guarantee came to collect them and sell them in other parts of town, from Chitsangani to Haborno, selling fish was what Guarantee was known for, he'd sell all the fish and come back with the exact amount of money agreed on, not a penny more nor less, I don't know how much All-Knowing paid him, they'd go off and talk business in whispers on the terrace or in the courtyard, they understood each other, I suppose, like two old foxes, they were two of the same and seemed quite happy and proud of what they did, All-Knowing showed great respect towards his old friend, he trusted him implicitly,

so as he was finishing up putting away his things, All-Knowing turned towards Voracious, tapped him on the left shoulder and said *"there, that's all done, all put away, sonny, I can't thank you enough, have a great evening, Voracious dear boy,"* Voracious bowed and as he turned to leave, without All-Knowing seeing, he shot me a last look to say goodbye to me too,

that evening I felt like a different person, as if something miraculous had just happened to me, the fact that I'd touched Voracious in the flesh was a great victory for me, the very same Voracious I watched at the beach, whose figure would appear before my eyes every time I closed them, and now I'd rubbed my skin against his, something which until

that moment had seemed utterly fanciful, I couldn't stop
thinking about him and I threw myself down on my bed to
carry on dreaming about it all for while, but I jumped up all
of a sudden when I remembered that I was supposed to be
getting the dinner started while we were waiting for Rattler
to come home, she always took her time coming home after
school, my father All-Knowing and I would worry about
her sometimes, he'd warn her about it but he was wasting
his time, his warnings fell on deaf ears, she and her friends
would start by hanging around at Missiri stadium for a while
and then they'd go and lounge on the grass in Mroni Park
or in some other park, All-Knowing would shake his fist
at her when she came home and give her a dressing down,
but she wasn't in the least bit bothered, the old werewolf's
threats didn't faze her at all, even when he threatened to cut
her off completely, it was all water off a duck's back to her,
she'd give him the same look she gave everyone else, as if the
name All-Knowing meant nothing to her,

Rattler had plenty of friends, she was very popular at the
lycée in Mutsamudu, as soon as she appeared at the school
gate everyone would call out to her and say hello, you'd
think she was a movie star or a world-famous musician,
someone like our very own Nawal, or Rokia Traoré or even
Céline Dion, who we'd hear about when All-Knowing was
reading his newspaper scraps, Rattler was like some kind of
Céline Dion at the lycée, whereas me, well, I didn't have a
single friend, girl or boy, I was all on my own, no one dared
to speak to me for that matter, people thought I was weird,
overly serious, yes, that was it, too serious, they thought I

didn't want to have anything to do with other people, pfft, what do I care, I didn't give two hoots about any of that, my job was to take care of my own rock in general and my Voracious in particular, nothing else, the rest of it was all just piffle,

in reality, everyone at school knew who I was but I knew nothing at all about them, so what, I wasn't bothered, maybe they needed to know all about me, but their business was no concern of mine, whoever they might be, I didn't mind being on my own, even in the midst of a crowd, there is one face I remember though, a girl who used to sit near me, she wasn't someone I thought about very much, in fact I paid absolutely no attention to her and she never dared utter a word to me, what was her name now, Desi, Desa, erm, no, it's on the tip of my tongue, Desi-rée, there we are, that's it, Desirée, yes, she was called Desirée, so how come I knew her name, well, because I'd hear all the boys calling out to her, whistling through their teeth at her, I used to wonder what she was doing at the lycée, that girl, with ten or more boys following behind her whenever she came into class, like some sort of queen, or a millionairess, a mad woman, or someone on the run that's about to be arrested, why not, you never know, and another thing, she used to douse herself in perfume and smear her lips and cheeks with a very risqué shade of lipstick, probably to maximise the harm done to her victims, who she wouldn't offer any kind of cure to, although maybe she cured them all in secret, she must have had her own rock somewhere, same as I did, she always came to school with nothing but a small notebook folded in

half like a rag, I'd see it when she took it out of the Chanel
bag she was always brandishing for all to see, I never understood what it was about Chanel, I wasn't really interested
and I'm still not, that bag of hers was her mascot, stuffed
with designer make-up all with logos that meant nothing
to me, I read them all though, with my eagle eyes, I'd spell
them out to myself while we were waiting for the teacher
to arrive, Désirée would set all her jujus out on her desk,
Dior, L'Oréal, Yves Rocher, Roc, Yves Saint-Laurent, and
whole load of other designer stuff she collected so people
would notice her, I used to hear her telling her friends about
how she wished she could dress in, I don't know, Christian
Dior, she'd say the name, Christian Dior, a thousand times,
like it was some kind of god, I'd think to myself she must
come from a family with plenty of money, only rich people
can afford that kind of luxury, or else they were crooks of
some sort, but it was none of my business, I kept quiet in
class, as I was saying a few minutes ago, I played the deaf
mute, I was quite content to sit and watch the others,
I loved it, I'd watch Desirée tarting up her eyes with her
Yves Saint-Laurent mascara, I'd watch people opening
their notebooks to demonstrate they were there to learn,
they really annoyed me, those show-offs, did they think the
rest of us were only there for decoration or what, I saw the
people who fell asleep on their desks, they deserved to be
pitied really, either they didn't have a mattress to sleep on
at home, a place where they could sleep in peace instead of
being grilled and hassled here in class, either that or they
couldn't stand up to their parents, they were too cowed
to insist they needed more sleep, they let themselves be

dragged from their beds to get to school, or else they were bone idle, yes, that's what they were, I'm sure that's what it was, I saw who was holding hands too, staring endlessly into each other's eyes, as if they were the only lovers in the world, burning with desire, the only ones without a place to go and revel in those feelings that give you wings and won't leave you in peace, oh, the poor creatures, weren't there any parks they could go to and have their fun undisturbed, instead of putting themselves through hell at school, along with all the rest of us and then, I'd look at myself watching the others and I'd wonder if I wasn't actually one of the worst characters in this tale and I'd chuckle to myself,

coming back to the differences between Rattler and me, as I was saying, I didn't have any friends but I did have my dreams, my private fantasy of a big strong man, not some fat slob, no, I'm not interested in great hunks, what I needed was a strapping young man, like Voracious, built like a man, not a boy with a body like a girl's, and there were plenty of boys who were very girly, all the boys at the lycée for a start, as far as I was concerned they were all wimps waiting for life to be served up to them on a plate instead of going out and working out for themselves what it was all about, I stayed away from them, but Voracious was a man, a real looker, he was hot, and not only had I spotted him, I'd seen him up close and touched him for the first time in my life, and that was a big day for me, I came alive that day, until then I'd been asleep, I lost my head completely to him, I was totally gaga, he'd put a hell of a spell on me, all it took was one look and I fell in love, yes, that's exactly it, fell in

love, funny isn't it, why do people talk about "falling in love,"
what kind of talk is that, why not "rising to love" or "flying
to love" or something like that, but "falling," it makes you
think of misfortune, it's a suicidal word, it's a very serious
matter letting yourself fall, you could bite your own tongue
off unintentionally, like a parrot, it's verbal suicide but
there's not much I can do about it, it's up to the so-called
Immortals to decide that kind of thing, I ask you though,
who are these Immortals of the Académie Française anyway,
is there anyone in this world who actually lives forever,
immortal, my foot, who do they take themselves for, shutting themselves away every Thursday in their green outfits
on the Quai Conti to talk about the meanings of words,
as if words were cars on roads in need of rules to keep the
traffic flowing, no, words are one thing and cars are another,
my friends, if it's words you're driving, you're not going to
crash so long as you're all moving in the same direction,
but driving a car is a completely different matter, you could
collide with another car at any moment whether you're all
going in the same direction or not, if you see what I mean,
so it's up to us to decide how we use our words in this three-
ring circus of a world, just as we're free to choose what to
do with our bodies, which is precisely what I'm doing at this
very moment, oh God, what am I talking about here, where
are you going with this, Eel, it's all because of that wretched
French teacher, isn't it, stuffing our heads with all those rules
about the correct way to use the French language, he was
another lying so-and-so too, that one, okay, I was doing fine
with my two images, it's the other ones that get in the way
though, wasting my energy, making me lose the thread of

my memories, but look, I still have my two birds in the hand and we have made some progress, even though I do keep going off on tangents, yes, I know, it's all a bit of a mess but there's nothing I can do about it, we just need to find out how I ended up in this plight, so let's continue, Mjihari and Mutsamudu, you're still there aren't you,

okay, so I'd fallen hopelessly in love, as they say, with Voracious, I knew it for sure that day, when I felt the cool touch of his skin, I got the cooking out of the way quickly so I could go and have a nap and dream about his hands, like that poet who wrote all those poems about how he was going out of his mind for his muse, whingeing on about her hands, saying things like *"give me your hands"* all the time, trying to get your sympathy, what was her name, that woman, oh yes, Elsa that was it, I can't stand poetry myself, poets always seem to have something wrong with them, they're never satisfied, they're all as miserable as sin, and then they go looking for solace off stage, they think they're too good for the hurly-burly of life, but I have to admit that I was fantasizing like a poet myself that evening, I kept seeing his hands over and over again, so fine and elegant, I'll never forget them, it was as if I'd claimed them for my own, his hands were my precious jewels, the apple of my eye,

I woke up the next day at first light to watch the fishermen setting off, hoping to catch a glimpse of Voracious, if only for a few seconds, All-Knowing was about to leave and I asked him if he'd like me to make him some tea but he said he still had some coffee left in his flask, and with that, he left and I was free to go up to the terrace,

dawn was a splendid symphony of crowing and clucking,
with all the hens and cocks in the neighbourhood joining
in one after another, like singers in a choir all trying to
outdo each other, I think we were about the only household without any chickens, All-Knowing had put his foot
down about it, as far as he was concerned all poultry were
an infernal nuisance, crapping all over the place all the time,
they were unhealthy creatures, he said, with a perpetual case
of the runs, and there was nothing we could say to convince
him otherwise,

that morning, on the terrace, I could hear the cats mewling
and purring, fighting or having sex as usual I supposed, I
wondered why they screamed like that, even when they
were having sex, I was dying to know if people screamed
like that too when they were making love, and of course,
that was something I was to find out soon enough, when it
came to my turn, I expect you want to know how that came
about, well let's not get ahead of ourselves, all in good time,
so the cats were having their fun on every terrace in the
neighbourhood, they had no sense of shame, not like us,
hiding ourselves away to make love, one day when I was
going up to bring in the washing I'd left hanging out to dry
on the terrace, I'd come across a tomcat on top of a female
cat, he was biting her neck and sticking something into her,
or so it seemed, and the female was screaming loudly, as
if she was being forced to accept it, when in fact she was
really enjoying it, anyway, they ran off like a shot as soon as

they caught sight of me, and as the tomcat ran by I caught a glimpse of that slender piece of meat like a pen between his legs and I wondered where he hid it when he wasn't all worked up, anyway, I was really sorry to have interrupted their fun, it was the best game of all they were playing and they had every right to enjoy it too, cats, they were everywhere, if there's one animal you find at every turn in our part of the world, it's cats, even under the bed, they don't wait to be invited and they never listen to a word anyone says, All-Knowing would often say to the cats yowling at his feet when he was eating *"if you thought there was any chance you might end up on my plate, I swear you wouldn't be quite so bold, but just because you know that no one's going to slit your neck and turn you into soup, you think you can do what you like and pester people to your heart's content,"* they'd wander into all the houses in our neighbourhood, whether people liked them or not, it made no difference to them, All-Knowing would be going on at them and they'd carry on mewling and demanding their share, but the old fisherman wasn't one for eating in company, he preferred not to be bothered while he was having his meal and in the end he'd say to them *"you're nothing but a bunch of wastrels, my friends, but here, take that,"* and he'd throw them a few scraps of bone, yes, bare bones, without an ounce of meat left on them,

so back to the terrace that morning when I wanted to watch Voracious as he left, it wasn't just the crowing, the cackling and caterwauling I could hear, there was the mooing of the cows on the beach too, and the bleating of the goats that hung around the medina all night long and on top of all that the birds would be twittering to their hearts' content with their dawn chorus, my favourites were the sparrows, I loved to listen to them chirping as they came flocking back from the cemetery and the nearby madrasas, and other sparrows would come from the badamier, the gigantic tree that had been witness to so much of the neighbourhood's history, you could see the top of it from all over Mjihari, and from Missir, Hamambou and Hampanga as well, when I turned and looked towards the east I could see the sparrows perched on the top of it, I'd see bats too, they'd electrocute themselves sometimes on the wires strung between street lights, poor things, they'd stay there stuck to the wires, rotting for days and nights, until all you'd see were their mangy feathers, but while we're talking about Mjihari, have I told you about where the name comes from, Mjihari really just means in the heart of the city, which is exactly where it is, and it owes its beginnings to the preacher known as Mussa Mudu, it was there before any of the rest of the city of my birth was built,

the badamier tree was the site of all sorts of occasions, weddings would be held under it and celebrations to mark the birth of the Prophet too, but there was other things too that gave this tree its special status, people would gather there to discuss fishing matters or to talk about business or politics while they played cards, drafts, dominos or backgammon, old men for the most part, some of them simply came to while away the hours on the benches there, All-Knowing didn't think much of any of them, he dismissed them all as idle loafers who weren't interested in making a living, the sea was right there, he said and it was free *"all they have to do is haul their backsides into a pirogue and go floating off on that giant treasure box,"* he'd say pointing out to sea, silly old fool, did he really think everyone wanted to be a fisherman like him, fishing is fine for some people, dad, but not for everyone, wait a minute, did I just say dad, well yes, he was my dad, and I do acknowledge him as my dad, even if he did throw me out of the house, but we'll get to that in due course, I don't want to jump the gun here,

so All-Knowing would come up with all kinds of things on the subject of fishing when he was trying to win people round to his way of thinking, he had his own way of talking about the sea, he was always saying things like *"the sea's a monster with a jewel in its belly reserved for the men with real balls, not for idle loafers who act like they're some kind of royalty,"* what a ridiculous thing to say, can you imagine coming up with that kind of stuff, it doesn't make any sense, however much you admire the prowess of fishermen, I think the old codger was losing his marbles, I mean, since when was the sea the judge of a man's worth, all I know is that the sea is like the land, a treasure trove for everyone, no more no less, both land and sea are vast reservoirs stuffed to the brim with a never-ending supply of dazzling treasures and it's all there for the asking, I fell in love with Voracious because I was in awe of his physique, not because he was a fisherman, no, he had a great body, but he could just as well have been a farmer or perhaps a docker, but not a schoolboy, no, they're nothing but sissies, schoolboys, they're pathetic,

ALI ZAMIR

All-Knowing was a regular at the card games under the badamier tree, he loathed and despised the smokers who came to watch the games fag in hand, he'd make disparaging remarks about them when the smoke became too much for him, but the smokers would have none of it and when he yelled at them one day and said to one of them "*hey, what do you think you're doing poisoning us like this, it's not like we asked you to, we have our rights too, don't we,*" the smoker, an old shopkeeper who was bigger than All-Knowing, told him he'd better keep his mouth shut unless he wanted to end up scraping his teeth off the ground, so our resident moralist held his tongue, silenced for once, he'd shout and yell at the kids too, and there were plenty of under-fifteens among the smokers, most of them would smoke at night, in dark corners where few people ventured, hidden away in the narrow unlit streets of the medina, but some of them were bold as brass and weren't afraid to answer back when they were told off by their elders and betters, however venerable they were, and then there were the kids who smoked in front of their parents to give them a dose of reality, to remind them they'd lost control of their offspring, sometimes when All-Knowing saw kids smoking under the badamier tree at night he'd try and talk them out of it, he'd warn them of the dangers of smoking and say "*you're killing yourselves kids, that cigarette is a stick of poison, it's an evil beast, a canker quietly eating away your insides,*" but if that's really the case, if they're going to die anyway, why upset them, it's their choice, they've signed their contract with the playwright, if that's the end they've chosen for themselves why not let them get on with it, have a bit of fun while they're swallowing their poison, let them enjoy their freedom, instead of picking a fight with them, everything in life is toxic, life itself is toxic, so why not be nice to those smokers, but All-Knowing always had to throw in his two cents' worth, and some of them would snap back at him and tell him *"you should stick to fishing Mister All-Knowing, your job is catching fish not dishing out lessons, unless you want put in your application to join the teachers over there, you'll have fun with them, especially the ones that bang on the most about morality, they're the biggest smokers of all, exhaust pipes on broken down old trucks they are, you'll have your work cut out for you there,"* and then others would join in to get him to succumb more quickly *"food's what we want, not lectures, you stick to what you're good at, Mister All-Knowing, all that here today gone tomorrow philosophising, you're not cut out for it, the fish are out there waiting for you, the sea looks lost without you, see how bereft it looks, quite sad really, don't you think,"* and then All-Knowing would leave and come back home muttering to himself, grumbling about young people blowing smoke in his face, on and on he'd go, non-stop, he'd work himself into a lather and proclaim *"there's no getting away from it, the whole world's going up in smoke, they're all at it, for God's sake, worms, blowing smoke rings out of nostrils they don't even have,"* I'd act like I was paying attention to him when he talked like that and I'd keep quiet most of the time, it was best not to interrupt All-Knowing if you wanted to be in his good books, all you had to do is let him think you saw him as a fount of wisdom when in fact he was merely crying in the wilderness, as far as I was concerned those smokers were simply enjoying life on earth to the full, they were free agents, how they lived their lives was their business, they could blow smoke out of their back sides for all I cared, and all this time I was dying for a smoke and for a drink, yes, I remember quite clearly, he had no idea that I was actually a heavy smoker, he wasn't the all-knowing person you'd expect him to be, his name did nothing for him, there was nothing magic about it, having a learned name doesn't mean things will be revealed to you, if it did the world would be full of people named All-Knowing, what's in a name in the end, a name is nothing but a silent wind blowing in a vacuum, it changes nothing, if you want to make an impact it's brain power you need, or shit power perhaps, it's no good relying on a name, you have to use your head to give your name resonance, or your arse if that's where your heart is, for it's the heart that's running the show, head and arse simply obey the heart's instructions, and just what does the heart want, well, it wants to be heard, to be listened to when it utters its cries of pain from deep inside, what it doesn't want is to be considered a degenerate just because it's not willing to listen to sanctimonious clap-trap that's got nothing to do with its troubles, are you following me here, for eel's sake, are you getting my drift, or are you plodding alongside me like a donkey, I'm not going to stop, you know, one way or the other I'm going to continue this adventure in words, what the hell, you can't stop in the middle of a ride like this, unless it's to flesh things out, there are no brakes on this, and when you don't have brakes, you need a free run, so I don't know if it's the mouth driving all these words or if it's the other way round, maybe you can tell me,

VORACIOUS MY LOVE

Voracious lived a few meters down the road from us, not far from his parents, who'd apparently reached their twilight years and could no longer do things for themselves, they were a frail, elderly couple who'd run their own business for many years and eventually handed it over to their children, Voracious was the only one not involved in the business and according to him, his brothers and sisters had abandoned their parents to poverty and illness, the family had fallen apart and he was the only one who was close to those poor old sixty-somethings, he did all their shopping and went to see them every evening, he'd talk to me about how important it was to look after one's parents, he said it was a way of showing you cared for your fellow human-beings, that you didn't shirk your responsibilities, people who took proper care of their parents would never hurt others, he said, they'd be too ashamed, I don't know if that's true or not, like the rest of the stuff that came out of his mouth,

yeah, well, a man can look good, he can seem polite and kind and handsome when he's trying to sweet talk a girl, doing his best to bamboozle her with his tales of heroism, there's no end to the things he won't make up about himself, I don't know if it was all just to win my trust that Voracious passed himself off as a man who held others in high esteem, yes, he claimed he respected everyone, and the respect he showed towards his parents was proof of that, I didn't know if he was making it all up or not, I had no way of telling, maybe it was all talk and he was doing one of those numbers where a guy claims to own all the cars in the car park when it's quite obvious from his scruffy clothes that he's no limousine owner, men like that don't care if you can see right through them, so long as they can get you to follow them into their net like a tuna once they've softened you up with tasty treats, yes, I did know about these things, but what happened to me wasn't like that at all, I don't think, I'm not a hundred per cent sure though, so be careful, don't put words into my mouth, and don't take everything I say literally, I'm all over the place here, completely at sea, drowning as I speak,

Voracious had several brothers and sisters but he was the youngest, his brothers were all shopkeepers and businessmen, they were greedy he said, all they cared about was profit, their parents relied on him much more than the others, they loved him and encouraged him in what he did, although they hadn't much liked the idea of him leaving school to take up fishing *"education, I tell you, is man's moral clothing"* All-Knowing would tell us endlessly, as if his warnings could protect us from the temptations of dropping out of school, it all went in one ear and out the other with me, I did as I pleased, we're put on this earth to lives our lives to

the full, don't you agree, I knew plenty of people at school
who didn't seem to wear this so-called moral dress, who did
he think he was, that white-haired old buffer, he had the
nerve to say these things to us when he'd dropped out of
school himself, I knew he regretted it but he didn't want to
admit it, he must have been afraid we'd go down the same
road, he defended himself tooth and nail and claimed he
had to drop out because his parents were so poor, he said
he'd been forced to take up fishing to provide for his parents,
what a joke, it made me laugh when he acted like he could
still go back to school, you could go to school at any time of
life he said, but I ask you at his age, I don't think so, listen,
old boy, what's done is done, there's no going back, otherwise you'd be able to stop yourself getting old, wouldn't you,
did you expect me to believe you could make the world turn
backwards, I mean, seriously, a man of your years, would you
really be up to studying, eh, Voracious was different though,
he was a fisherman and proud of it and he had no regrets,
he'd dropped out before he even went to secondary school,
which took some guts, he was certainly bold, I'll say that for
him,

anyway, I was telling you about how I'd woken up at the
crack of dawn the morning after we'd looked each other
in the eye and made that first physical contact, I'd got up
to watch him going out to sea, I positioned myself at the
best spot on the terrace to see all the pirogues preparing
to take to the waves, I could see several fishermen getting
ready to push their boats out into that vast ocean, but to
my surprise, Voracious wasn't among them, I thought maybe

he'd already left, yes, I told myself he'd gone out before the others so he could come back early, which he often did, even before sunset sometimes, but I'd always assumed it was just because he had a motorboat, anyway I'd never actually seen him leaving because I'd never had any reason to go up to the terrace that early in the morning, I was always busy with the dishes and getting ready to go to school, but that morning I felt I absolutely had to go up there, a complete change had come over me since that one moment the day before, I'd become a different person, I was lost to the world, everywhere I went I saw Voracious's figure, I had to see him in the flesh that morning, whatever it took, I'd already talked myself into missing my classes for him, I needed to lay eyes on him, even for just a few seconds, maybe he'd flash that smile at me again, one smile from him would be enough to fill heaven and earth with dazzling light, I'd be floating on cloud nine, so I looked everywhere, turning my head this way and that, towards the beach, behind the badamier tree, towards the port, I listened for every movement, every echo, thinking perhaps he was away from the beach, or behind me even, it was madness, wasn't it, I worshipped that Hercules, I admit it, I was frantic, where in God's name had he gone,

it's hard falling in love, especially if you're the type to go completely off the rails, I started to lose patience, I was chomping at the bit, the fishermen had left, the beach was emptying out, all I could see were the cows and a few pirogues that probably weren't being taken out that day, they were left there, parked like cars in their usual spot on the promontory, carefully positioned to attract jealous looks from those who didn't possess a boat, I stood there on the terrace for ages, consumed by worry, I barely noticed the breeze wafting up from the sea, and then the sun began to appear lazily on the horizon, rising tentatively as if it too was unhappy, as if it wasn't sure it was the right time, anxious that it wouldn't find the thing that mattered most to it, I was at a loss for what to do, thrown off course by my emotions, I had just a few seconds left to decide if I was going to go back down and get ready to leave for school, when I suddenly spotted a tall figure in the distance, like a giant on the road, striding silently beside the low wall that divided the road from the beach, walking towards our house, oh good heavens, it was Voracious, he was heading for our house, yes it was definitely him, but what was this, he was looking at me the whole time, or maybe I was wrong, no, I was right, he was definitely looking straight at me, and then as he came closer he glanced right and left, every which way, what was he doing, he looked almost like a thief checking to see it was safe to strike and then all of a sudden he stopped and gave me a furtive look, I was shaking, the fact that it really was Voracious looking straight at me was starting to sink in, what did he want with me, for eel's sake, I had to do something didn't I, but what could I do, little scaredy-cat that I was, my lips were quivering, as if they might actually be capable of saying something useful, and in an effort to get hold of myself I turned round to face the citadel, with my back on Voracious, talking to myself the whole time, with an inner voice haranguing me and saying *"think fast, you've only got a few seconds to make up your mind, or you'll lose him for ever,"* and with that, I spun round to face him again,

I knew I didn't want him to go, he was still there and it looked like he had something he wanted to say to me, he signalled to me to say hello, I was shivering like a little girl waiting for her punishment and suddenly I could feel my bladder full to bursting, I thought I was going to wet myself there and then, in my knickers, but when someone greets you, you have to respond somehow, don't you and well, I don't know exactly how I did respond, all I know is that I made some kind of rapid, clumsy gesture but he understood what I meant, that was what mattered, it didn't seem to make any difference that I'd waved at him like an idiot, I was eaten up by panic, I didn't know where to put myself, so I decided to act like he wasn't there, yes, I tried to get ahold of myself by pretending I didn't realise he was there, but it was no good, I could still see him there, even when I tried to close my eyes, so I decided I'd keep my eyes wide open, he flashed me a deadly smile, full of *je ne sais quoi*, a knowing grin and then he gestured to me again, asking me, if I'd understood correctly, if he could join me on the terrace "*maybe he's having me on*" I said to myself, I nodded in agreement though, without a moment's hesitation and by God he took me seriously, he was walking towards the door, I felt my heart pounding in my chest, the old door creaked noisily as it always did and I was really scared then, the noise might have woken Rattler, I mean if it'd been me I'd have got straight up to see who was there, but she's a lazy-bones, Rattler, even if she did hear the door creaking she wouldn't get out of bed, she always slept really hard, which explains why she never made it to school on time, so I heard Voracious coming into the courtyard and I rushed towards the stairs and there he was, in the flesh, I couldn't believe my eyes, my heart was in my mouth as we carried on communicating in sign language, I don't know why, maybe it was because neither of us could muster the courage to actually speak to the other, I signalled to him to come up the stairs, and as he climbed the steps stealthily, it wasn't his footsteps I heard, it was my heart hammering like it would split my chest open, shame on you Eel, I thought to myself, it's not enough just to have a big mouth, you have to have the courage to act too, but I didn't know what to say so I stood there at the top of the stairs, speechless, watching Voracious coming up to join me, and what ran through my mind was a question, what if Rattler were to wake up, I'd have to be on my toes and make sure she didn't find me with Voracious, she'd probably think he was there every day, I was sure that was what she'd think, or maybe she'd have been happy to discover that I wasn't the sister she thought she had, yes, that she'd been a sucker all along, maybe she'd have carried on spying on me and not necessarily said anything to my father, or maybe she wouldn't have cared, given that I still gave her space and pretended not to know what she got up to at school, I don't really know how she would have reacted, she might have made it worse for me, you never know, who knows if she would have dared tell my father All-Knowing about all this, she was full of hot air, Miss Rattlesnake, which makes me think of one the catchphrases All-Knowing would come out with when he was pontificating about something or other, as he was most of the time "*do a donkey a favour and all you get by way of gratitude is farts,"* but I wasn't going to change my mind and I certainly wasn't going to tell Voracious to go away, I wasn't that stupid, I can tell you that, I wasn't going to cheat myself out of my real life, I mean has an eel ever been known to turn its back on something that's good for it, you fishermen out there, have you ever seen such a thing,

I'd be killing myself laughing about all this if I weren't under such pressure to wrap up these reminiscences, I'm trying to understand what happened to me, I mean, when I think of all the people with shit for brains spouting crap all the time, I don't know whether to laugh or cry, but I haven't got the time for that now, I have to crack on, find out where this is all leading, that's just the way it is, *voilà*, hey, wait a minute, where did that come from, I'm certainly not going to get sidetracked into talking about that old drunkard by the name of Voilà, we'll get to him later, come on Eel, get your shit together, try and be serious,

so I pulled myself together, I welcomed Voracious in a state of delirious rapture, but I was still shaken to the core, that hadn't changed at all, he'd shown up unannounced and I hadn't been expecting to meet him like that, we were very careful and tried not to make a sound, not that the pounding of my heart, like claps of thunder in my chest, wasn't loud enough to wake the dead, I was convinced it was going to give us away, well, why not, stranger things have happened, so Voracious joined me on the terrace and sat down on the ground, it struck me at the time that he was taller than me, he was trying to stay out of sight of the neighbours or of anyone who happened to be passing, in the street, or on the beach, I stood there gazing at him as if he were a Martian, wondering what to say to him, whether we even spoke the same language, if we'd be able to communicate at all without gestures, I stayed where I was at a safe distance, dumbstruck, I was in my favourite spot and I turned to I watch what was happening on the beach, my mind suddenly far away, Voracious noticed I was acting weirdly and called me over to him, I pulled myself together quick as a flash, as if I'd been woken from the deepest of dreams and I did as he said without a word, I sat down too, still at a good distance from him, he gave me a sidelong glance, almost as if he was trying to read my mind, and then he looked me up and down, oh the look in his eyes, it was wild, he was devouring me with his gaze, I couldn't take it, I looked down and then I heard him make a sound, he was clearing his throat, as if he was about to make a speech he was completely unprepared for, I wondered if he thought he was at some kind of meeting, he was talking to me, choosing his words carefully, asking me if I was well, I nodded to say yes and then he was hesitating again and saying *"you're probably surprised to see me here first thing in the morning, coming up here and taking an interest in you,"* another moment of hesitation, he looked down for a few moments and then shook his head and went on *"I thought your father probably wouldn't be around at this time in the morning,"* and I was thinking to myself *"aha, so you're afraid of All-Knowing too,"* I didn't realise people were so scared of him, even the big, strong types, I'd thought it was merely out of respect that Voracious did his best not to wind him up, after all he could have spoken to me right under All-Knowing's nose if he'd wanted to, like one of those cocky so-and-sos that talk to girls in front of their parents, those feckless types who take advantage of parents' lack of vigilance, some parents simply give up on their children, they turn a blind eye to all kinds of things, their children never listened to them anyway, I'm telling you, there's not much a parent can do if the things their children learn on the street are the opposite of what they're taught in class and they certainly can't watch over their daughters right up until the final curtain, it's just too much, plus they're scared of making things worse and while we're on the subject of getting things wrong, maybe I'm barking up the wrong tree myself, this isn't the way an eel's life is supposed to be, it's meant to be straightforward, without a care in the world, surely there's only so much an eel can take, but back to the question of parents, they weren't all downright negligent, some were simply afraid of getting too mixed up in their daughters' lives, they knew it would just stir things up and cause an almighty storm, girls who were kept under lock key got fed up with it, they thought they were smarter than their mothers and knew better than their elders, and then there were the parents who were so enamoured of the western way of life they were quite happy to see their daughters constantly in the arms of their so-called intended, they thought it was a sign of being highly civilised, yeah, right, we all know that what those boyfriends were really after when they agreed to get engaged, a wolf knows perfectly well how to nail his prey, doesn't he, but I don't need to waste our time here lecturing you about wolves and their habits, I chose Voracious and I did it my own way, we weren't married and we didn't get engaged and we were happier than any engaged or married couple on earth, well, maybe that's going a bit too far, I can't really say there were no regrets later, that it didn't all end in tears, but we'll get to all that in good time I still don't know where this is all going to lead and I'm not sure I even care,

but going back to where we were, Voracious was well aware that if he'd dared to speak to me in All-Knowing's presence that would have been the end of their friendship, the old man would have chased him away from the house like a dog and bombarded him with filthy looks every day after that, so I did understand what Voracious was saying, especially when he suggested, his voice still full of reticence *"I don't know if this is going to get you into trouble, you only have to say the word, I mean I do know what your father's like,"* he obviously knew what a risk he was taking but that doesn't mean he was being as honest as you might think, if he was really worried about making trouble for me why had he come up to join me at all, it was a pretty canny thing to say to me, wasn't it, he wanted me to beg him to stay, I'm sorry but it's the kind of thing men do when they're trying to hit on a girl, all they have to do is act like they're looking out for her and she won't have any idea she's being sold a bill of goods, poor thing, seriously, but I didn't say a word, I stayed completely mum, Voracious buttoned his lip abruptly, as if he was thinking about what he'd just said and wanted to see if he'd made any progress in this game of words versus silence, his mask against my rock, he looked up and took in his surroundings and said *"it's nice up here,"* he's trying to find something else to talk about, I said to myself, although in fact I was thinking that he was absolutely right about our terrace, the sun was already starting to cast its first rays, the terrace was transforming before our eyes, the concrete floor was turning into a mattress of sweet-smelling flowers, the walls were becoming pillows of jasmine, the sun's rays were as dazzling as the gaze of the man standing beside me, and then coffee smells began to waft in on the morning breeze, the old ladies were brewing coffee for people to drink on their way back from the mosque after morning prayers, I could smell the madeleines baking in the ovens, just as they did every morning in Mutsamudu, I could hear the brooms swishing across floors, the plip-plop of water dripping from taps into basins, the clicking of knives and forks against plates as they were placed on tables, the happy shouts of children leaving for school, all the sounds of a typical morning in Mutsamudu, old people and children, the usual early-risers, but that morning it was all muted, Voracious's presence eclipsed everything else, when he aimed that piercing gaze at me and spoke to me there was nothing I could do, and what he finally said was *"hey, aren't you going to school,"* and I suddenly looked up, I'd kept my head lowered until that point, and said *"yes I am,"* and he muttered *"OK, well some other time,"* he was going to say something else but I cut him off and told him it wasn't time yet, I was lying of course, it was time for me to go, I had to go downstairs and get ready but I wanted to stay there for ever, even if I never managed to say what my heart was crying out to express, that's right, my lips were sealed but my heart was chattering nineteen to the dozen and to break the long silence weighing so heavily on my heart, I asked him if he wasn't going out to sea, and he replied that he'd go later, that it could wait, this was a perfect opportunity for him to spend a bit of time with me, what counted was the here and now *"the sea can wait till later, I'm on land now and when you're on land you have to follow your heart, that's what matters, but if I was out at sea, I'd be going where the boat takes me, that's for sure,"* is what he said to me, I wondered what he meant, what exactly he was expecting of me, what was it about this particular moment that was so important to him, what he was saying was crazy, and then all of a sudden he changed the subject, maybe he realised I was trying to work out what he meant, perhaps he was too, because the next thing he said was *"I saw you up here every day as I was coming back to shore, I didn't want to make you feel uncomfortable so I pretended I hadn't seen you,"* my heart started beating even more wildly, I was flabbergasted yet again, completely stupefied, how was it possible, just when I thought everyone on the beach was far too busy minding their own business to pay any attention to me, when I thought they were all actors just playing their own parts, only speaking when they were on stage, it turned out I was on stage too, I had a regular audience, unbeknownst to me, it had never occurred to me that Voracious might have noticed me when he was down on the beach, and then he said he'd been feeling antsy ever since I touched his hands the night before, he'd thought about coming back that same night, I couldn't take it seriously, surely it was all talk, a fine example of a silver tongue, how could he just walk into a house guarded by a lion twenty-four hours a day, huh, I ask you, had he forgotten about All-Knowing, who never actually slept as far as I could tell, he just lay there wide awake, listening to every movement, God knows what kind of creature I was living with, and then Voracious told me he'd been feeling something quite extraordinary since last night, something really powerful, he'd decided he couldn't go out to sea until he talked to me, he absolutely had to tell me before he set out, he was prepared not to go out that day so he could spend more time talking to me about everything, yeah right, give me a break, was he really going to sacrifice a day's work for the sake of a girl, was a girl going to give him the catch he went in search of every day, and what about that mask of his, sooner or later that mask was going to come off and scare the life out of that girl, wasn't it, so no, it was all poppycock, a man can always come up with some malarkey or other to spout when he's trying to lure a girl into his lair, but malarkey or not, the fact is I'd fallen for that man and I let him know he'd made himself clear, that I understood what he'd been saying to me all this time, that he didn't need to go into detail "*so what are we saying here, what's the answer I get to all this*" he asked me, gazing languidly at me, and then he added "*a conversation isn't over until you've had a response to all the things you've said,*" I wondered what else he expected me to say to him, me, in a state of complete discombobulation, unable to utter a word, when suddenly he asked me "*do you come up here every day,*" and I said no and he went on "*so this morning you needed to chill out apparently, to get some air, I mean,*" I still said no, he was surprised by my answers, as if he didn't believe me and he thought for a moment before concluding with "*ah, I see, well this time, you can't say no, unless you want to shut me up for good, you came up here to watch me leave, right,"* I hesitated for a moment and then I couldn't help laughing, I wanted to really laugh out loud but I was afraid the neighbours would hear me, I needed to be careful, I couldn't stop myself though, I roared with laughter, I don't know what came over me, I felt completely at ease, Voracious was laughing too and he kept asking me *"so, go on then, I'm right, aren't I,"* I couldn't stop laughing and then I said that yes, he was right, he'd guessed what it was I wanted that morning, I asked him how he knew and he told me that he wasn't really sure about what he'd said himself, he'd been meaning to say he assumed I'd gone up to watch the boats heading out but it'd come out wrong, he didn't really mean to imply that it was him I wanted to see, he was just kidding, well, it may have been a joke for him but that wasn't how I read it, and then he came out with *"just as well I said it though, I wasn't expecting you to be interested in seeing me too, I'm deeply touched to hear it,"* he stopped short and then he was looking at me as if he was trying to read my mind, his eyes darting this way and that, and then he asked me *"are you sure you meant what you said just now,"* I said yes, I did, I told him I'd been feeling a bit restless too, I'd come up to the terrace to catch a glimpse of him on the beach, he was right, I'd been watching him admiringly every day on the shore, I wasn't expecting to hear the feeling was mutual, especially with him standing there, right next to me, killing me with that look, I admitted I'd been walking on air when I saw him the evening before, that by the time he left, I was going nuts, and then, as I was talking, Voracious reached out and touched me, he patted me gently and gazed at me, giving me affectionate little strokes without taking his eyes off me, until I couldn't go on speaking, I closed my eyes to make it easier to talk but it didn't help, my heart was pounding, I was trembling from head to toe, I tried closing my eyes again to let my heart do the talking, for as I've said before, when the body is silenced the heart will always speak out, especially if it's just starting to find its voice, I let Voracious run his hands over mine and all the way up my arms, gentle strokes that gradually became caresses, his hands hovered all over my body like butterflies on a rose, Voracious was coming closer and closer to me, his hands were working their way up to my face, I felt his touch on my temples, I tried to resist, hoping to break free, and just as my spirit was about to take off and soar towards another planet I heard a voice of doom calling me from below, I flinched and Voracious quickly pulled his hand away and we both listened, staring wordlessly at each other, I was drained of all energy, worn out by the ardent cravings of my heart but I managed to identify the voice calling my name, it was Rattler, she'd woken up and yelled out to me, wondering why she hadn't been woken by me as I left for school no doubt, she must have been surprised, especially since she could see my things were still in our room, she'd guess that I was up on the terrace, my obsession with people-watching was no secret, so I pulled myself together quick as a flash and gestured to Voracious to keep still, Rattler mustn't see him, I grabbed the washing off the line to make it look like I'd gone up to the terrace to bring it in and ran helter-skelter down the stairs, and there was Rattler in the courtyard, standing there with her hand on her head, an absent look about her, she looked as if she'd fallen into a reverie after she'd finished yelling and when she saw me come down the stairs she was thrown off balance again *"oh, so that's where you were,"* she exclaimed, I told her I'd been looking out to sea, well why not, Voracious was an ocean too, wasn't he, I didn't want her interrogating me, I hated being treated like I'd been taken in for questioning, I pretended I'd lost track of time and she turned round and went back into the bedroom without saying a word while I started to make my way up the stairs to help Voracious get away, I signalled to him to come and join me on the stairs and he crept stealthily down behind me, the door creaked loudly and then slammed shut, that damn door had a mind of its own, it was determined to get me caught red-handed, but I managed to come up with a way out, I remembered the peddlers who went from door to door selling bundles of sticks, they'd often come knocking at the door, bothering you when you were trying to sleep, people would get really angry and jump out of bed full of fire and brimstone ready to give the wretched vendors a piece of their mind, so when the door slammed that day, I managed to trick Rattler into believing it was someone selling bundles of sticks, I'd just thought of it when Voracious sneaked a crisp kiss on the back of my neck and left, laughing at the performance I was putting on, yes, I was actually shouting *"no thank you, we don't need any sticks,"* and since Rattler was in the bedroom she didn't suspect a thing, by this time I was definitely running late for school so I quickly gathered up my things to try and make it to the second lesson, which had probably already started, I hurried through my routine of getting washed and dressed in under fifteen minutes and left Rattler taking her time, as she always did, before even starting on her toilette, it never failed to surprise me how slowly she got moving, imagine spending an hour stretching and yawning as if you have nothing at all do, it's worse than laziness, it's more like some kind of disease,

in class I just sat there dreaming, yes, my mind went wandering off all over the place, until my head started to spin, I couldn't stop dreaming, dreaming, dreaming, I couldn't get that stolen kiss out of my mind, the teacher, my classmates, the board, the desks, none of them were real, they were figments of my imagination, a cartoon show playing out in front of my eyes, I laughed to myself and then all of a sudden the teacher was transformed into Voracious, and the other students too, all of them, even the wimpy boys, there was a chubby Voracious, a scrawny Voracious, a potbellied Voracious, a haggard Voracious, a Voracious with big feet, a pipsqueak, a weedy specimen, so many of them, the lessons on the board were declarations of love, winding around all over the walls, like eels out of water, the classroom became a magnificent beach, the desks were cliff-tops for our delectable trysts,

that afternoon I came home to an empty house, as usual neither All-Knowing nor Rattler were there, I rushed up to the terrace, desperate to catch a glimpse of Voracious, it was like a drug, at one point all the fishermen on the shore merged into Voracious, he was everywhere, every time I heard a motor rumbling in the distance I went back upstairs to watch the boats coming in and in the end I saw him, out on the waves, it was already getting dark but I recognised him and he saw me too, he raised his head from time to time to make it clear he could see me, I signalled to him to come up, God, the sheer nerve of it, what if someone were to see and tell All-Knowing *"what's the matter with you Eel, what's got into you,"* I said to myself but things had changed, I'd had enough of being a puppet on a string, we all have our own part to play in this world, you have to be your own person and not just repeat the twaddle you hear from others, you have to improvise, not so you can make a name for yourself and go down in the annals of history but to make it clear it's not as easy as just walking on stage feet first, you have to make an entry, head first or arse first, I'm no star but nor am I a robot and I won't be conned into following the crowd, oh God, I'm rambling again aren't I, and I've still got a long way to go, shit, what is it with me, why does everything have to be such a production, maybe it's just the way things are when an eel's in her death throes, making the biggest splash of her life before she leaves the stage and there's no one here to tell me what's what, oh well, you'd have understood it much better if you'd been there at the time, putting your mind to the question, all you fishermen who pride your-selves on your wit, I'll have to answer my own questions because there doesn't seem to be anyone else around, not that anyone would have anything to say anyway, except for the fools who think they know it all, oh why can't I just go straight to the point, damn it, instead of getting sidetracked all the time, time's running out, Eel, you nincompoop, so get on with it,

okay so I'd spotted Voracious and signalled to him, and he'd understood that I wanted him to come over, he reached the shore and left the catch with his mates, which was what he usually did, he was like the boss in a way, he never sold his own fish, I went downstairs to the door to meet him and we stood there talking for quite a while, right by the door, where I could see if anyone was coming, I didn't want another encounter like this morning's with my sister, I said to myself that he shouldn't stay too long, I knew when to expect Rattler, although she was pretty late sometimes, she never came straight home from school, Voracious asked me if he could come the next morning and join me up on the terrace before I left for school and of course I said yes, how could I resist, I needed to see him too, he seemed really pleased and he kissed me on the mouth, a long slow, tender kiss that gradually became more insistent, I could feel his tongue wiggling around in my mouth as if it was looking for something, my tongue probably, I didn't know what I was supposed to do, what did I know about kissing on the lips and wagging tongues, all I can say is that with that kiss I learned a simple truth, that a tongue wriggling around with another tongue is happier than any eel under the sea, I inhaled the smell of the ocean and relished every moment of that kiss, and then we smiled at each other a few times and off he went,

at dawn the next day, after All-Knowing left, I washed and dressed as quickly as I could, gathered up my school things and went in to wake Rattler and tell her I was leaving, she was lying flat out in bed like a sack of potatoes and opened her eyelids for just long enough to see that I was ready to leave, I

called out goodbye and then headed noiselessly up the stairs
to my spot to see if Voracious had arrived and there he was,
outside, waiting for me, I called down to him and went back
down to open the door, I held it open for a few moments
and then let it creak and make the same noise it did every
day when I closed it behind me, and all without stepping
outside the courtyard, I told myself Rattler would think I'd
left and she had the house to herself, and now Voracious and
I were alone together on the terrace, with silence reigning
around us, there was no turning back now, it was a beautiful
morning, blissful and unforgettable, although the sun was
almost too much at one point, intruding on our moments
of ecstasy and frazzling our skin with its celestial rays, but
our kisses cooled and soothed our overheated bodies like
fresh water quenching a thirst, with no obstacles in our
path we gave full rein to our feelings and when Rattler left
for school Voracious and I went downstairs together into
the bedroom, and that's how it went on for more than a
week, we'd go into the bedroom after Rattler left for school,
and what did we do there, well, we did all kinds of things,
what do you expect, we did all the foolish things a man and
a young woman get up to when they shut themselves up
in a room alone together for more than three hours at a
stretch, what else are they going to do but talk, touch each
other, caress and pet and kiss and set out eventually on a
long journey that will leave them battered and bruised, yes,
that's the right word for it, bruised, because at the end of the
journey you suddenly find yourself out of breath, weary as
a marathon runner arriving unexpectedly at the finish line
with no idea how you got there, and sometimes the journey

is disappointing, don't ask me to go into detail, if you haven't found these things out for yourself there's not much I can do, I'm not here to give life lessons to people who can't keep up and besides, I don't have the time,

I even stopped going to school, we'd spend our time staring longingly at each other and smiling, we'd kiss with wild abandon, long kisses, we didn't speak, we had no need of words, our bodies did the talking, discovering new delights every day, we'd lie there, pressed close together and Voracious would let his fingers wander slowly and lightly over every inch of my body, he'd start with my arms, then my face, my eyelids, my temples, the swell of my backside, he'd gaze at me sweetly and nibble on my shoulders, the back of my neck, I could feel the prickle of his stubble as he pecked at me as if I was a bunch of grapes, I felt like one of those paintings by Arcimboldo, I wondered sometimes if Voracious looked at me and saw a bunch of fruit, and what I found really strange was when we were making love and Voracious would lick me all over, like a cat lapping up milk from a saucer, it seemed really silly to me when I thought about it afterwards, a funny way to make love, where had he learned all this, all these peculiar moves, they were like some kind of drug, if this was what love was it was even worse than a drug, you get intoxicated to the point of ecstasy and then you'll do anything, you don't know what you're doing, I'd feel a glow of warmth and tenderness spreading from my belly up to my brain whenever Voracious stroked me with his nose, I did nothing to him at first, I lay there writhing and moaning like a patient in the hands of her doctor, and

110

I wondered why you had to moan like that when you're on this journey, did the cats I'd seen doing it on the terrace feel the same sensations, but whatever, we weren't purring like cats, we opened our mouths to moan, as if we'd swallowed a mouthful of pepper, yes, love is a kind of pepper too with a different sort of sting but it has the same effect as hot peppers, that first day when I felt that strange sensation my heart was pounding wildly, I wanted to go on but something didn't seem right and when I realised I was taking wings and starting to fly, I was seized with fear, like an actress attacked by stage fright as she was about to go on, I tried to empty my mind and think of nothing, I didn't want to let Voracious down, I didn't want him to see me as a stupid little twit who knew nothing about sex, I was ready to do everything and learn all there was to learn, so I let myself be carried along, with no holds barred, like a soldier stripped of his weapons, ready to obey orders, and from that day onwards, I lost all interest in school, Voracious wouldn't go out to sea until the afternoon and we'd spend all morning dozing, eyes half-closed, kissing and fondling after our moments of ecstasy, and so the days went by until one day Voracious suggested I come to his place in the morning before going to school, it was too risky to spend every day in my room he said *"it'll be safer for you at my place,"* I mulled over his suggestion for a long time, going into a man's bedroom wasn't something I could do lightly, people might see me and tell All-Knowing as soon as they had a chance, sitting under the badamier tree, for example, revealing their secrets to each other, those two-faced blabbermouths, they'd start by saying sarcastically *"ah, she's already learned how to conjugate all her verbs, that one, all of them, even the irregular ones,"* walls have ears in Mutsamudu, there were spies everywhere, it didn't take much, a fly only had to flap its wings and someone would make a story out of it *"once it's out of the bag, you can smell it everywhere, right up to the tops of the mountains,"* as All-Knowing used to say, he warned us to be wary of the people of this town, a person's private business could go from mouth to mouth and end up broadcast for all to hear in every public place, like the squares of Mroni, Uvoimoja and Jaf, the crossroads of Foukoujou, under the badamier tree, in Mpangahari, Minadzijou and on and on until there was not a single person who didn't know that Monsieur So-and-So or Mademoiselle Such-and-Such had farted in this place, on that day, at this time, that's right, after all that whispering in all those places the whole town would be awash with the news, people would go out of their way to belittle others and poke fun at them, most of the jokes were at the expense of men whose wives had kicked them out, people would make up names for them, point at them whenever they caught sight of them, their affairs would be the hot topic, on everyone's lips, I can't stand people who poke their noses into things that have nothing to do with them, life is what it is, we're all in the same boat, it's up to us to tread softly and not kick up a storm, leave the birds to twitter and let sleeping dogs lie, people who have nothing better to do than bang on about other people's affairs know nothing about life, I've got no time for them, they're sick in the head,

so I did wonder if I'd be creating a stir by going to Voracious's house, but at least in my family no one knew what was going on, our home was an eel pond with no ripples, I was protected by the fact that we didn't have any regular visitors, except for Tranquil and she only came very rarely, once a month and always at weekends, when we weren't at school, it was only Rattler and me she seemed to be interested in, but be that as it may, when it came to agreeing to Voracious's request, I didn't really have any choice, I was madly in love with him, I was even ready to give up going to school for good if it meant I could spend more time enjoying myself with him and in the end that's what I did, I stopped going to school, just like that, I was besotted with him, he'd come round in the morning and not go out fishing until later in the afternoon and after he'd left I'd get stuck into working around the house as if there was nothing unusual going on, and when my father All-Knowing came home I'd be in the kitchen, cooking, he'd start in on his interminable harangues and I'd laugh, same as I always did and then Rattler would come home, late as usual, and so the days rolled smoothly by with magical nights spent dreaming only of Voracious, until the day came when I decided to accept Voracious's offer and told him I'd come to his place, he was over the moon when I said that, that's right, he acted like he'd heard he'd passed his exams with flying colours, he kissed me over and over again and the next morning I was in his house, I expect you're wondering how I managed to pull off such a feat, well, slipping from one stone to another is a piece of cake for an eel, all you have to do is slither along discreetly making as few bubbles as possible and slide silently underneath the stone, I carried on with my morning routine as if nothing had changed, taking my time and calmly getting on

with all my chores, I made All-Knowing's coffee and he got
ready and went off to work, then I washed and dressed and
left the house, covered from head to foot in my *shiromani,*
the two-coloured cloth with its six patterned squares that
women wear here, they were the cause of many a marital
squabble in Mutsamudu, husbands and wives would be at
loggerheads the moment a new consignment of *shiromanis*
appeared in Mamadaly's or La Chance or any of the other
larger shops and even if a husband promised his wife he'd
buy her a *shiromani* as soon as he was paid, the wife would
still sulk and make a fuss and he'd have to put an end to
the crisis with a trip to La Chance, where there'd be usually
be a scrum of women pushing and shoving like little girls
squabbling over the same doll in the supermarket, you had
to be ready to fight for your purchases, everyone would be
in a lather, sweat running down their faces, and when they
succeeded in buying the coveted cloth the women looked
as happy as if they'd just won the World Cup, while their
husbands strutted around in front of their mates, the envy
of all the wives, but that's a whole other story,

so, getting back to my assignation chez Voracious, I was
wearing a black and white *shiromani* when I went out that
day, I set off through the medina down a long street which
led to a series of several alleys, it was a world of its own,
the medina, it was a rock where anything could happen and
the medina would give nothing away, people didn't realise
this, but I'd understood it the day when I looked down on it
from the citadel and realised that although you could look
down on the medina's hidden alleyways from there and gaze

into its secret heart, you could only guess at what went on in its depths, and that day I didn't want to run into any students going to school or any old men on their morning walk around the medina after their morning prayers, so I followed the route Voracious had worked out for me that took me through alleys I'd always avoided before, I'd just walked past a small wooden door next to a large house when I heard a voice behind me whisper my name three times, I turned round with a start and saw Voracious, gesturing to me to meet him outside that tiny little door, the alley was strangely quiet but I double-checked all the same to make sure no one had seen me, and then I turned round and plunged through the door straight into Voracious's bedroom, he closed the door and as he double locked it the sound of the lock clicking into place resonated in answer to the questions hammered out by my heart, I tried to pull myself together but my heart wouldn't stop thudding in my ears, I stood there gawping at my surroundings like a prisoner eyeing her cell for the first time, my heart pounding so hard I thought it was going to smash through my chest, I gazed around at this cell that bore the mark of Voracious, scanning the walls, with their ancient paint peeling off here and there, and the high, beamed ceiling, and then I looked at the contents of the room, an old linen cupboard, a cotton mattress on top of threadbare rush matting, a rickety chair with legs of different lengths that wobbled constantly, an antiquated table in need of attention with an old-fashioned radio cassette-player sitting on it, and with the exception of a scrap of bread from Badrane's, the island's best bakery, and a bottle of orange juice on that excuse for a table, everything in that dilapidated dump looked to me like a left-over from before the flood, and there wasn't much light to speak of in there either, Voracious offered me a seat and I collapsed onto the chair like a felled tree, I felt tired all of a sudden, out of sorts, I was doing my best to pull myself together so as not to upset Voracious, and then I was hit by the smell, a strong penetrating odour, there wasn't a single window in that room, no way to get a gulp of fresh air, I couldn't breathe for the smell, Voracious took two glasses out of the cupboard, put them on the table and poured juice into one of them, as usual he didn't have much to say, he seemed weary too, his eyes were red, maybe because he hadn't slept, or perhaps he'd been drinking, what with that overpowering smell, I hadn't realised Voracious was a drinker, so I asked him what was the matter, and he said he was a bit tired, he was worried about Voilà, his best friend, Voilà was his right-hand man, or at least that was what I thought at the time, it was Voilà who usually helped Voracious sell his fish, everyone knew him as a legendary drinker, he'd wander through the streets of the medina babbling incoherently and putting on quite a show, it was really very funny, every time he opened his mouth he'd come out with "*voilà, there you go,*" as if that was the end of it, and then he'd carry on, although most of the time he was simply repeating himself, I remember one day I was on my way home after school and I came upon a crowd of people in the middle of the street at the crossroads at Foukoujou, which wasn't particularly unusual, but I couldn't get round them so I drew closer to see what was going on, they all seemed to be fascinated and I wondered what this irresistible scene could be,

I stuck my head into the ring and all I saw was an oldish man sitting on the ground with his legs wide open, like a kid waiting for his mum to give him his bowl of soup, he was a puny little thing, with a bony face, in fact he looked more like a skeleton, a walking human skeleton, you could count every one of his hundred and ninety-eight bones, you think I'm exaggerating but I'm telling you there are people like that, God's honest truth and in fact it was Voilà, lips puckered, yelling at the top of his quavery old voice, babbling absolute drivel and shouting *"voilà"* all the time in his raspy voice, I peered intently at the whole scene, trying to work out why all those people were crowded around this old lush, he was farting the whole time too, which really bothered me, God knows what he thought he was doing, he couldn't get up off the ground and people were having a good laugh at his expense, they were betting him he wouldn't be able to get up without pushing himself up with his hands, and the old blabbermouth sat there on the ground blathering on, thinking he was some kind of Hercules, until he eventually made a pathetic attempt to get up, bending his legs first like an invalid to get himself into position with his hands on his legs, and every time he tried to pull himself up, he'd let out the most extraordinary farts, one after another and the crowd would roar with laughter, but Voilà took no notice of them and kept trying again and again, and every time he managed to barely lift his stinking backside he'd start yelling *"voilà"* and immediately collapse onto the ground like a rotten papaya, I realised all of a sudden that my nose and eyebrows were twitching, I could hardly breathe, well, I don't need to spell it out for you, I mean, when you fart, what is it you're letting out, eh, we're not talking about essence of ylang-ylang flowers from Tranquil's field in Hombo here, let's face it, a fart is a fart, as we all know, and although some people are bold enough to make free with their farts, most of us realise there's an art to it, you have to make sure you squeeze your buttocks at least seven times before letting the slightest smell escape, like you do when you're talking, otherwise you could do yourself an injury, or do damage to other people who are just minding their own business, it's a gas we're talking about, let's be honest, and the gas that comes out of a person's backside is always going to be full of germs even if it comes out of an angel's bum, and even without the smell, it's still bacteria you're letting out, and as for Voilà, when it came to his farts, oh yuck, it smelt worse than a dead rat, God help me, I'm telling you, all the time that old wino was trying to go for broke a vile stench was emanating from his backside, engulfing the crowd like a cloud of teargas, but the surprising thing was that even with those farts stinking up the whole area, there were only a few people holding their noses and spitting on the ground, the rest of the crowd seemed utterly unfazed, in fact they were encouraging Voilà, egging him on, I'm telling you, they were crying with laughter, you'd think they didn't have noses to inhale that ghastly odour, which really did reek to high heaven, what on earth did Voilà eat, poisoned fish-gills, rotten innards or what, Christ, he nearly poisoned me that day, I didn't want to be suffocated so I made sure I got out of there pretty quick, those people always had to find some clown to laugh at there, that was how they got their kicks,

so where was I, oh yes, we were talking about that old wino,
Voilà, that's right, Voracious's right-hand man, and that first
day in his bedroom, Voracious was telling me something
about him but before he carried on with his story, he stood
up again and took a packet of Gauloises out of the cupboard
and asked me if he could smoke while he told me what had
happened between Voilà and his wife, I couldn't really say no,
I wanted to hear what had happened with Voilà and I was
in Voracious's house after all, it was up to me to accept him
as he was and get used to doing things his way, it seemed
fair enough, so he lit his cigarette and started talking, telling
me first how Voilà had been kicked out of his house by his
wife the night before, in the middle of the night, it turned
out he'd been getting too aggressive with his wife, he'd been
completely out of order for a while and his wife was fed up
with being beaten and threatened all the time, Voilà may
have had his reasons, fine, that's his business but whatever it
was it was no cause to beat up the mother of his children, I
mean, come on, you morons, who do you think you are, aren't
you ashamed of yourselves, sullying the rose and stripping
it of the very perfume that drew you to it in the first place,
talk about being ungrateful, shame on you, destroying the
essence of life, for when you abuse one woman you endanger
all of us, a woman's not a drum you can beat any time you
feel like it, women are life itself and when you're tired of
life, what do you do, you simply walk away from it, however
much it hurts you, when the time comes you have to walk
away from it, you don't try and destroy it, unless you want to
drag everyone else down with you,

Voracious was saying that Voilà suspected his wife of cheating on him with various tradesmen, he'd been confiding in Voracious every day and telling him all his troubles, he said his wife had changed, that she went out all the time and came back looking flushed, she'd taken to wearing so much make-up she looked more like a doll than a woman, he said Madame Voilà went to great lengths to primp and beautify herself, she was always dressed to the nines, and on top of all this, she ignored her husband, it had driven him to drink, so he'd have a few every evening while she was out, and then when she came home they'd argue, and eventually he'd call her a strumpet and start hitting her, he was a jealous creature that old wino, his jealousy made him aggressive and when his wife started screaming, the children would wake up and join in, squealing like kittens, there were seven children in that family, the eldest was barely fifteen years old and he'd already started hitting the bottle and he could hold his drink a whole lot better than his father, he'd left home and gone into business, wheeling and dealing, although always with the greatest of scruples, he dealt in cigarettes and hung around with a group of local drug dealers, you'd see him at the port of Mutsamudu, poor kid, with all the alcoholics, old and young alike, propping each other up as if they were all the same age, and there were two more of Voilà's children who didn't live at home, one was a petty thief who stayed away from the medina and spent his time pilfering bananas and breadfruit in broad daylight from the cemeteries at the madrasas or from the fields around Bandrankowa, the other was a little thug who was quick to lash out with his fists, he saw himself as some kind of superman when it came to fistfights and he'd even mix it up with adults, he'd start fights with the kids playing in the streets of the medina, blocking their way and taunting them until they fought back, the two daughters were the only ones in the family to go to the primary school in Missiri, whenever they yelled in protest at their father beating their mother, Voilà would direct his brutal threats at them too and then the babies would wake up and start crying and Voilà would issue warnings to all of them, little girls and babies alike, if they opened their mouths one more time they'd get a beating too, he'd say, and not with the belt but with his bare hands *"you shut your mouths, all of you, or you'll get what's coming to you, you're a pain in the arse, the lot of you,"* the poor little things had no choice but to keep quiet and they'd bury their faces in the mattress to muffle their cries, eventually Madame Voilà realised what her husband was like when he'd been drinking and came up with a plan to put a stop to the constant threats and beatings, her husband usually drank at his friends' houses, Voracious's for example but he kept a private stash for drinking at home by himself, so when she found a small bottle with white wine in it one day, she flushed the wine down the toilet and filled the bottle with baby piss, from the youngest one that was only a few months old, she filled the bottle right up, forgetting that it hadn't been full before and then she put it back where she found it and went out as usual, and when Voilà came back from Voracious's place he was already three sheets to the wind, staggering around, as he did on so many other nights, like a man on his last legs, you'd see him slamming into walls around the medina, falling on the ground and crawling along like a reptile with spit drooling out of both sides of his mouth all the way down his front, people would laugh and children would throw rocks at him, he'd curse them and continue on his pathetic way, farting freely as if he had no control at all of his back passage, people would ask him if perhaps he'd had something rammed up his arse, some said that was how he liked it when he'd been drinking but he'd say nothing, he just went stumbling on, and that night when he got home in that abject condition, what did he do but go straight to his stash to get his bottle of wine, he started glugging the contents, thinking it tasted rather bland at first and then it struck him that the taste wasn't what he was expecting, he tried another mouthful to see if his taste buds were tricking him and it still didn't taste like wine, so he took the bottle over to see Voracious, intending to dispel his doubts and get confirmation that it wasn't wine in the bottle but something else, Voracious had been drinking too but the smell hit him the minute he opened the bottle, he announced straight away that it was urine, a baby's probably, as it was so clear, well Voilà had already swallowed half the bottle, he felt deeply ashamed and humiliated and started mouthing off about his wife, saying she was nothing but a whore *"she'll soon see what she's got coming to her, that tart, staying out till all hours of the night,"* he shouted, and with that he went home, still staggering and crawling through the narrow streets and when he got there he found his wife in their bedroom, getting undressed, so he started hurling insults at her, he called her a degenerate, grabbed her nightdress from her and tried to lay hands on her but his wife, who was dressed in nothing but her lacy bra and panties, backed away from him and he edged closer to her and said *"so you put the baby's piss in my wine bottle, you filthy bitch, get your arse over here,"* his wife said nothing and carried on stepping backwards while Voilà, still clutching the nightdress, fell over a few times, and as he struggled to get back on his feet, he kept on yelling furiously *"voilà,"* while his terrified wife said nothing and then he started goading her, brandishing her nightdress, babbling incoherently and edging closer to her *"look at this, that's what you want, isn't it, you want to go around dressed like a white woman, God knows where you get the money to buy this shit, and on top of that you change your shiromani like underwear every day, if you call that thing you're wearing underwear, what is that supposed to be anyway, that G-string thing, it looks more like a fishing line than anything else, I can see there's a good catch in there, why not hang a neon sign too, fish here, you're ready for any pecker that comes your way, aren't you, well, what do you have to say for yourself, a nice snug fit, that's what you want, isn't it, always ready to go out and spread it around, that's right, what is all this shit, say something you filthy bitch, or I'll finish you off right now,"* and while he was still in full flow, his wife suddenly kneed him between the legs, he dropped the nightdress, let out a sharp cry, grabbed his crotch and stood there, doubled over in agony, moaning and groaning, clutching his privates and screaming pathetically at the top of his voice *"Christ, she's ruined her favourite toy, her magic wand, what is it, seen too many bigger ones, is that it,"* and when he realised his wife wasn't going to pay any attention to him, he moaned pitifully *"she's a murderer, I knew it, help, I'm dying,"* his wife picked up her nightdress, put it on and left the room, and when she came back a few minutes later she was holding a big fat stick for crushing manioc leaves, she looked at her husband trying to crawl towards the door for a few moments and gave him a great thwack on the head, a knock-out blow that floored him completely, well, he didn't remember anything that happened after that blow, he passed out and when he came round, he found himself at Voracious's place wondering what had happened and Voracious told him his son had loaded him onto a trolley from the docks and brought him there, the kid who went around beating up all the others and fancied himself the strong guy of the neighbourhood, Voilà was completely unhinged when he heard this, swearing like trooper and whingeing through clenched teeth *"in a loading trolley, that goddamn kid, I'll kill him if I find him,"* he had an enormous bump on the forehead from the blow from the pounding stick but he couldn't feel a thing, he only knew it was there because Voracious told him about it, he carried on hurling abuse and then announced *"they were in it together, her and the boy, sly bitch, I'll show them, I'm off home right now,"* Voracious did his best to persuade him to stay and wait until the next day, it was getting late he said and he'd be feeling better in the morning but the fool wouldn't listen to him and set off home to find his wife, but when he got there the door was bolted and all his clothes lay scattered on the ground outside, Voilà growled furiously and banged on the door, demanding the rest of his stuff *"you carry on snaring men with that thing between your legs if that's what you want but I want my table back and my cassette player and while you're at it you can give me back my plates and my forks too, and my glasses and spoons, it was me that bought them from Madjikha's, not you, shameless hussy,*

124

why don't you tell your fancy men to go and buy you some new ones, we'll soon see who the real men are," he went on like this for over an hour with no response and in the end he had no choice but to pick up his clothes and go back to Voracious's, where he spent the whole night blabbering and heaping scorn on his wife, Voracious told him to forget her and not go back there at all, but Voilà kept on all night and neither of them slept a wink and Voracious finally told him that he had an important meeting that morning before work, so Voilà left at daybreak and went back to his wife, which really surprised Voracious, it took some courage, he said, to go back to a house you'd been chased out of like a dog, but Voilà wasn't about to roll over and accept defeat, his wife's message had fallen on deaf ears,

anyway, all this had completely passed me by, even though it happened right under my nose, I was too busy watching what was going on at the beach or on my route to school to pay attention to life in the medina, I saw that part of town as a rock, pierced by a series of corridors where anything could happen in absolute secrecy, at its summit was the citadel and that was where you had to go if you wanted to understand anything about the medina, when you looked down on all the rooftops beneath you, everything became clear, it all made sense, but the foreigners who came to visit the town approached the medina with caution, they feared getting lost in its depths and it did often happen that tourists went astray in the medina, Europeans like to think of themselves as real daredevils, don't they, those white people love to stick their necks out and some intrepid couples would chance it and go wandering about in the medina without a guide, you'd see these ladies and young girls with their companions, all dressed in shirts and baseball caps, drooling over the old doors in the heart of the medina, there were doors of all kinds, Indian, eastern, western and the Arabo-Islamic doors and ornamental windows in Ujumbe Palace, which according to All-Knowing was built in Hamoumbou in 1541 by Sultan Idarousse, the one considered by certain founts of wisdom, otherwise known as historians, to be the first Islamic Arab ruler of the Comoros, I don't usually believe a word those historians say, as I think I've already told you, it's all a bunch of lies, they think they know everything but they don't realise they're only seeing things from their own perspective, like a camera lens, it only captures the scenes it focuses on, oh shit, where am I going with this,

so the tourists would be squinting peculiarly at the doors and windows, taking pictures, touching them sometimes, caressing them as if they were hopelessly in love with them, they'd buy vanilla, nutmeg and ylang-ylang from street sellers, some of them would get so carried away strolling about the medina they'd forget all about getting back to their ship until the sound of the ship's siren brought them back to reality, it was impossible not to hear the racket from those cruise ships bellowing out all over town, the medina itself would tremble and the tardy tourists would be taken by surprise by the sound of the hooter and start running around all over the place trying to find a way out, it was hilarious, sometimes children would offer to guide them and everyone would guffaw but in the end they always managed to get back to their cruise ship in time, only very rarely did the ship's crew start to cast off or actually leave the port and then our harbour master had to make them turn round and come back to pick up the stragglers,

so let's come back to my lover's bedroom with Voracious telling me the story of Voilà, by this time he'd already smoked almost the whole pack of Gauloises, the room was full of smoke and I was having coughing fits, I'd put up a real fight against smoking in the beginning, it made my eyes sting, my eyelids would flutter all the time and my eyes would start watering but in the end, I came to like the smoke too, I liked the smell of it and I imagined myself smoking, I really wanted to try it and see if I could get used to it and in the end I blurted out the question that was on the tip of my tongue *"can you pass me a cigarette,"* Voracious gave me a quizzical look and held up the packet, peering at me as much as to say he couldn't believe what he was hearing, I knew he didn't believe me, he thought I was just trying to be funny but eventually he opened the packet and when I reached out to take it he held my hand and told me to take off my *shiromani* first and sit down beside him, I did as he said and he lit the cigarette for me, I started spluttering as soon as I took a drag, I didn't know how to smoke properly then, I'd snatch at it and do nothing but cough and I certainly wasn't ready to blow smoke out of my nose, I loved watching Voracious do that when he smoked, I couldn't get enough of it, but every time I tried to do it myself I'd start coughing, he told me to watch carefully and see the way he breathed in the smoke through his mouth and let it out through his nose, you had to take your time inhaling, so I did as he said, I copied what he did and in the end I was smoking just like him, I wanted to smoke and smoke and never stop, I made myself dizzy with smoking, the craving was insatiable, and that day in his room I was puffing away and drinking my juice, Voracious had laced his drink with white wine from a bottle he'd taken out of the wardrobe, he said he had to hide it from Voilà, who was a total lush and would drink everything in sight, I asked Voracious what the taste of alcohol was like and he said it depended who you were, it was different for everyone *"I don't know how to describe what it tastes like, I can only tell you what it does to me, when I drink I can be myself, I can talk openly, I can say what I really think without beating about the bush,"* those were his very words, he could say what he really thought, and yet he never told me what he really thought of me, but at that moment I wanted to know what was going on in his head, so I asked him and he immediately replied *"you,"* and then I asked him to let me have a sip to see if it had the same effect on me, if it made me think about nothing but him, I was curious to see if he was exaggerating, well, all it took was one sniff and I was tipsy, it went straight to my head, so I drank and drank and Voracious started kissing me lovingly, I kissed him back passionately, holding his head between my hands to make the most of my kisses, just like I used to hold the green coconuts Tranquil would bring us, I'd suck out the cool, sweet liquid and swill it around my mouth, but smooth and sweet as that juice was, it was nothing compared to the lethal nectar of those kisses, they were paradise on earth, I ran my fingers, scissor-like, through his hair, I explored his

ears, and so it went on, I'd come to know his weak spots
during those early days at my house, I'd seek them out and
he'd go all quiet and then he'd let loose and go crazy, especially when I ran my fingers over his rock hard, muscular
chest, I'd start by feasting on his nipples, caressing them all
the way to the tips, and when I'd done everything I needed
to do I'd push him back until he was lying down and then
I'd go for the inside of his elbows and the backs of his knees
and he'd grab me frantically and pull my clothes off and I'd
try and escape, slithering out of his grasp with lightning
speed until I grew tired and he'd get the better of me, holding
me down as if I was a wild cat, and that first morning at his
house we slept for a long time, he snored atrociously, like the
motor boats I heard every day at home, I thought my head
was going to burst, I'm telling you it sounded exactly like
one of those boats, as soon as I started to fall asleep there'd
be a loud, rhythmic exhalation that made me jump out of
my skin every time, I don't know why he snored so horribly
like that, was it the wine or was he worn out from work,
those were the only moments I didn't enjoy being with him,
I was used to sleeping in the peace and quiet of my own
home, but it was up to me to adapt, I loved him and I had to
get used to his snoring, I'd have to join in and snore with
him and add my own notes to that discordant racket, so I let
Voracious sleep in peace, what else could I do, and of course
I said nothing about it to him, I couldn't, I wanted him too
much, when it comes to matters of the heart there's no room
for wavering, you have to give your heart what it craves,
trying to thwart your own deepest desires is nothing but a
waste of time and energy, so while Voracious was snoring

loudly that day, I heard someone banging at the door, yelling his name over and over again, I woke Voracious and as soon as he heard the shouting he said it was Voilà, he'd told him not to disturb him that morning, but Voilà, being the pain in the neck he was, couldn't stay away, there was no chance of having a few hours' peace and quiet with that voice piping up every so often, spouting some tom-fool nonsense, so we lay there in silence, cuddled up together completely naked for another half-hour until Voracious said he had to go out to sea and told me to go home, we threw on our clothes and he opened the door and took a look outside before ushering me out, I walked as quickly as I could through the narrow alleys of the medina, people were out and about but they all seemed preoccupied with their own business and when I got back to my lair the house was empty, there wasn't a fly about, as we say around here, evening was the only time the whole family was there as a rule, after work or school, but it was too late for me to go to school that day, I'd even missed the afternoon classes, that was when I started bunking off school completely, neither All-Knowing nor Rattler had any idea, and I carried on with my amorous wine-soaked assignations, I'd go over to Voracious's place in the morning before he went out to sea, we'd smoke like chimneys and knock back the wine until we were drunk as skunks, we'd sleep for a while and then I'd get up and go back home, still feeling groggy, I'd have a quick bath, brush my teeth and gargle to get rid of the cigarette smell and then I'd relax and sleep, All-Knowing would come home in the evening and find me fast asleep, what else could I do, I ask you, it was the only way I could avoid being found out, he thought it was school knocking me out like that but all that time I was dead drunk, I'd been at my own secret school, one that I'd never tire of, so he left me sleeping like a log, poor old All-Knowing, he thought he was so smart, he'd wait for Rattler to come home and tell her not to disturb me and I'd wake up late in the evening, feeling anxious and unrested, I'd wonder what the time was and ask Rattler and she'd tell me it was already past bed-time and I should make sure I'd eaten something, we used to go to bed really early in those days and be up with the lark, sometimes when I woke up All-Knowing would come and ask me if everything was alright, if I was managing to study, just like any normal parent does when their children are preparing for their exams, he'd enquire after my health, and I'd reassure him and tell him I was fine, I was just a bit tired, school was getting more and more exhausting but it was nothing to worry about and then he'd ask me *are you sure,*" and I'd nod my head and he'd leave without saying anything else, I was really worried he'd find out I'd been drinking and smoking before I came home, surely he'd be able to detect the heady smells of Voracious's room on me, especially the tobacco, the odours would cling to my clothes and my whole body, even though I changed clothes after my warm bath and before I fell into a dead sleep, in the end I decided I was probably worrying too much about it, he couldn't possibly know what was going on, he thought he knew everything but for all his high-blown claims, he was nothing but an old fisherman who'd spent his life reading scraps of newspapers, whatever he might have believed himself to be, within a few days I'd begun to develop a taste for alcohol, I was on my way to becoming a real wino, oh, when I think about it now, all that wine I drank, I was a late bloomer there too, it was almost as bad as my obsession for Voracious, I'd gaze with frenzied longing at the glass of red wine, I loved watching those dark reflections in the glass glinting like the skin of an eel, even the glass itself seemed to radiate excitement, I'd hold it lovingly between my fingers and caress it as I did my lover and then I'd take little sips and savour the aroma, I hadn't realised wine could be so seductive, I'd always spend a few moments gazing at my new love in admiration before I took my first sip, letting it appeal to my senses, sight, touch and finally smell, just as I did with Voracious as a prelude to our daily session of that game known as love, with its kick of pepper and spice, I got to know almost all the wines that Voracious splashed out and squandered his savings on, he'd tell me about his family, his parents mostly, he'd recount tales of Voilà too and we'd both have a good laugh, he told me it was Voilà who'd introduced him to the great French wines, his friend would boast about the expensive wines he'd drunk, he'd talk to him about red wine, white wine, rosé wine and its lighter cousin, *vin gris*, he claimed to have drunk Beaujolais and all the Burgundy wines, as well as the very best Bordeaux wines, including Médoc, Graves and Sauternes, not to mention Chablis and Pommard, he liked to make out he was deeply knowledgeable on the subject of wine and never tired of dropping all those names, Voilà was crazy about wine, he'd go without clothes and spend his money adding to his list of wines he'd memorised, he'd urge his friends to consult him on matters related to wine and give the other drunkards lectures about the correct way to drink *"savour what you drink, my friends, discerning men like us know how to appreciate our drink,"* most of the time he didn't have the money to buy the wine he drank, he had to get others to pitch in and then he'd try and cheat his friends and keep the best wine for himself and then other times he'd drink cheap home-brewed palm wine, yes, some of those lush-heads would brew their own palm wine and sell it when times were hard, and Voilà would proclaim *"the only reason I'm drinking this stuff is to stay alive, to keep myself afloat, someone has to drink it, it's all about staying afloat, that's all there is to it, voilà,"* oh God, I can see it all now, and so every day I'd spend the morning in delirious rapture with Voracious and then I'd go home and he'd go out to sea in the afternoon, I wonder if his friends were surprised at his change of schedule, and once I got home, I'd sleep all afternoon and evening, good heavens, I'd become lazier than Rattler, I could see she was surprised by the change in me but I pretended I hadn't noticed,

the days drifted by, I forgot all about school, my classes, the wimpy boys and Désirée with her daily dramas, yes, before long it was all a distant memory, no one at home had any inkling that I'd stopped going to school, well, no, that's not quite right, think about it Eel, how can you be so sure no one suspected, would you really have known, so let's just see what happened next instead of blathering on like Voilà and, as it turned out, I was the one who had no idea, for by God, Rattler was spying on me, it seems obvious now, she gave me quite a shock one day when she did something completely out of character, she got up with me at the crack of dawn, All-Knowing had already left, and as I was getting ready to hurry off to my morning assignation there was Rattler sitting on the side of the bed yawning so widely I thought for sure she'd dislocate her jaw, I could see she'd forced herself to get up early, she could barely keep her eyes open, she looked like she was stoned, she sat there, yawning and saying nothing and looking like she was half asleep and then she jumped up and started getting ready to go to school, washing and dressing really quickly, it was all very worrying, where was the Rattler who took more than an hour to get ready in the morning, but whatever, I was already leaving as she was getting dressed and I hurried out so she wouldn't see which way I was going, we never went to school together anyway, not since she'd been held back the year before, we didn't have the same timetable and we went in at different times, so why this sudden change, what was she playing at, I was just about to open the door and leave when I heard a great crash, she was in such a hurry she was dropping everything she touched, her comb, the chair, her bag, what on earth was she was on that morning I wondered, but I went out the door and thought no more of it and then when I'd barely taken ten steps I heard a door creaking, Rattler must have decided to come with me I thought to myself, but where to, was she planning to go school with me or follow me to my rendez-vous or something, I certainly wasn't looking for a companion but when I turned round there was no one behind me, so I assumed she'd gone no further than the door and went on my way, I had to go straight ahead at first down a long street before turning right towards Voracious's house but just as I was coming up to the turning, I looked back to check behind me one more time, it was almost as if someone was telling me to, and what did I see but Rattler creeping up on me, she was quite a way off but she had a clear view of me, she was dragging herself along, head down, looking like an old woman, except for the fact that she wasn't actually limping, and then a group of cows appeared at the turning, six of them at least, although I didn't stop to count them, I was too busy thinking about Rattler following me, wondering what she had in mind, I had no choice but to keep going straight down that street, I passed a second turning to the right and then a third, but I didn't take either of them, I didn't want Rattler to think I was going to school by a roundabout route, so I carried on walking straight ahead, to wipe away any doubts she might have, the only turning I took was the one to the left that led straight to the Foukoujou crossroads where I used to see Voilà making a fool of himself after he'd had a skinful, I always thought of him every time I passed that spot, and when I reached the crossroads I headed for the road to Missiri, where the lycée was situated, I was in a state of panic, my heart was pounding like crazy, I couldn't stop wondering what Voracious would say if I didn't turn up, he might just go off to work and not wait for me and then I had a brainwave, I'd get to school as quickly as I could and then I'd turn round and go back the other way at top speed, I'd noticed that if I walked faster Rattler did too, so I picked up the pace and strode towards Missiri, like a student intent on getting to school on time, I was in good company, there were plenty of others hurrying to school, they probably wanted people to think they were serious about their studies but I ask you, just because you're in a hurry, what's that got to do with taking school seriously, I mean I was certainly in a rush but I was serious about something else altogether and it had nothing to do with school, so think about it, weren't you all just trying to pull the wool over your parents' eyes, what was there to say you weren't hurrying to your date, like I was, with your backpacks or your hand-bags, I mean, I had my bag too but mine was just a disguise to make me look like a student, and the rest of them were as bad as I was, I'm sure they all had assignations too, we were all skiving, some of them sauntered along as if they'd been forced to go to school but no one was forcing me, no one could make me go to school, why go if you feel you're being dragged along by the scruff of your neck, no, I had more respect for the students sitting on the walls around the madrasas, the ones who parked themselves on the benches in public squares, clutching their bags, chatting calmly and watching the world go by, the way I saw it, they were the ones who had the right idea,

I made it to school in under two minutes, and once inside the school gates I heard a noise behind me that sounded like cheering followed by waves of laughter, girls were shrieking as if they were witnessing something momentous, I turned round to see what was going on and all I saw was Rattler surrounded by a group of students, other people were walking towards her looking all excited, I realised they were amazed to see her at school on time, she'd never arrived before the bell before, so it was a big event, all the girls wanted to give her a hug, the boys to show their respect, some of them were actually bowing to her, I seized the opportunity to make myself scarce and headed towards the other gate behind the building leading towards Chitsangani, I scurried out of there like a rabbit and slipped away from the lycée before you could say Jack Robinson, I retraced my steps at top speed, racing through the same streets I'd taken before, moving at such a good clip I could barely make out the figures walking along beside me, I became aware of all the people hurrying to work once I was inside the medina but I paid no attention to any of them, all that mattered to me was getting to where I was going,

I knocked on Voracious's door just once, he looked taken aback when he opened the door and then he let out a deep sigh, as if he'd just been relieved of a burden, as I walked in he told me he'd just started to wonder why I was late *"I've got a little surprise for you today, you see,"* he added emphatically, well, let me tell you, I hate surprises, I liked people to be straight with me, for eel's sake, surprises are for soppy romantics and I'm not soppy, I'm not one for romance either, when I was with Voracious I always did my best to be honest, okay, there were times when I did get all lovey-dovey, it's true, but you can be in love without being all starry-eyed, love is a kind of madness and I'd rather be mad than soppily romantic,

I wondered what this surprise could be, what did Voracious have in store for me, I couldn't wait to see and then he opened the old wardrobe and took out a small blue box, which he opened to reveal an enormous, gleaming gold ring, he took it out of the box, held my left hand and slipped the ring on my finger, it was quite a weight that ring, I have to admit, and it was very shiny, I asked him what he was doing, I could see this was no little surprise as he'd suggested, this was a very big surprise, the ring was heavy and must have cost an arm and a leg, the thought of wearing it scared me, I had no desire to follow in Désirée's footsteps, I had my own path to follow, Voracious explained that it was a gift, a way of proving that he loved me, I replied that the real proof of love was intangible, like the air we breathe, you can feel it and hear it in the beating of your heart, that's how you know, your heart is your best friend, it's no good being fooled by material things, I mean, people who confuse gifts with love, oh God help me, love is something else entirely, completely different from a token someone gives you, even if they give you the sky, or the whole universe, it's still got nothing to do with love, we're talking about two totally different things, a gift can flatter your body but only love can nourish your soul, so tell me, which do you think is more important, gifts or love, body or soul, it's important to choose wisely my friends, I'm not saying anything but which one is easily broken and which one stands the test of time, it's up to you to work it out, I just wanted to make it clear that when it comes to love, you have to be certain you're not walking into a trap, don't make the mistake of saying the first thing that comes into your head, like Voracious did, I told him that if he wanted me to accept his gift he'd have to take back what he'd said, that's right, either he was giving me the ring because he wanted to give me a present, full stop, with no strings attached, or he'd have to keep his gift to himself and leave me to my mixed-up ideas, which are a far cry from all that Romeo and Juliet stuff, please don't put me in the same bag as those pen and ink creations, I'm alive, I move, I act and I'm more interested in making an impact on a heart than on a body, Eel is my name and that's who I am, some might say I'm empty-headed, yes, or that I have shit for brains, that's up to them, Voracious said I was weird, he said he'd never heard such things, that I thought very differently from other girls he knew, he tried to explain to me that giving a thing as a gift was a way of showing you love someone but I was having none of it, only idiots believe that love isn't real unless you have a material object as proof of its existence, as if their very being depended on the things that slip through their fingers every day, they forget they have a soul they've never seen and never will see, even though they think it's their very own, enough said, those people drive me nuts and I said so to Voracious, to which he eventually replied emphatically *"listen Eel, my favourite fish, you're right and now I can see what's so amazing about you, you're as wonderful inside as you are outside, you make me think of a night sky full of twinkling stars but please let me give you this ring, not because I want to make the moon and stars even more beautiful but just because quite simply I'd like to see my name in the stars, if that's possible,"* well, I really liked that, much more than the gift he wanted to give me, his words brought a tear to my eye, unlike the ring which had left me dry-eyed, there are plenty of two-faced girls who pretend to be touched by the fact that someone has given them jewels or precious stones, baubles that have nothing to do with the heart and its secrets, people will have the nerve to tell me that words will fly away and it's true, words do have wings, but locking them up won't contain them, they are born free as birds, only if you nourish them with sincerity can you make them your own, make no mistake about it, words are very powerful indeed, they take aim and hit the target spot on, in the hands of a skilled marksman they go straight to the heart and that's where they lodge themselves, permanently, that's where they do their work, feathering a nest with pleasure or with pain, they leave their mark for ever, so you have to know how to use them wisely if you don't want them to fly off into thin air, you have to know how make the most of them when necessary, and if they reap no rewards, as some of you will insist, you have to throw them back in the face of the person addressing them to you, or else block up your ears as soon as you can, before they lodge themselves in your heart, because they might do that and take pride of place there and then, no matter what you do, they'll end up damaging you,

so, not wanting to disappoint Voracious, I placed a kiss on the ring and another on his lips, which he returned with a lingering kiss and then we talked about why I was late, I told him I was worried that Rattler suspected something and Voracious said I was probably wrong, I was scared of her, that was all, and I was imagining things, I should relax, but how could I ignore what I'd seen and act as if I hadn't noticed anything, he said if I was so keen to throw Rattler off track, I could always cast suspicion on her, well, she certainly had something going on in her little head, I knew my sister, even if I didn't know exactly what she got up to hanging around the streets with her friends but until now, she'd known nothing about how I spent my time, she'd never shown the slightest interest in what I did all day, she'd go to school all dolled up to perfection and she knew lots of people, everyone knew her too and she was up to speed on everything about her friends' lives, girls would tell her their problems and ask her for advice and people would help her out by doing her homework for her, that's right, someone would do her assignments for her every day, I'd take a look at her notebooks when she was studying at home and I'd see all kinds of different handwriting, I didn't think anything of it at first and then I realised it was her friends' writing, a fact which she confirmed later when she meekly confessed everything to me, but looking at that hodgepodge of scripts I thought those people must be nuts, either that or Rattler had been plying them with wine somehow, I mean how on earth did she manage to get that level of service from people, I don't think even the Queen of England gets that much attention,

when I got back home, I was in for a real surprise, for the first time ever, by God, Rattler was already home, she seemed to be waiting for someone and that someone could only be me *"there you are,"* she said *"at long last, I've been waiting for you here for over two hours,"* strange, don't you think, since when did she come home early and wait for me to come back, and what did she think she was doing talking to me like that, as if I had something to explain to her, I'd always been the one waiting for her to come home and I never spoke to her like that *"just who does she think she is,"* I thought to myself, I was all fired up from drinking wine but for once, I hadn't overdone it and I managed to control myself, I went into the bedroom without saying a word to her and put my bag down as if I'd come home worn out from a long day at school and went straight into the bathroom to have my daily bath without batting an eyelid, I kept my mouth shut and didn't utter a word, for fear of letting her see I'd been drinking and when I came back into the bedroom she was still there, sitting in the chair as if she'd been waiting for me all along, I pretended I was really tired so she'd leave me alone and maybe she understood what I was doing as she came right out and asked me this odd question *"so where were you then,"* what on earth did she want from me, it was bad enough having to put up with All-Knowing and his questions and now she wanted to put me in the hot seat too, I felt like I was being addressed by the old windbag himself, I mean, I ask you, for eel's sake, since when did we ask each other where we'd been *"All-Knowing put you up to this, didn't he, he told you to follow me,"* I thought to myself, yes, I had quite a conversation going on in my head *"since when do you talk to me like that, Rattler, what exactly are you getting at my girl, it's none of your business sweetheart, you keep your paws to yourself,"* after which I decided I had to think of something to say to her to shut her up once and for all, otherwise she'd never leave me alone, so I told her firmly that I'd come straight home from school *"you weren't at school,"* she replied curtly, and added *"you haven't been to class at all for almost a month,"* which stopped me dead in my tracks, how on earth did she know, so I thought for a moment and told myself that Rattler couldn't have known for a month and not said anything to me, she must have just found out, so I tried to get more out of her, remember I told you how we love to ask questions in my part of the world, it's considered a great tradition, so I asked her *"who told you that,"* just like that taxi driver, or like All-Knowing trying to justify himself after one of his long monologues *"we're all crazy,"* he'd say *"make no mistake, not just the madmen throwing stones, we all have our own bats in the belfry, the blind leading the blind, you're better off with a crazy streak in your veins than a dose of stinking helleborus, which is what you'd get in a madhouse full of lunatics who don't even know who they are, rather like the one we're living in here,"*

Rattler gave a lengthy sigh when I asked her this question and then said she didn't need anyone to tell her I wasn't going to school *"I go into your classes all the time and you're never there,"* well, that was hard to believe, I decided she was hiding something, that one of my classmates had told her, I mean for a start, why would Rattler suddenly start taking an interest in my life, no there was something fishy about it and even if what she was saying was true, that she went looking for me in class and never found me there, I didn't think it was any of her business since she hardly ever went to any of her own classes, she went to school alright but spent all her time hanging around outside, I didn't care what she did, why should she police me when she didn't do what she was supposed to herself, anyway, I wasn't listening to a thing she was saying, it all went in one ear and out the other, if she thought I was going to say anything to her, she was wrong, and I flung myself down on my bed, keeping my lips sealed and pretended to go to sleep, I could hear her still trying to get me to talk, banging on about how she was worried about me, that I had a reputation for being serious, she realised that now and she didn't want me tarnishing my image, she said that she wasn't trying to poke her nose into my affairs, she just wanted to warn me, that I should be careful and think about what I was doing, well, what was I doing exactly, why should I be wary, how could she say such things to me when she knew nothing at all about me, she said *"I think you know very well what you're doing and what you want,"* well of course, Rattler, what did you think, and then she started telling me all about herself, that little rattlesnake who thought she was so smart, all of a sudden I became her confidant, Rattler, who only ever spoke to me when she had to, about practical household matters, she poured her heart out to me that day, what was I supposed to do with her secrets, me, Eel, a marine creature, not a landlubber like her, there's a world of difference between an eel and a snake, I'm sure you know what I mean, she started telling me about how she wanted to change, to be a different Rattler because she'd realised you had to struggle to be true to yourself, she said she'd turned her back on all the foolishness she'd been mixed up in for so long, that's right, she wanted to change her behaviour, this all came as a shock to me, hearing her say all this, it was like some kind of dream *"what do you mean, change, just like that, what's come over you Rattler,"* I said to myself, Rattler was claiming that people had her all wrong, that people misunderstood her because of the way she behaved and she'd made a decision *"the important thing*

*is not to follow such and such a path but to find your own way,
to negotiate the rocks and all their dangers with skill, in other
words to get through life without falling into any of its everyday
traps and ending up a wreck,"* Rattler was saying in a calm
voice, I thought she was still trying to be clever and I was
enjoying it and laughing to myself, because, whatever she
said, she'd never be able to deflect me from my path,

to tell the truth, people at school found Rattler hard to
fathom, and I didn't want to get caught in her net, so I trod
carefully and let her plough on *"life is in front of us, we're
holding it in our arms, like a child that needs to be cradled, we
have to be able to cradle it just right, and make it smile,"* my
goodness, she was good, I didn't disagree, since that was
exactly what I was doing, cradling my life in my own way,
and that child in my arms was having a good laugh, well
what did you think, she certainly wasn't in floods of tears but
I had to give it to her, I realised that day that All-Knowing
had his rattlesnake completely wrong, he thought Rattler
was nothing but a waster, he had her down as reckless and
headstrong, it was his way of letting himself off the hook
for her refusal to obey him and for his own negligence too,
but now I think she was hiding something all along, she put
on a good show but she knew exactly what she was doing,
she was pretty smart, that pig-headed girl, her friends were
right to come to her for advice, you'll see what I mean soon
enough, she really had become a different person and all
because of one incident, she'd been watching me, keeping
ominously quiet, acting like nothing had changed but the
whole time she was secretly preparing to rear up, she really

was a rattlesnake after all, and why not, we're all playing a part and we each have our own way of going about it, some players try to fool their audience by hiding down in the murky depths while others reach out and try to haul themselves to the surface,

SHH, RATTLER'S COMING

Rattler was acting like she needed to get something off her chest, talking to me as if she had great faith in me, as if she was hoping I'd understand and be supportive of what she had to say, she was telling me all about her friends and her friendships with boys as well as girls, talking about me and all the things she'd heard people say about the two of us at school and around the medina, it was all too much, I lay there on my bed, overwhelmed by all this information, pretending to be asleep, but in reality I was all ears, yes, I was weighing up every word that came out of her mouth, it's best to listen to what these people have to say, you have to be on your guard, if they take you for a bigger fool than they are before you know it they'll be worming information out of you, a strategy we eels often use, but you're probably not too interested in all that, so let's move on,

so she'd started talking to me about school, saying she was late to school on purpose, she wanted to be noticed by everyone, even the most die-hard latecomers, she didn't want her appearance at the school gate to be marred by the arrival of even a single student after her, she liked being greeted by cheers when she showed up, it made her feel good to be popular, she knew she could hold her own with all those girls who thought they were the bee's knees, like Désirée, who as far as Rattler was concerned was all show, trying to gain popularity by getting gussied up all the time, putting on a display of luxury and passing herself off as rich, which is definitely not the way to make friends, Rattler's friends were like brothers and sisters to her, she said, she'd hand out advice to them and they'd do her homework for her, she didn't even need to ask, but she realised now that she'd been wrong all these years, neglecting your studies is no way to make friends either, popularity comes when you set an example, when you're courageous and smart and considerate, when you're big enough to be tolerant of others, Rattler said the important thing was to take school seriously, to really want to learn something at school *"all those teachers there deserve our respect, even more than our parents,"* she said, and then she started telling me about all her failed love affairs, all the times she'd been threatened, how she'd been constantly disappointed by what boys expected *"they all think love is just a matter of shutting yourself up in a bedroom, stripping off and thrashing around like an animal, there must be more to it than that but getting laid is all they think about, all the time, getting laid, nothing but getting laid,"* and just what did you think love was all about, Rattler, did you think it was simply a matter of lolling around on the grass, gazing longingly into someone's eyes, wrapped in each other's arms, huh, well you were wrong there my girl, thinking you could rule out going into the bedroom with a boy, apparently

152

Rattler ended up losing every boy she went out with *"if that's what love means, shagging all the time, no thanks, that's not the kind of love I'm looking for,"* she said over and over again, I wanted to ask her what kind of love she did want but I told myself it was better just to listen and give her time to get it all off her chest, and then she said she didn't want to get involved in relationships any more because she realised more and more that people thought she had crazy ideas, one boy even asked her if there was something wrong with her *"what's the point of bunking off school if you're never going to let anyone touch you, what game do you think you're playing at, getting people to follow you and then going all coy and acting like you don't know what's what, I mean, are you nuts, or what,"* is what he said, people couldn't understand why she didn't sleep around, as far as they could see she was free to do as she pleased, she could have sex with whoever she wanted to, and then she started telling me about how this so-called realisation had come to her, life was a precious jewel, she said, it was very fragile, most people didn't understand that you had to cherish it, you had to make sure you didn't take a wrong turning and let it all slip away, and then she told me what had made her start thinking like this, she said that she was standing at the school gates one day, chatting with her friends about where to go and hang out, which was what they usually did after school, when a young man came up to them and said hello, he introduced himself and said his name was Cobra, he was dressed in jeans with a black Lacoste tee-shirt, a red baseball cap and a pair of sunglasses that hid his eyes completely and as Rattler put it, he'd let his jeans slip down a bit on his hips so you could see the top of his underpants, people always said that was the fashion, but personally, when I saw people wearing their trousers falling down like that, I thought it was because they had the runs and never knew when they might be caught short, I mean you pull your trousers down or hitch up your skirt to go to the toilet, don't you, or else when you want to spice things up with a bit of you-know-what, if you see what I mean,

Cobra didn't go to school, he was like all the other boys who dropped out of school and frittered away their days hanging around on benches in public squares with full-grown men, they said they couldn't see what their elders had gained from going to school, the people with the most education were the ones who worked the hardest and earned the least as far as they could tell, well, I'd dropped out of school too but not for the same reasons, what a stupid excuse, don't you think, it doesn't make any sense, it's cowardly, they're just trying to cover their arses, the truth is they're scared of failing their exams, especially since girls always do better than they do, it's always the girls who get the top marks but people can't accept it, you can't even mention it, the whole subject is taboo, it's just too much for some men, no, the reason I quit school was so I could get on with my life, that's all, my eel-shaped existence, I wasn't afraid of anyone or anything, even though I acted like I was scared of All-Knowing, and I certainly wasn't scared of exams, I always did well in them, I beat almost all the boys, those pathetic wimps, that's just the way it was, an eel is an eel after all, she's made for life on the rocks at vertiginous depths, so Cobra had his eye on Rattler and wanted to get to know her, her friends all knew him already, they said they'd seen him around the medina although they didn't know exactly where he lived, the important thing for us here is that after he introduced himself he invited the gang to go to Pangahari with him to see the *tam-tam de boeuf*, and if you're wondering what a *tam-tam de boeuf* is, it's a show, where men face up to a ferocious bull and dance in front of it while the *tam-tam* players stand behind a flimsy wooden fence playing their drums, the dancers wear a long piece of fabric called a *sambi* around their neck and move together in step with the rhythms drummed out on the *tam-tams*, it's a traditional dance, sometimes the dancers all make the same movements with their hands and feet, and sometimes they make a rapid movement of one foot after the other, the only place in Mutsamudu to put on these shows was the square in Pangahari, an imposing site of great symbolic importance that was built, according to All-Knowing, in the seventeenth century, a place where Comorean culture, traditions from all over the Islands of the Moon had always flourished, dances like the *chigoma*, the *hambaharousse*, or perhaps the *zifafa*, it was especially beautiful at night when strings of lights would float above the heads of the audience, you'd see the women all dressed up in their *shiromanis* taking up their positions on terraces, balconies and staircases around the square to watch a show, or a wedding with its celebratory songs and poems, the lights would cast a glow over the mosaic of the *shiromanis* filling the whole place with all the colours of the rainbow, and so that was where Rattler and her friends went with Cobra that day, to Pangahari to see a *tam-tam de boeuf,*

after that, Cobra would often come to the school gates to
wait for Rattler, they became almost inseparable and then
one afternoon Cobra invited her for a drink at a refreshment
stall near the lycée, and there in those blissful moments in
that tranquil setting, in the course of a lengthy and rather
romantic conversation, he whispered in her ear that he'd like
to invite her to his place, Rattler declined, saying that she had
never set foot in a man's bedroom, Cobra tried everything
in his power to persuade her, he told her he wanted her
to see where he lived, nothing more, it would make him
really happy if she agreed to come but she stuck to her guns,
saying she'd consider anything except going in to someone's
bedroom, I don't know what my sister was afraid of, being in
someone's bedroom doesn't necessarily mean you have to get
your kit off, but I think I understand now why she wouldn't
go home with her boyfriends, when she was in an enclosed
space like that the silly girl felt vulnerable, she really was
the feeblest girl in the world, as far as she was concerned, a
man's bedroom always meant having sex, if she ever found
herself in a bedroom with a man she'd no longer be a bird on
the wing, she'd be trapped, her wings clipped, imagine, she'd
be an easy target for any self-respecting bird of prey, she'd be
helpless, like a puppet on a string, ready to be turned every
which way, no positions would be off limits, if you see what
I mean, and I'm not mincing my words here, I'm not afraid
to call a spade a spade, I'm assuming you're all adults so I
don't need to give you all the details, you know what I'm
talking about, you can picture the rest, just think of it like

the homework assignments they used to give you at school when you were told to imagine what happens next, I always wondered what that was all about, dear teachers, I wanted to ask, what exactly do you want me to say, you knew what was going to happen, it was just a way of getting up our noses with your so-called assignments, what a joke, I never gave two hoots about any of that stuff, I'm telling you, but what the hell,

it was true, what Rattler was saying to Cobra, when she loved someone it was platonic as they say, sweet talk, kisses exchanged in words, by telepathy, whatever, so long as there was never any touching, you know the score, it does exist, that sort of love but Cobra didn't want to know and he took off, like all the other boys she'd met, and from then on, he even stopped coming to see the girls at the school gate, you can't blame him, why waste petrol needlessly, petrol or energy, they're one and same after all, no need to split hairs here, I let words take me where they will, I'm a driver of words, I go where I want, with or without petrol, wherever my fancy takes me, and where I'm headed is for the far reaches of my mind, who knows if I have enough time left to make the journey, but I won't stop trying, that's the way I am, it's in my nature, it's all part of my eelness,

rumours were flying around at school, Rattler found out from a friend that Cobra was being teased by his mates for failing to get Rattler to come to his place, word had it that Cobra had had a bet going with them, he'd boasted that he'd succeed where so many others had failed, and then when

he realised he'd made a laughing stock of himself, he got
all riled up and started putting it about that he'd dumped
Rattler because she was an airhead, Cobra was one of those
creeps who turn everything into a competition, they were
all the same those jerks, they all thought they were the cock
of the walk, keeping tally of all the girls they'd been with
just to show off and prove they were hotter lovers than the
others, but when Rattler found out what he was up to, she
told a friend to go and tell Cobra to come and meet her at
the lycée, maybe he thought Rattler had changed her mind
and was finally going to give in to him because he went
to the gate to wait for her, and that's where they met, like
two old friends, not lovers, just friends, and Rattler told
Cobra just what she thought of him, she started by letting
him know that she'd heard the lies he'd been spreading
about their relationship, not that they'd actually been in a
relationship and that's exactly what Cobra said to her too
*"oh yeah, we were having a relationship were we, you and me,
well I don't remember anything like that, in your dreams, sweetheart, you've got hold of the wrong end of the stick if you think
I'd have a dumbshit bimbo like you for a girlfriend,"* but Rattler
wasn't going to let herself be provoked, she told him he'd be
better off going to school and getting an education instead
of letting his brains fester, at which Cobra took offense and
told her she wouldn't presume to talk to him like that if she
knew who she was dealing with, she thought she was so
smart but she had another think coming, everyone knew she
was nothing but a slag, who did she think she was, trying
to pass herself off as a serious student, he threw it all back
at her, everything, all the classes she skipped, all the time

she spent lolling around in public squares, strolling under the trees, it all just proved what a lousy student she was, he told her she only hung around in those places to try and get picked up and he made a point of saying to her *"it's what they all say about you, everyone knows,"* he was pushing it a bit but why not, can you blame him for trying his luck,

all this yelling had attracted the attention of several other students, people were stopping to listen to this altercation, laughing out loud, and within a few minutes a whole crowd had gathered at the gate to see the show, it was like some kind of pop-up song and dance, people kept on coming, cheering as they approached and Cobra carried on saying the same things over and over again, that everyone in the medina thought Rattler was nothing but a whore, that she was the queen of slags and didn't belong in a lycée, and then he started talking about me, he told Rattler her sister was the only real student in the family, stupid sod, talking about me as if he knew who I was *"she's the smart one, not you, you're wasting your time trying to fool people, I don't try to be anything other than who I am but you, you're making a fool of yourself, trying to cover up who you are, coming to school with a bookbag like someone who takes school seriously, when all the time you're just another screw-up,"* Rattler felt like she'd been knifed, so she hit back, she accused him of a being a thug and said *"you're nothing but a lowlife, you're not fit for anything but breaking rocks, you'll never catch me anywhere near your dump of a place, lowlife scum,"* and when Rattler said that, Cobra, who was ready to snap, raised his hand to strike her but some passers-by saw what was going on and rushed over to come to Rattler's aid, they broke up the crowd of students and pulled her attacker away from her and for the first time in her life Rattler felt really stung by what had been said to her, and in front of a crowd of people too *"because it was all true,"* she said *"everything Cobra was saying to me, I had no choice but to accept it, it wasn't easy for me, it's dangerous to look directly at the sun but it's up there every day, you have to make an effort if you want to get over something,"* so after all this time, that little twittering sparrow saw her feathers being pecked away one by one, our little starlet had to step out of the spotlight and take a good look at her own behaviour, does this make sense to you, is it worse to be publicly attacked than have your parents harangue you, is it really more of a punishment, how can it be, Rattler, I didn't realise you were so sensitive, that you'd fall for all that, and it was that very same day that one of my friends, who was trying to debunk what Cobra had said, asked Rattler if I was ill *"because we haven't seen her in class for quite a while and that's not like her,"* what a moron, why did he have to drag me into it, huh, who asked him to go sticking his nose in everywhere, even into my eel-shaped life, to tell the truth, I was listening intently to Rattler while she was telling me all this, trying to take it all in, feeling increasingly bitter and exasperated, I'd dug myself into a hole and I was ready to explode *"so that's why you were skulking around following me this morning, you were trying to crack my secrets, huh, that's what it's all about, well you won't get anywhere with that, you can't see beyond the end of your own nose, there's no way you can get to know my eel-shaped secrets,"* I said to myself secretly, Rattler was absolutely stunned when the boy told her I hadn't been at school, she wanted to find out if it was really true but I'd been very careful while she was following me, she didn't know where I went all day, I was still pretending to be asleep while she was telling me all this, I made out I didn't hear a word she was saying, she claimed she wanted to start taking school seriously *"for my own good, not for anyone else's sake,"* she declared as she was getting up to go into the kitchen, so she was changing her behaviour as a result of a row with a boy, was she, I wouldn't have changed a thing if it had been me, you can't conquer a disease with a one-size-fits-all treatment, what cures one person's malaria won't necessarily have any effect on the next person, there's no shame in being given a public dressing down, not for an eel, Rattler was just being weak but there you go, that was the effect it had on her, I wasn't going to let it affect me though, no way was she going to influence my behaviour,

every day when All-Knowing came home in the evening, he'd find Rattler either in the kitchen making the dinner, or in our room doing her homework, we didn't have a TV or a radio, all we had in those days were our books, and there I'd be in the kitchen with my notebooks open to make it look like I was doing my homework, oh, when I think back to it, the only reason I opened them was for All-Knowing to see, sometimes I just sat there drawing fish, I loved drawing the ones that looked most like me, eels of course, what do you expect, did you think I'd draw a cowardly creature like a turtle, trying to keep a foot in both worlds, wasting time on land and missing half of what goes on at the bottom of the sea, no, eels stay where they belong, in water, under the sea, in streams, lakes and rivers, where their secrets are safe, so I stuck to drawing elongated eels, shamelessly making love every day, spending their time drinking wine and smoking, yes, living a life of decadence, my eels were long and tapered, they slithered along, weaving about piteously from all the wine, doing their best to avoid making waves when they felt under threat, what they feared most were the robbers of freedom, the predators waiting to lure them from the seabed with their bait and devour them, and I'd sit there drawing secretly, sinking down into the depths and creating never-ending fantasies, I'd make up stories that took place under the sea, the place where all the world's most beautiful stories unfold, which most people don't realise, even those who call themselves All-Knowing,

so where was I in this never-ending saga, damn it, can someone tell me where I was, for eel's sake, oh yes, with Rattler, that's it, I have to stop losing the thread all the time, I have to concentrate on finding out just how I got here, how I came to be thrashing about in my death throes here in these black depths in this seemingly empty ocean, so I knew All-Knowing was surprised by this sudden change of behaviour taking place with Rattler, he was probably very happy to see it, he couldn't help coming out with things like *the sun that rises sluggishly is quick to set, our forefathers knew what they were talking about,* he'd say it wryly, as if he had it all worked out, we just kept quiet, we'd listen to his pronouncements and pretend we didn't understand, and ever since Rattler's confession to me I was trying twice as hard to make sure she didn't notice what I got up to, especially when I came home drunk, but I came up with the solution of coming home earlier and making sure I wasn't too wasted,

and then the day came when Voracious presented me with another proposition, a most unwelcome idea, one that would be repellent to any eel, he suggested we meet on set days during the week *"it's the best solution, to avoid suspicion, you have to understand, I don't want to create problems for you,"* he said, and when I tried to get him to see that what I did was my business, that it was of no interest to anyone else, he replied *"that's the last thing I want to hear, what do you mean no one's interested in what you do, that's ridiculous,"* I hated the whole idea, I couldn't believe he'd even think such a thing, it wasn't like him at all, I thought to myself *"has it only just occurred to him that this whole business is a sordid affair, everything we've been doing,"* it was very hard for me to accept his suggestion, I'd already made up my mind to drop out of school, I hadn't been for almost two months and I didn't see any reason to go back, it would be like swallowing something I'd thrown up, a disgusting thought, don't you agree, eating your own vomit, and when an eel refuses to take the bait, live or otherwise, there's no chance of catching it with a hook and line, no, you'd have to find some other way of getting me to go back to school, put a chain round my neck for example and pull me along like a cow, otherwise all your hard work would just go down the tubes, into the lake, and when I thought about Voracious's idea I realised I'd die of boredom at home, I'd be without my two, no, my three great loves, I wouldn't have my Voracious with me, or my slug of wine, or even my packet of Gauloises, I couldn't bear the thought of saying yes to his plan, and then Voracious tried to sweeten the pill by telling me he'd give me a pack of Gauloises every time we saw each other to help me get over the hump, but it wasn't enough, I'd still be without the things that mattered most, him and the wine, him most of all, I certainly couldn't put him in my bag and take him with me any more than I could the wine, it would be too much of a risk taking a bottle of wine into the house, I could hide the cigarettes without any trouble, that would be easy enough but it was torture thinking about how much I was going to miss him, I scowled and pulled a face but in the end I said yes, it was a bitter pill to swallow but I had to accept the agony of being imprisoned in my own house, sitting immobilised on my bed, staring at the ceiling, arms folded on my legs, far removed from the frenzied daily diet only Voracious could feed me, so we agreed to meet three days a week, on Wednesdays, Thursdays and Saturdays, and I had to endure four days of suffering, four days in a row almost, Mondays, Tuesdays, Fridays and Sundays, and it wasn't easy for me, you know, I'd start thinking about Voracious and get really wound up, and then I'd sneak up to the terrace for a smoke, but smoking whole packets of Gauloises was no substitute for the real thing, I'd be up there, smoking like a chimney, even when Rattler was home, I'd risk going up for a smoke because she never went up to the terrace, she'd sit inside hunched over her notebook like a prisoner and I'd puff away on my Gauloises until I burned my fingers, I'd smoke them right down to the end and chuck the butts away outside, as far away as I could throw them, I couldn't let anyone know I smoked, and sometimes I'd have a craving for one in the toilet but smoking in there was a risk I wasn't prepared to take, our toilet was a tiny little room that didn't even have a window, it wouldn't take much to turn it into a den of smoke, just like Voracious's place, you can imagine what would happen then, someone would fart in there and things would be very difficult for me,

with all those Gauloises, my voice was changing, I could feel it getting deeper and becoming like Voracious's but it didn't bother me, you can get away with saying all kinds of things with a deep voice, it adds gravitas, which is just what an eel needs, the main thing was that no one saw me smoking, Voracious was the only one who knew, well, no, wait a minute, I say no one had seen me but I do remember one morning after All-Knowing left very early in the morning as usual, I'd forgotten about that day, I remember now that Rattler started coming up the stairs to the terrace to tell me she was leaving, I was up there having a smoke when I heard rapid footsteps on the stairs and I panicked and held the smoke in my mouth and pressed the burning end of the cigarette into my palm to hide it, I closed my hand around it and the pain went right through me, all the way up to my brain, but I had to keep my hand tightly closed, in my panic I'd missed my chance to chuck the cigarette away and now it was too late, Rattler was already there and I had to hold my breath for fear of letting even a wisp of smoke escape, I sat there squirming and wriggling, trying not to feel the excruciating pain in my hand, I clenched my jaw and ground my teeth, I pretended I was trying to hum a tune I couldn't quite remember, Rattler was telling me she was about to leave, because, as I think I mentioned, she left earlier now that she'd changed her ways, and after telling me she was going out, just as she was about to leave I saw her sniff the air for a moment as if she was trying to pin down a smell she couldn't quite place, she frowned too, I felt exposed, I had to say something so I quickly swallowed the smoke I'd been holding in my mouth all this time, it really smarted, it felt like pepper in my throat but I went ahead and swallowed it, and breathing out noisily I said *"okay"* as quickly as I could, because in reality I was choking and that was the only thing that came out of my mouth, and she went back downstairs without another word, I knew she was worried about the way I was acting but she couldn't find a way of broaching the subject in a sisterly fashion and I kept avoiding her, I didn't want to find myself in the hot seat, I didn't owe anyone anything, but I paid for it once she'd gone, my hand hurt like hell and I was left with a huge swelling from the cigarette burn,

three days went by and I knew something was wrong, my period didn't come, oh, when I think back to it now, I was just about going out of my mind, it was three days late, mark you, three days of ever increasing anxiety and I said to myself that I had to do something, I couldn't stop myself thinking *"what's going on here, am I pregnant or what,"* I wasn't scheduled to see Voracious that day, it was Monday, I wasn't supposed to see him the next day either, not until the following day, Wednesday, but I couldn't possibly hold out until Wednesday, I had to see him, by hook or by crook, I had to talk to him about it before it was too late, I absolutely had to find a way out and it needed to come from both of us, well, what do you expect, I didn't get into this position by myself, it takes two people to make a pregnancy, there was a little creature starting to form in my belly, taking shape all the time, an embryo, then a foetus, a pregnancy and the end product would be a baby, a pregnancy isn't the same as a baby as I see it, there's no baby yet, just a pregnancy, a creature in another world, well that's Eel's view, you might see it another way, you people out there, it makes no difference to me though if you don't see things my way, it's not a baby in my book until it's actually born,

so I was planning to leave at first light, after All-Knowing went out, I needed to go over and see Voracious before the situation got any worse, I had to leave as early as possible and catch him before he went out to sea, don't forget that Rattler would leave before me in those days, but that Tuesday I was the first to leave the house, Rattler had given up spying on me by this time and it was all smooth sailing, right up to Voracious's door, I knocked quickly three times and then another three times and then again three more times, there was no sound from inside, I listened hard, hoping to hear some sign of movement but there was no response, which surprised me because I knew that Voracious didn't leave at the crack of dawn like All-Knowing did, I said to myself that maybe he was dead drunk and couldn't hear me knocking, so I banged on the door again and by now I'd stopped knocking politely, I was hammering on the door so loudly it was ear-splitting, I was sure the neighbours would hear it and wake up, unless they were the kind who slept really hard, in the end an old woman opened her window to see where all the noise was coming from, they're always nosy, old women, have you noticed, they wake up sometimes just to go and have a look at the cats enjoying a romp and caterwauling, so I'd just decided I'd better leave when all of a sudden the door opened, and there was Voracious, standing stock still in the doorway, a haggard look on his face, he stared at me, his forehead contracted in a tight frown, he seemed nervous, edgy, I apologised for waking him and made a move towards the bedroom, I was just about to go in when he stopped me with his right hand, I stepped back and gave him a questioning look and then he said *"listen, I'm really sorry, but you can't come in,"* I asked him why not and he hesitated for a moment before saying *"it's not one of our days today,"* what the hell, how could he say that to me, you don't talk like that to the woman you love, if you really do love her, who did he take me for, and I asked him *"you do realise who you're talking to, how drunk would you have to be to act like this, tell me I'm dreaming, do I have to have an appointment to come here,"* he lowered his head and gave me a despairing look, he said nothing so I told him I had something very important to tell him *"can't it wait"* he asked me furiously, I was dumbstruck, and then I heard him say, with his very own lips *"it can wait till Wednesday, can't it, it's not your day today,"* I was flabbergasted *"what did you say, repeat that please, the words that just came out of your mouth, not my day, what is that supposed to mean, not my day,"* to which he replied in an urgent whisper *"listen, there's someone asleep in here, you'll wake her up,"* he paid no attention to what I said and just carried on trying to provoke me into giving up and leaving, he knew I wasn't going to give in that easily and then I yelled at him at the top of my voice *"what do I care if there's someone asleep, who is this person anyway, what do you mean 'you'll wake her up,' who the hell is this bitch, is this the way you"* I didn't get a chance to finish my sentence, for God help me, I'm telling the truth, as if in answer to my question, I saw a girl standing just behind Voracious, she was wrapped in a dark blue sheet, my favourite sheet, the very same sheet Voracious and I lay under as we slept, I'd picked it myself out of the cupboard and there she was, dressed only in that sheet from her chest down to her knees, I felt a sharp sting of jealousy at first, she had bloodshot almond eyes, bright red, her face was rumpled, her hair dishevelled, she'd heard me shouting and woken up, she didn't say a word to Voracious, she just stood there staring at me and said *"who is this person, what's she doing bothering everyone and handing out threats to people she doesn't even know,"* Voracious looked thrown off balance and turned to her and mumbled *"you go back to bed, I'll explain later,"* but she didn't budge, she just stood there, staring harder than ever at me and said to Voracious *"I want you to explain this before I get really mad, but you'd better start by telling her who I am, or you'll be sorry,"* Voracious let out a long sigh and stared at me despairingly, as if someone had aimed a gun at his head and told him what to say *"okay, fine, this is my fiancée, Bream,"* and with that, the despicable swine turned and gave her a look of regret as if to ask forgiveness for everything he'd done with me, I peered down my nose at the little cow standing blatantly behind him, what I wanted to do was tell them both what I thought of them right there and then, I wanted to jump all over that girl but I was afraid of waking the neighbours, a sure way of causing a scandal and then All-Knowing would be the first to know, but my God, when I think about Voracious answering to that girl's beck and call, that bitch who claimed to be his fiancée, I wasn't going to fall for that one, there's more than one way of being engaged in this world, especially if you spend your life swimming about in the depths of the ocean, I was engaged to Voracious too, if being engaged means sleeping with a man in his bedroom, but that cow had got herself out of bed to lord it over me and Voracious was dancing to her tune like a performing dog, that was what hurt so much, this wasn't the Voracious I knew, all that muscle meant nothing, he was nothing but a poodle, a performing dog who couldn't stop himself drooling at the sight of a girl, he didn't think twice when that girl blackmailed him like that, he looked at me one last time and said *"you'd best go back home,"* that's all he said, and then he slammed the door in my face, me, Eel, after humiliating me like that, and I was humiliated by all of it, I said nothing, I stood there at that door, frozen to the spot, I never imagined I'd be spurned by him one day, not for a single moment, he didn't even want me to tell him why I'd come to see him that day, he treated me like he didn't even know me, like I was nobody, and in front of another girl what's more, a girl who was no more than a floozy, a tart, you can say what you like about me, you people out there who probably can't hear me anyway, you can say it was just jealousy but it's all water off a duck's back to me *"he had the nerve to spurn me in front of that hussy,"* is all I could think as I hung my head, feeling like someone had just thrown a

great lump of mud in my face, that really was him, that was
Voracious, I still can't make sense of it to this very day, that
was the man who told me he didn't think much of people
who showed a lack of respect towards others, who claimed
that people who took good care of their parents were the
only ones who'd never harm anyone else and there I was,
mortally wounded by him, crushed to the bone, I'd thrown
myself into the jaws of a shark, yes, that's what he was, Voracious was nothing but a shark, a skirt-chaser hiding behind
a mask, yes, well, beware of pretty faces with their seductive
charms, why hadn't it occurred to me before, why hadn't I
seen that Voracious was a shark, there are plenty of them
roaming the earth, although they really should be in the
sea, yes, there are a whole host of creatures on *terra firma*
carrying on as if they were in the depths of the ocean, I
thought I was the clever one, able to put on a disguise and
make life easy for myself, but there are disguises lurking in
every nook and cranny of this globe, in silent, secret, hidden
places, like the depths of the oceans, we don't even know
what goes on in our own stomach, no one does, it takes a
whole fleet of instruments to explore it and a stomach is
a small thing, it is part of us, so how are we ever going to
understand the immensity of the seas, and I'd forgotten that
I actually lived under the sea, which goes a long way towards
explaining how I was taken in,

people talk about having a good name, as if a name could be
bad or ugly in some way, or they say they were born under a
lucky star, as if that was all it took to have the world at your
feet, and then there are the ones who say they are descended

from kings, that they have royal blood, it's all a load of rubbish, you can call yourself whatever you like but the fact remains that you all have a secret name, one that even you don't know, or maybe one you prefer to keep to yourself, who knows, it's nothing to brag about, there's an equivalent for all of you under the seas, either you're a shark like Voracious, or maybe a bream like that hussy in his room, or a tuna perhaps like All-Knowing, or a dolphin like Tranquil and her husband, or a rare specimen like Rattler, or a sea snake like Cobra, as I said, we all have our real name that we keep secret, there are lobsters too, and shrimps and turtles and crabs, the list is so long, I could keep going until the end of time, listen to me, what am I saying, the end of time, is there really an end to this play, will the show finish or keep going for ever, oh, cut it out, Eel, you're going off the rails again, I was saying that whatever names you choose to give your brothers and sisters in this ocean, this sea I'm floating in, talking to you at this moment, or wittering on to myself, whatever, it's all the same to me, I could be swallowed up by a whale here and that would put me out of my misery because I'm not worth a thing now, I'm a washed up eel, my life is hanging by a thread, I need to hurry up and deal with these memories before they all vanish, when an eel's been fatally smitten by a powerful force, away from her own territory, she has no alternative but to sneak back quietly for a crash-landing, back to her own domain, under her own rock if you like, but let's not forget that whatever she does, the effects of that venom injected her into will eventually be visible to those around her, and whatever happens, an eel is still and eel, even when she's mortally wounded,

UNRELENTING SCANDAL

I had to go back home and think, I needed to mull things over in my head, look at it all from every angle, I was searching for a spark, a solution that offered some hope, a way to settle my fate without delay, I didn't want anyone to know I was pregnant, nor did I want an abortion, every time the thought of it crossed my mind I batted it away, why would you throw away something you'd actively pursued, I'd got what I wanted, hadn't I, why else would I have sought Voracious out, we'd gone after each other of our own free will, there was no doubt about that, we had to take responsibility for what went on in our bed as well as in our heads, you have to be honest about these things, all the time, I mean it's no good playing the victim like some girls do, those spineless creatures who get a taste of this eel's life only to rain curses on it once they've eaten the fruit, never for one single minute will I play the victim, the lovers of Verona don't exist, they're fiction and always will be, that's just the way it is, no point in making a fuss, there are snakes lurking under stones everywhere in this theatre, surprises that feed on silence, a silence that shuns noise, it doesn't pay to be seduced by eye-catching images, fiction may look good but that's exactly why it's the source of so much misery,

as I was saying, when you love someone you have to love the souvenirs they leave you too, love's fruit, good or bad, sweet or sour, bitter or salty *"this is where I am, I'll live with it, what the hell,"* I said to myself, I love this being that's going to die with me here before too long, just as I loved its father, yes, he did betray me but I'm still free to live my life as I please, to hide under any rock I choose, and with that thought, I felt silence wrap its comforting wing around me, I felt protected from harm and free to follow my own desires, to go where I wanted, his betrayal couldn't stop me from taking my destiny in my own hands and looking ahead to starting my own family, my son and I, we'd be a family, wouldn't we, so that was it for the idea of a termination, I wasn't one to throw in the towel, not this eel, abortion wasn't the answer, ending the pregnancy out of fear, what's that all about, it's cowardly, that's what it is, trying to get rid of something you were happy enough to create, shame on you, I'll admit that I panicked when I found out I was pregnant but that doesn't mean I was scared, there's a world of difference between fear and panic, I'm sure you don't need me to tell you that,

all the same, I did have to decide what to do, everything hinged on that one question and the answer was a long time coming, which is why there was such a scandal, I was worried sick and I wasn't thinking straight, ideas were spinning around in my head and I ended up mired in confusion, there were moments of darkness, like rainy days, I needed to smoke to sort my head out, to dot the i's and cross the t's, as they say, or something like that, whatever, it's all smoke and mirrors, all these sayings but that was the problem, I didn't have any smokes, and no money either, that was always Voracious's department and I was determined not to give in to the temptation of going to see him, it was a tempting thought though and it did cross my mind *"get thee behind me,"* I had to say, every time it popped up, I didn't want to see that man cross my path ever again, that snake in the grass, we weren't together any more, it was all over, which meant I'd have to give up the wine, and Gauloises too, well that wasn't going to happen, I couldn't possibly go along with that line of reasoning, there had to be a way, remember, there's always a solution to an eel-shaped problem, necessity is the mother of invention and all that, it's not enough to look at things and think logically, you have to use your gut too, it's easy to get thrown off course by other people's opinions but you have to be true to yourself if you want to get what you need, take me for example, I'm an eel and the answers to an eel's problems are usually right there, within our grasp, but we're blind to them most of the time, we get led into believing we can think our way out of a mess, we're stubborn, we're like people who've lost their sight but still insist on leading other people around, even if we keep tripping up, and how ridiculous is that,

I was convinced All-Knowing was squirreling money away somewhere, he was a hoarder, that one, although he was always haranguing the other fishermen, accusing them of being misers and saying things like *"people who hang on to*

*things they don't know what to do with are no better than rats,
helping themselves to things just because they're there,"* well, let
me tell you, you were one of those rats yourself, old man, I
needed some smokes and I knew he had a pile of money that
I'd be able to help myself to without actually robbing him
blind, so of course I decided to steal a couple of coins from
him, what do you expect, do you think I was going to go on
being miserable, who knows I might have ended up making
myself sick, no, the world had to be saved and after all, an
eel's life is a whole world, so this is what I came up with,
I'd go and steal from that penny-pinching old so-and-so,
he'd been making money from his fish for longer than I'd
been alive and what did he do with his money, he was no
different from the rest of them, fishermen are unbelievably
tight-fisted, they don't think like other people, no one ever
sees the colour of their money, even though they have plenty
stashed away, and I remembered there was a tin, a large
cylindrical tin where All-Knowing kept his money, he'd go
up to the terrace with it sometimes so he could count up his
cash in private after he'd done the day's reckoning with his
side-kick Guarantee, he'd sit there with his Nido dried-milk
tin for ages after Guarantee left and then he'd come back
downstairs with a sigh, as if the effort of counting up such a
massive amount of cash had worn him out, there must have
been a tidy sum in that tin, I thought to myself, I'd have to
sneak into his room to get it while I was alone in the house,
when Rattler wasn't there, I was pretty scared, who wouldn't
be, it's only natural, we're all the same, all of us actors on this
stage, we all feel anxious when the next act is about to begin,
so let's all take up our positions and carry on with the show,

I walked into All-Knowing's room, the bedroom where we never dared set foot, we had to stand outside the room and talk to him from behind the curtain whenever we had something important to say to him, there was no actual door in his doorway, just a curtain, same as in our room and he never gave us permission to step through that doorway, but he was out that day and I took my chance to help myself, all I did was take a few coins, or rather, I stole them if you must, I was a thief, it's true but I had to have some money, I was shaking as I tried to find the tin, I don't know why, I was rummaging around on a table with newspaper pages on it and I stopped to look at the headlines *"Israel-Palestine: the wait for a new American plan"*, *"Sudan: 6000 child soldiers in Darfur"*, *"Burma: Aung San Suu Kyi held in Rangoon"*, *"French Comoros Islands: Mayotte says yes, UN, League of Arab States and African Union say no"*, I didn't go any further, I didn't want to see the rest, I was fed up with hearing the same old stories in the news for as long as I could remember, it didn't stop people dying like rats everywhere, so I carried on with my search, I bent down and there on the floor under the table was a large box stuffed full of pieces of newspaper, full to the brim, so that was where he kept all those scraps of paper he'd been collecting all this time, ever since he was bitten by the bug for reading absolutely everything that came his way, I swear he'd even peer at a pile of dog shit to see if there was anything written on it, well, you never know, stranger things have happened,

the last thing I wanted was to waste my time reading those ancient dusty newspapers all over again but as I was lifting a pile of them, I was stunned to see a series of horrible scenes, pictures of the Rwandan genocide, it was written there in black and white "Rwandan Genocide" in big letters, bodies, mutilated and bleeding, piled up like rotting tomatoes on a road in flames, it was terrible, I couldn't look at it, it was all wrong, what kind of a performance was this, we'd strayed a long, long way from the play we'd agreed to produce on this stage, there were dead bodies in the next image too, oh God, that's all there was, nothing but killing "*Apartheid in South Africa*" it said beneath the picture, I quickly lifted another stack of pages to see if All-Knowing had buried his tin at the bottom of the box under this mess of papers, and I saw a whole lot of other shots that made me think of school, photos of Martin Luther King, Mohandas K Gandhi, Nelson Mandela, Yasser Arafat, Charles de Gaulle, René Cassin and so many others I'd learned about at school in my history classes, all those lessons destined to end up covered in dust like those newspapers, but I haven't forgotten what I learned, God knows what All-Knowing did with all those articles from way back when, I suppose it was all grist to his mill, he really was obsessed, what an old fool he was, I came to the conclusion that the tin wasn't hidden there, All-Knowing wouldn't want to go through all the bother of sifting through those ancient pages every day, my hands were already filthy from them, so I turned round to look under the bed, nothing but old shoes there that belonged to him and my dead mother, then I looked under the wardrobe, still nothing but dust and an enormous spider's web with a wretched fly caught in it, the fly was a pathetic sight, all dried up, I saw a spider go scuttling away, I shouldn't have been bothering it while it was contemplating its scrawny catch, I straightened up to take a breath and see where else I needed to look, the top of the wardrobe for a start, I stood on tiptoes to get a good look up there, still nothing but dust, it really was dusty that bedroom, just like its owner, the only place left to look was inside the wardrobe, I thought it might be locked but no, it wasn't, the door didn't have a lock, just a handle, not that All-Knowing trusted no one would open the door, no, he was simply too stingy to buy another lock, the house already had one door with a key and to his way of thinking, one lock was enough for a house, he was careless about things like that, so I opened the wardrobe and peered at the three shelves, each with a few clothes neatly folded and stacked, some of them smelt musty, I wiped my hands on my *pagne*, like most people I usually changed into my sarong when I got home, then I began to take out the clothes that had been in there for God knows how long, I moved them very carefully, one at a time and there, right at the back of the first shelf I saw the tin, it was a stroke of luck, I was ready to rummage through all three of those shelves, the tin was certainly well hidden, you wouldn't see it at all unless you took the clothes out and it was heavy too, I had a hard time lifting it and I didn't have a chair to sit on while I opened it, I took off the plastic lid and found bundles of notes folded in half, stacks of them, but it certainly wasn't those notes making the tin so heavy, there had to be coins too, I could hear them rattling around when I shook the tin, a few coins were all I needed so I started taking out the notes to get my hands on the coins, once the notes were out of the way I stuck my hand into the tin and got hold of a handful of coins, I didn't stop to count them, I didn't really know what I was doing, I'd decided I'd only take coins because All-Knowing probably didn't know exactly how much he had in loose change, or maybe he did, who knows, we're talking about All-Knowing after all, all I cared about was getting hold of my pack of cigarettes, I didn't have an exact sum in mind, and then I put the tin and the clothes back as quickly as I could and scooted out of there,

I needed to buy my cigarettes from a shop where I wouldn't have to answer all sorts of awkward questions, everyone's a reporter where I live, and it's hard to know which newspaper they're working for, that's the problem, I mean if all those people poking their noses into other people's business really were reporters, it would be fine but I'm not exaggerating when I say they were worse than paperazzi, not that I was scared of a bit of bad press, all that's just water off a duck's back to me but I didn't want to get funny looks and be subjected to questioning just because I was seventeen years old and buying a packet of cigarettes, for example, so I decided I'd go further afield, go somewhere outside our neighbourhood to buy my cancer sticks, as All-Knowing referred to them, but then I had another idea *"what if I sent someone else to get them, a kid for example,"* I thought, I'd have to find a child who was a loner, but how would I know the kid wasn't curious about what grown-ups got up to, I'd be taking a risk, I mean some kids are even worse than adults on that front, I stood at the door thinking about what I should do, looking this way and that, when I caught sight of a child dragging a toy along on a string, a little truck made out of a plastic bottle with wild almonds for tyres, I had to flag him down to get his attention, I didn't want to shout, so I waited a bit and then I saw another kid coming over to him, he said something to him and the little kid with the truck seemed absolutely terrified, it looked like the newcomer was going to grab his toy away from him but the little kid ran off with his toy towards Hamoumbou and the would-be mugger turned to watch him, making sure his victim really had got away, and then he crossed the street and started to walk towards my vantage point, I waited until he was close enough and signalled to him to come over, I kid you not, I waved him down, he stopped and stared at me, checking me out before he came any closer and that was when I recognised him as one of Voilà's children, the one who went round threatening all the other children in the neighbourhood, just as I'd seen him do with that little kid a moment ago, so when he was close enough I asked him a question *"you're one of Voilà's kids, aren't you,"* he glared at me suspiciously, frowning nervously before nodding in agreement and looking down at the ground, so out of curiosity I asked him where he was headed and he fired back without looking up *"nowhere,"* well, I could see this conversation wasn't going to go anywhere either, I didn't see how it was possible to spend all day just hanging around, doing absolutely nothing, some people might think it could be done but they're in cloud-cuckoo land, along with plenty of other inhabitants of this wretched planet, it's ridiculous, I knew he wasn't telling the truth, telling me he was going nowhere was just a way of shutting me up, so then I asked him if he'd go and buy me some Gauloises and he immediately said yes, I did think twice about sending him on this errand though, why was he so quick to say yes, how could I be sure he'd come back, and then I saw what a scrap of a child he was and I said to myself that except for bothering other children he might not be such a bad kid, I didn't really know how much to give him, I still had all the coins in my hand and when I counted them out and gave him the lot I noticed that he seemed worried, so I said to him *"what's the matter,"* and he asked me with the same sullen defiance *"is that all for cigarettes,"* so I said yes, it was, and he asked me how many packets I wanted and I said *"just the one,"* and then what did he do but count out the money like an adult, and he took just five hundred francs, that's all, five one hundred franc pieces and the rest he gave back to me, and then I saw him vanish into the backstreets of the medina, I took a moment to count the money left in my hand, I still had eight hundred francs, how did he know the price of a packet of Gauloises I wondered, he looked much too young to me to be smoking, by the look of him he couldn't have been more than ten years old and although, as All-Knowing liked to say, even a worm knows how to smoke a cigarette, I just couldn't believe this little kid was a smoker, I turned the idea over in my mind, wondering whether he actually smoked and trying to work out where he'd be at that moment, when it suddenly occurred to me that someone might ask him who sent him, I hadn't thought to warn him about that, maybe it hadn't been such a good idea after all, what if someone decided to put him on the spot, he'd have nothing to fall back on, and then I thought what if he just ran off with my money and never came back, he didn't seem to be afraid of anyone, I mean let's not forget, this is the kid who loaded his own father into a cart to help his mother kick him out of the house, what was to stop him cheating me, after all, he didn't know me from Adam, and just as I was mulling this over who should I see but the kid skipping down the road, batting his hands around in the air, as light-footed as a cat, he came bounding towards me and it occurred to me all of a sudden that the hands he was waving in the air were empty *"oh my God, what's he done with my money,"* I thought, which is the kind of thing a person who gets rich from taking advantage of others would say, the world is full of people like that, which reminds me of the story of the three friends, Hand, Ear and Fly, and how they fell out, there's always some poor insect that gets ripped off, or even crushed so the hand can do exactly as it pleases,

so Voilà's kid came back after all and I breathed a sigh of relief as he pulled the packet of Gauloises out of his pocket, he turned out to be pretty smart that little waif, and as he was about to turn round and walk away I invited him to come into the house with me, I said there was something I needed to tell him, he hesitated for a moment and then made up his mind to follow me, we sat down side by side on the bottom stair like two old friends and I asked him if he smoked, I needed to get the conversation started somehow, he said he didn't so I said I knew who he was, I told him everything I knew about Voilà, all the tales Voracious had told me in his bedroom about Voilà and his wife, I even repeated the story about his wife thwacking him with the pounding stick and knocking him out, I recounted the whole episode as if

187

I'd seen it all with my very own eyes, and then when I said *"and you're the one who put your dad in a cart and wheeled him all the way to"* he cut me off and snapped *"he's not my dad,"* I didn't know what he was talking about *"what do you mean, he's not your dad,"* I said and the kid replied that he wouldn't have bundled his dad into a cart like an old piece of trash like that, well, if Voilà wasn't his dad, who was, and when I put that question to him, he looked down and eventually said *"Voracious,"* I still didn't get it, so he explained that his mother had told him that Voracious was the one who took care of them and that he was his real dad *"what do you mean,"* I said, feeling more and more thrown off balance, as you can imagine *"Voracious takes care of our food and gives money to Mum, that's what I mean,"* he said, so I went along with it and said, as if I was taking it all in *"so he's your dad because he provides for you, but actually, he's not really your dad, right,"* I'd barely finished saying this when he interrupted me again with a categorical *"no"* shaking his head slowly from one side to the other as if he were explaining to me what the word no meant, so I pushed him further and said *"maybe your mum's just saying that, to make you forget about the awful way Voilà treated her,"* to which he responded by tapping me twice on the hand with his finger and lowering his voice as he continued, in all innocence, to blow the lid on his mother's secrets *"Mum sends me over to Voracious's every evening to tell him she's coming as soon as she's got the baby to sleep, and then Voracious sends me out to buy his Gauloises,"* and I finally started to believe everything this sneaky little kid was telling me, painful as it was, I realised it had to be true but as I said before, it was hard for me to believe it, that his mother was actually involved with Voracious, I was completely stunned by this revelation and I sat there dumbfounded for quite a while, I didn't even listen to the rest of what he had to say, although he carried on anyway, he was asking me a question I hadn't heard, tapping me to wake me up, and when I came back to my senses I asked him to repeat his question *"what about you, do you smoke,"* he asked me, nosy little thing, what business did he have poking around in my life, I lied and said I didn't, I made him believe the packet of Gauloises was an errand for a friend of mine, I couldn't stop thinking about what he'd said, I couldn't believe my ears, that Voracious was sleeping with his mother, I just couldn't get my head around it, it was certainly clear that the kid didn't like Voilà, I cast my mind back to the way he'd reacted when I asked him if he was one of Voilà's children, he'd seemed resentful, as if my question was an affront to him, I could see now why he'd been so reluctant to tell me where he was going, so I tried a different topic, thinking that perhaps we could have a civil conversation now that he'd spilled the beans about Voracious and his mother, I asked him about the little boy I'd seen run away from him earlier, why did he want to take his toy away from him *"the kid should have been at school instead of playing in the street,"* he said *"and what about you, you're not at school, are you,"* I asked, wondering what on earth he could mean, and what did that strange kid reply but *"no, I'm not, I don't want to go to school, but that kid should, all children have to go to school, except me,"* he said it was different for him, he didn't like school but he wasn't going to let other kids get away with not going, the back alleys of the medina were his territory, if he saw a child carrying a school bag he'd leave him alone, but any kid he found hanging around his streets would either have to scram or get ready to fight, some kids were scared when they saw him, he said, they'd quake and pee in their pants *"even if they're with their parents,"* but if a kid did wet themselves in front of him he wouldn't lay a finger on them, he'd let them go, he said he'd come across a kid wandering about the medina one day who started crying pathetically and farting as soon as he saw him, he hadn't even touched the kid, and while he was telling me this, the cheeky little beggar came out with *"farting just like Voilà, he was,"* and of course the whole thing made me laugh, the kid too, he was laughing along with me, so I made the most of it to ask him again where he was headed earlier, to see Voracious was his reply, and with that he leapt up, as if he'd just remembered something, and said *"I have to go, my mum told me to catch Voracious on the beach,"* and he waved goodbye and took off without another word,

I went up to the terrace to see if what this kid was telling me was really true, I won't deny that I was driven by jealousy, I looked out at the beach where a handful of fishermen were getting ready to go out, the ones who set out around mid-day, and then I picked out Voracious's figure among them, bending down to check something in his motor, he'd removed the casing on the top part and I saw him pulling the cord to start the engine, I could hear it from where I was and there was their child walking towards him, I say "their child" because there were at least two men who could claim to be his father, I don't know exactly how many of them there were, but I wouldn't be surprised if there were

more than two, the boy looked like he was muttering something in Voracious's ear, they carried on chatting for a while
and then I saw Voilà in the distance, coming over from by
the badamier tree, the kid saw him too and slipped away at
the opposite end of the port and up onto the road before
disappearing into the medina while Voilà went over to help
Voracious repair the motor, and then Voracious replaced the
casing and set off, alone, as usual,

observing all of this, I felt like I was watching a show,
the kind of show that chills you to the bone, was it really
happening before my very eyes or was it all a dream, I hope
you realise I do know the difference between what I've seen
and what I've dreamt, I've never been one to confuse fact
and fiction, unlike those charlatans who don't know the
difference between truth and lies, although maybe there's no
such thing after all, maybe there isn't any difference between
truth and lies, oh, it's all a load of rubbish, it's not worth
getting all hung up about it, what matters is yourself and
everything around you, the things you're aware of, the things
you can see, feel, smell, that's what's real, what else do you
need to know, which means that the things I could see with
my own eyes had to be the truth, yet another truth to add to
all the other truths I'd been oblivious to before,

so Voilà hadn't suspected a thing, and I found myself
wondering about his so-called friendship with Voracious,
since when did friends treat each other like that, I want to
screw your wife so I get close to you, it must be a new kind
of friendship, something you find in that silent world where

eels and sharks flourish and change shape, like turtle eggs
hatching, they're barely recognisable at first but before long
they're good imitations of the real thing, and then they crawl
forth from the depths so others can take their place, but to
go as far as betraying your close friend, God help us, that's
why I was never interested in having friends, no thanks, you
ladies can keep your girlfriends, just be careful you're not so
busy indulging the pleasures of the flesh that you end up
with nothing in your head, you have to be able to use both
your heads, and it's you men I'm talking to now, you have
two heads, as you well know, and if you let the bottom one
rule the top one your brain turns to mush and you're left
with an empty head up top, which means you're nothing
but a brainless beast, don't you agree, which is exactly what
happened with Voracious and that's all I'm saying, I'm not
here to make judgments, it's just an observation, you can't
blame me for calling him an animal, it's not my fault, it's all
because of that second head of his, or else it's my eel-shaped
arse, I'll let you be the judge of that, just this once,

after I found all this out and saw how Voracious acted
towards his closest friend, I stayed there on the terrace,
smoking, lost in thought, I didn't even see where Voilà
went, the beach was deserted, it was only when I heard an
ear-splitting voice that I was startled from my reverie, the
voice of the muezzin at his microphone, it made me jump,
first it was the muezzin from the Friday Mosque and then
other muezzins from all the other mosques joined in, rever-
berating all round the medina as if they'd conspired against
me, just to wake me up, I didn't know which one to listen

192

to, the muezzin from the Friday Mosque or the other ones, there are twenty mosques in the medina alone but the Friday Mosque is the only one big enough to hold a crowd for Friday prayers, it was the first one to bring the whole town together for Friday prayers and the name stuck, and then as the population grew more mosques sprang up, the Friday Mosque is huge, it has two storeys and a tall minaret that towers majestically over the whole town, All-Knowing said it was built in the seventeenth century by a brilliant woman called Sayyidat Karima Binti Saidi Akili, daughter of Sharif Bin Abdallay Tuyur Djamalilaili, she was highly educated and she commissioned this enormous structure in 1670, it was more a testament to her artistic taste than a symbol of power, she's buried beside her father in a pyramid-shaped tomb right behind the mosque,

titles like Sharif mean nothing to me, they don't tell you anything, take poor old All-Knowing for example, you can't learn much about him from his name, people put on all kinds of airs and graces because of the name they have, or because they're rich but it's all piffle, what matters is the way we treat each other, the casual harm we do to one another day in and day out without giving it a moment's thought, we trample all over each other, beat each other up, make each other suffer, we treat people like dogs and claim we're trying to help them, but don't think people can't see through you, of course no one's going to tell the emperor he's not wearing any clothes, they don't want to spoil the show, if we all told each other the truth the play would be over and then we'd all be condemned to a life of boredom, I don't know what the answer is, it's not so easy, is it, who knows what we want in the end,

it's certainly true that if you looked down on the medina from the citadel you couldn't help but notice the height of the minaret in relation to the rooftops, rather like a lone coconut palm in the middle of the desert, but it's the citadel that dominates everything in the medina, including the minaret, goodness, here I am blathering on about minarets and citadels and history, I was talking about the muezzins snapping me out of my reverie, it all gets muddled up in my mind, what I really wanted to say was how shocked I was by this display of so-called friendship, it made me feel that life wasn't worth living, it was worse than when I found Voracious with that hussy Bream, men, I ask you, it's not that I'm against men in general, no, why would I hate men just because I was cheated on, that's not what it is, no, it's the brazen lack of shame, I'm not the jealous sort and heavens above, I'm not a man-hater, but men seem to want to treat women like their playthings, it's in their blood, and when they're not doing that, they're making clichéd judgements so they can attack women and throw them off balance, they're always saying women are impossible to understand, they name natural disasters after them, for heaven's sake, Elina, Catherina and goodness knows what else, but it doesn't stop them chasing after these incomprehensible creatures, fighting over them, grabbing them for themselves, slaughtering each other like beasts, they'll wheedle and manipulate, they'll abuse women and then stand back and subject them to all sorts of insults, they're always claiming they're smarter and stronger than women, don't make me laugh, if you men are so clever, why are you always drooling at the sight of a woman in a miniskirt, is that what you call intelligence, a man who looks at a woman's legs, her breasts, her backside and can't think straight, is that intelligence, tell me that, let's be honest, you men like to twist things, just who do you think you are, you need to look reality in the face, it's right there in front of you, every day, wherever you go, it's men who are the stupid ones, chasing after women, consumed with desire for them all the time, they'll do anything to try and get a woman in their power, they'll even get down on their hands and knees and crawl, what else do you want me to say, well, that's all I have to say on the subject, I'm sure you think I'm just being jealous or that I'm deranged or something, I can just imagine what you think,

a few days after I found out about the affair between Voracious and Voilà's wife I was starting to feel worse and worse, I wasn't smoking enough to satisfy my cravings, I didn't want to keep sending someone to get them for me so I had to cut down, then I started feeling sick whenever I was cooking, the sight of all that food made me feel constantly nauseous, I wasn't hungry for anything, I didn't eat for fear of throwing up in front of everyone, and then one day I had to cook some manioc leaves for a dish we call *mataba*, a traditional favourite we have with rice, you make it with crushed leaves and coconut milk, some people simply can't eat rice without *mataba* where I come from, All-Knowing wanted it made for him at least three times a week, and on Sundays, his day off, we absolutely had to make it for him, so, it was Sunday that day, I wasn't feeling well but I was doing my chores as usual, it was my job to pound the manioc leaves while Rattler was grating coconut, All-Knowing must have been out somewhere, under the badamier tree probably, the usual Sunday noises drifted in from outside, people clattering about, children having a good time, which made me wonder where that kid with several fathers had got to, letting all those children run around outside for so long, you could hear adults chatting too and street vendors going past with their barrows, calling out their wares, it was all very chilled, a typical Sunday and there I was, feeling dizzy every time I raised the pestle to pound the manioc leaves, the voices were starting to seem further and further away, blending and blurring into one and then disappearing into the void, I forced myself to listen, trying to distinguish the individual voices until my head began to spin, and then as I carried on pounding the pestle into the mortar over and over again, I felt everything going black, it all went quiet, I couldn't see and then I don't know what happened but I ended up toppling over like an uprooted tree, I couldn't keep myself upright, it was stronger than I was, like some kind of infernal machine, it dragged me down and flung me to the ground with great force, I couldn't stop myself, I passed out, still clutching the pestle and when I came round I was lying on my bed, I could hear people murmuring somewhere in the distance, All-Knowing's voice was clearly recognisable but there was a second voice I couldn't make out, a woman's voice, I tried to sit up, which wasn't easy, but I managed to do it somehow or other, I realised my head hurt and I put my hand up to touch it and that was how I knew I was injured, my forehead was wrapped in a bandage and my head burned when I touched it, I still couldn't make out what they were saying, it all sounded like gibberish, I wanted to know who it was talking to All-Knowing in hushed tones, I wanted to know what they were saying, whether or not they were talking about me, I managed to drag myself out of the bedroom and I caught them off their guard, locked in conversation in the doorway to the living room, All-Knowing and a woman who lived in a different part of town and worked as a doctor, I recognised her face, she worked in the hospital in Hombo, that was all I knew about her, they stopped talking, the woman had a black bag in her right hand, she glanced in my direction and then back at All-Knowing for a few seconds and then muttered *"well, Monsieur All-Knowing, I'd best leave you with your offspring, I'm sure you'll do what you think is right, I'll be available in case you should need me,"* All-Knowing said nothing, he didn't even look at me, he was silent the whole time, his head bowed and hands crossed behind his back, like a man manacled and burdened by the shame of his crime, he merely nodded by way of acknowledgement of the doctor's remark and I knew then without a shadow of doubt, it was all clear as day, a light had been shone on my belly, my innermost secret was out in the open and the woman who'd revealed it was heading for the door to leave, I looked over and saw Rattler sitting on the bottom stair, staring at me with a look of furious worry on her face, the door creaked slowly shut and slammed and then All-Knowing turned to me, and came right out with it, he announced in a stern voice *"get yourself ready to leave this house, this minute, I don't want to see you here again, find*

*yourself somewhere to go, your lover's house for example, I want
you out of my sight, right now,"* I stayed there, rooted to the
spot, Rattler got up from where she was sitting, seething
and scowling, she could barely stand up straight, and I stood
there, stiff as a post in the courtyard, while All-Knowing,
realising I hadn't moved, got more and more worked up
and started to rail against me impatiently *"I think I've made
myself clear, so don't stand there waiting for me to give you a
push, I'm not going repeat myself, if I have to tell you again you'll
be on the receiving end of a slap, I'll give you a good thumping,"*
he said in no uncertain terms, I turned round resolutely to
go and collect my things from the bedroom, I could hear
him still holding forth, for as we all know, he was nothing if
not a squawk-box, once he got started he'd never stop, angry
or not, but this was a new side to him, he told me to go and
get my things and for some reason followed it up with *"you
needn't take anything at all from in there, there's nothing here
of yours, this is my house, and everything in it belongs to me,"* I
didn't need to hear any more, he'd made it clear I only had
a few minutes to get myself together, so I started by picking
up my handbag, the one I used to take when I went over to
see Voracious instead of going to school, I grabbed a few
bits of clothing too and a pair of shoes in a plastic bag, and
all the time I was gathering up the bits and pieces that really
mattered to me All-Knowing was badgering me, venting all
his bile *"hurry up and get out, I don't owe you a thing,"* he
yelled from the courtyard, Rattler was trying to talk to him,
saying *"give her a break, dad,"* but as soon as she said it he
snapped back *"who asked you, I don't want to hear a word from
you, you mind your own business and keep your mouth shut,*

do I make myself clear," I was just about ready to go when I remembered the ring Voracious had given me, I had to open my bag to check it was still there, it was, and I could see I had a few bits of change left too, the money I'd been pinching once every third day from All-Knowing, thank God, I wasn't completely empty-handed, I walked briskly towards the door with my bags, I could hear All-Knowing sounding more and more infuriated by the fact that I wasn't responding, I knew my silence would incense him further, and then he started complaining, bemoaning his fate like a man condemned *"you've put up a wall of silence around your-self just to put me through hell, go on, get out of here, I should have listened to what people say, after all I've done for you and this is what I get, I've sweated blood for you to succeed, both of you, I thought you were the intelligent one, Eel and all along I was harbouring a viper in the nest, you've dragged my name through the mud, how could I have been such a fool,"* I can't stand people who question their own decisions, when you make up your mind to do something you don't talk about it as if you're not sure you're doing the right thing, I couldn't see that any of what he was saying mattered at all, success, intelligence, reputation, I don't give a fig about any of that stuff, none of it, you should have kept your mouth shut, my dear All-Knowing, instead of banging on like that, battering me with all those words, none of it meant anything to me, I couldn't have cared less,

I was already outside in the courtyard getting ready to leave when I saw him looking at me like he was about to explode, he glared at me and said *"what have you got in that*

199

bag, you're taking nothing from here, didn't I make myself clear, am I speaking Chinese or something, Bambara, Lingala, Double Dutch, did you not understand what I said, huh, answer me," he came up to me and furiously grabbed the plastic bag I'd put my clothes and shoes in, he was about to go for my handbag too when Rattler jumped in and came to my aid and not a moment too soon, no way was I going to let him get his hands on that bag and certainly not with that ring in it, I'd rather have died that day by his hand than let him get hold of my present, he could have the bag and the money I'd stolen from him but the ring, no way, I'd show him what this eel was made of, but I didn't have to, thanks to Rattler, the two of them got into a tussle, both of them pulling on the plastic bag until the contents spilled out onto the ground, they ended up each clutching a piece of the bag, breathing hard like runners, I'm telling you, they were completely out of breath, Rattler was trying to pick up the clothes and All-Knowing was grabbing them from her and refusing to let them go, and he said to her *"you want to fight to the death here, is that what it is, huh, you think this is some kind of madhouse here, are you trying to kill yourself,"* I told Rattler to let him get on with it, it was no good going against him when it came to his possessions, although of course it was completely unfair, as I'm sure you'll agree, I walked out the door with nothing but my handbag, just to show him that I didn't need his things, the bag and the money were all I needed, I could hear All-Knowing as I left, still yelling furiously after me *"those clothes were all paid for with my money, have you no shame, go and find the one who got you into this mess, get him to buy you some clothes, I don't know who he is and I don't want to know, whoever that moron is, you let him stick his pecker inside you, you've made your bed, now you can lie in it, "* his words washed over me, it was all hot air, meaningless phrases, people say the first thing that comes into their heads where I come from, nothing but baloney, everyone seems to have their own repertoire and I have a few sayings of my own too, when people have nothing to say they spend all their time bleating about something or other and then when they do have something to say they do nothing but spout shit, if you're super smart the shit comes out of your mouth, if you're not so smart it comes out of your arse, you can be daft as a brush and everyone will love you but if you're worth anything at all you'll get nothing but abuse, I could go on if you like, I've got lots more up my sleeve, all you moralisers out there, I hope you're listening to this,

to tell the truth, I didn't know where to turn at that point, I'd acted as if I had all I needed but I didn't, I left that house with my head held high though, All-Knowing had every right to decide who he wanted to live in his house, didn't he, it was his house after all, that eel tank, what's the good of staying if the owner doesn't want you there, and he thought he'd managed to keep me on a tight rein, but he was wrong there, I mean I ask you, can you imagine keeping me tethered like a goat, me, dream on,

outside, I stopped by the door to collect my thoughts, there I was, with nowhere to call home but I was free as a bird, at long last I had free rein to do as I chose, I had to make up my mind about where to go, I can't stand drifting around like a stray dog, as I think I've already told you but it was hard to think straight with All-Knowing still hollering, blathering on, yada yada, pouring out all his rage and Rattler making even more of a racket, I could hear them both, Rattler was blubbing and snivelling like a little girl who's hurt herself, what's the good of crying like that, it's not worth tuppence, you should never let yourself wallow in misery, it might spill over into someone else's life, someone who's teetering on the edge of a cliff, I was determined not to let them get to me, I had my own path to follow, but the two of them were beginning to get on my nerves, the madman and the little girl, the blabbermouth and the cry-baby, and just as I was getting ready move away so as not to hear them, I saw Guarantee walking towards me, he seemed surprised to see me and started interrogating me *"what on earth are you doing, you've had a nasty fall, barely an hour ago and now you're going out, where do you think you're going, why are you standing there gaping at me, what is it, do you need a hand,"* I didn't know what to say, he'd obviously heard about me passing out, he must have been the one who went to get that woman, he'd left me with All-Knowing and gone to find her, Guarantee was like that, he never did things by halves, but I could see he didn't know what the doctor had discovered, he didn't have the full picture, he wasn't there when that woman dropped the bombshell, and then he realised he wasn't going to get an answer out of me and barged into the house, I grabbed my chance to slip away out of the neighbourhood as quickly as I could and it wasn't until much later that I stopped somewhere at a safe distance to see how much money I had in my bag, I counted it all up carefully, one thousand two hundred and fifty francs, and just as I finished I heard a child's voice calling out to me, it was Voilà's kid, the one who'd told me Voracious was his father, he wanted to say hi to me just to show people he knew me, and then he asked me where I was going, I had the feeling he was getting back at me for my nosiness, I thought about how I'd persisted with my questions that time out of sheer curiosity and ended up unwittingly dragging the truth out of him, how was I to know I'd uncover such earth-shattering revelations, but as far as I could tell, I was the only one who knew, or there again, maybe it had always been common knowledge, maybe I was the only one who wasn't in on the secret, who knows, as I've said before, walls have ears where I come from, you never know what people are saying about you, it's all hush-hush, whispering in corners but they're quick enough to point the finger the minute they see you coming, what I do know is that no one was going to get my secrets out of me, they might hear it from Voracious but not from me, no way, they'd have to kill me first, no one could make me talk, I'm telling you, if I hadn't fainted that day, I would have vanished without All-Knowing ever finding out I was pregnant, I mean he never realised I was drinking and smoking, or that I was stealing his money, so when I saw the kid, I was in the middle of concocting a plan, I knew I had to decide where I was headed first of all, oh God, listen to me, what am I doing spilling everything out here in a vacuum, I don't even know if I'm alive or dead, I'm on my last legs, I know that much, but I can't afford to dwell on all that, let's get back to where we were, I don't want to die on you before we get to the end of this interminable tale, what a let-down that would be, if I left you to make up the ending yourself, like one of those tedious teachers that like to befuddle students with all sorts of fantastical nonsense, don't you think,

so I answered the kid's question without thinking and told him I was going on a trip and then he asked *"where,"* good question but I came up with an answer straight away *"to Mayotte,"* which, when I thought about it, was a better answer than I realised, it was just what I needed, a life-saver in fact *"why don't I get on a clandestine boat to Mayotte,"* I said to myself, there were all sorts of ideas spinning around in my head at that point, I decided I needed to sell the ring and make the journey that very day, why not, there was no time to waste, in Mayotte I'd be able to live my life on my own terms, that's what I told myself, I'd live there with my child for the rest of my days, I'd forget all about Voracious and his mind-numbing depravity, it'll destroy him in the end, he'll be dragged down into the pit of infamy, for all his bravado, he has no idea what a wretch he is, he's smart but not smart enough to understand how crippled he is, to realise his handsome features are nothing but a front for a withered heart, if I went to Mayotte I wouldn't have to put up with All-Knowing lording it over me and constantly bombarding me with his highfaluting pronouncements that have no relevance to my life as an eel, I wouldn't have to endure Rattler prying into my affairs, naïve child that she was, hoping people would think she was smart and asking all those infantile questions, the kind of questions you'd expect from a kid, like that one with several dads, poor kid, although he seemed happy enough, oh God, that poor little boy, still, it's got nothing to do with me, the more I thought about it all the more I realised I wanted nothing more to do with anyone who tried to hold me back, there was no room in my life for people like that, what I wanted was a life without hassles, to be free to bring up my kid, and when I get to where I'm going I'll work day and night, I'll do anything, I'll clean bathtubs, wash basins, I'll mop floors and clean windows, anything, no more pursuit of pleasure for me, I'll work like a dog to earn money of my own and I won't let those crooks in the banks get their hands on it, I'll have my own bank under my mattress until the day I die, I'll get there, by God I will,

you might make so bold as to ask how I propose to live on this island where they stop you all the time and ask for your papers, you'd think it was the Garden of Eden, I mean it's not as if the same sun doesn't shine on all these islands, what's so special about the island of Mayotte, well I don't give a damn about papers, I'll worry about all that later and anyway, who's going to stop me and ask me for my papers, huh, some guy with papers of his own, that's right, well, he'll have to tell me where his papers are, the real ones that is, I'm not talking about forged documents here, because the papers he'll be asking me to show will be forgeries wherever they were issued, a person's true papers are nowhere to be found on this earth, you know I'm right, what's with all this asking for papers, I mean no one knows what's written in their own papers, the real ones that is, people think they can depart from the script in the middle of the show but the

author is watching all the actors making fools of themselves
with their attempts to skew the plot, the one who wrote the
whole show has all our papers, with reams of information
about every single actor, it's a waste of time trying to make
up your own lines, it'll never come to anything, and as for
the paper fanatics, I'll tell them they can see my papers when
they've found their own, if I knew a way to get my hands on
some legal papers, I'd obviously carry them with me all the
time but I'm the same as everyone else, my papers must exist
somewhere but I have no idea what's in them, so let's put all
that aside, we'll leave it as a side-dish for the moment, it's
time to get serious, enough of this joking around,

while all this was going through my head, the kid was sitting
next to me talking to me, asking what'd happened to me, he'd
seen the bandage round my head, even though I'd pulled my
shiromani up over my head, I told him I'd banged my head
on a wall and he smirked, the cheeky little sod, I could see
him sniggering while he told me I should look where I was
going, people were staring at me as if I was a creature from
another planet, I wanted to get out of there so I asked him
to come with me and show me the various jewellery shops
in the medina, he spent a few minutes counting them all
off and then he pointed out to me where they were, I told
him to take me to the closest ones first, I needed to sell my
ring to a jeweller as soon as possible, so we went into the
first one, where the young guy in charge gave my ring a
withering look that said he thought it was a worthless trinket,
but he still fondled it as if it were his wife, the pervert, I
watched as he turned it this way and that, weighing it again

and again on his scales, no way was I going to put up with that, he was wasting my time, so I grabbed it out of his hands, I could imagine what he was going to say to me, I wasn't fooled by his snooty attitude, he was dying to buy my ring, I could tell by his shaking fingers and the frown on his face, he wasn't going to admit it though and I knew he was getting ready to pull one over on me, so I hightailed it out of his shop, I hate that sort of hypocrisy, we went into the next jewellers where I had to negotiate with an old man who was deaf as a post, God it was awful, I had to repeat myself at least three times, shouting loudly to get my message across, in the end I told him to give me back my ring and walked out, he was really starting to annoy me, I'd already spent ten minutes trying to get him to understand that I wanted to sell the ring, we hadn't even started to talk price, God almighty, and there was another old man in the third shop, I showed him the ring, and he acted like he was looking for something, his hands wandering all over the table, I watched him fumbling around, exploring every object with his fingertips, in the end he found what he was looking for, his glasses, and I realised he was blind as a bat, he put them on and waited a moment or two before asking me to hand him the ring, he said he didn't put much value on that kind of gold but he'd be able to buy it anyway, he asked me how much I wanted *"a hundred and fifty thousand francs,"* I said *"what,"* he exclaimed with a look of shock and I lost control and screamed my price at the top of my voice, thinking that he was probably hard of hearing too, he looked affronted and replied curtly *"I am not deaf, young lady,"* he informed me that the ring was not worth that price, that he wasn't even sure it was gold at all but if I wanted him to buy it, he could give me fifty thousand francs, I'd had enough and told him to give me back the ring, I'd leave him in peace, I wasn't going to sell my ring, it was all a mistake, not for that paltry sum *"are they all crooks, these jewellers,"* I wondered, and just as I was stalking off, the old man called me back and offered me seventy-five thousand francs, I told him my ring was worth well over a hundred thousand francs but I might be able to let him have it for a hundred thousand and not a cent less, he pondered for a moment, I really didn't feel like waiting around but at the last minute, he asked me to give it to him again and he weighed it one more time before counting out the hundred thousand francs in cash, I knew he was perfectly well aware of the ring's true value, but he wanted to try and cheat me, good God, that's the way these crooks operate, so off we went, me and the boy with two fathers, looking for something to eat, I asked him if there was anything in particular he wanted, he said no, so we each had a croissant and a glass of ginger juice at a roadside café and then we said goodbye, and as I still had a bit of change left from the money I'd stolen from All-Knowing, I bought a packet of Gauloises too,

I'd crossed the Rubicon, I knew exactly what I was doing, I was headed towards Missiri to leave, from there I'd be able to get a bus to Doroni, where I planned to find out about picking up a *kwassa-kwassa,* as we call them here, one of the boats that go to Mayotte, and then, as I was striking out towards Missiri who should I see heading towards me but Guarantee *"not him again, what does he want now,"* I said to myself *"I've been looking for you everywhere,"* he announced, gasping for breath, I wondered if All-Knowing had had a change of heart and sent him to find me, what a turn up for the books that would be, he wasn't likely to show any compassion though, All-Knowing wasn't one to be tender-hearted and in all honesty, I wasn't about to abandon my plans whatever Guarantee had to say, as it happened All-Knowing hadn't changed his mind, he could never do that, but Guarantee had cooked up a plan of his own, he'd come to tell me that he wanted me to go to his place first, to stay with his wife and children for a few days *"until your father comes to his senses,"* he added, he'd tried to talk All-Knowing round but the old curmudgeon refused to calm down, he was still fulminating and swearing by all the gods that he'd never allow me to set foot in his house again, he'd actually said to Guarantee that he'd never forgive me, those were his very words, and to think he'd had the nerve to tell us it was wrong to cut off the hand that offends you, so much for his integrity, the way he acted that day proved he was incapable of practicing what he preached, I told Guarantee there was no point in hoping All-Knowing would think again, he'd shown his true colours, I explained that I'd made my decision and I intended to stick with it, no way was I going to turn my back on my eel-shaped life, it would be a terrible mistake, in my heart I'd always be longing for it, he tried pleading with me but I told him there was no point *"where are you going to go in that state,"* he asked me, and I told him what I was planning to do, I spilled it all out, and he said he had brothers and sisters who'd done well for themselves in Mayotte, they'd be able to take me in, he gave me their

names and addresses and I wrote them down in a notebook
I'd only ever used for eel sketching at home, Guarantee had
been to Mayotte when he was young, he'd spent fifteen years
there and he knew the island well, he gave me the names of
people in Domoni who operated the clandestine boats, he
said I had to make sure the owner of the *kwassa-kwassa* was
someone to be trusted, there were two names he said several
times that stuck in my head, Miraculous and Survivor
"Miraculous and Survivor, they're the best for the job, although
Survivor did get lost at sea coming back from Mayotte once, he
turned up in Mozambique three months later," and then in an
effort to reassure me he added *"but that was a long time ago,"*
and with that he left me to go my way,

I was headed for the ends of the earth, I gazed at the medina
behind me, two big tears welling up in my eyes, the first
tears I'd shed since I'd turned seventeen, I was leaving my
home, the place where I'd always felt safe, where my eel's life
had taken shape, I knew I'd never come back, it was a voyage
of no return, the die was cast, but I hadn't expected to end
up here in this fathomless void, adrift in the ocean wastes,
not that I regret any of it, please try and get that into your
head, I know there are people who can't understand something unless they've seen it with their own eyes or heard
it with their own ears, and then there are the people who
have their heads up their arses, they're the worst, and they all
think theirs is the only way to understand the world, but for
heaven's sake, if that's the best you can do you're never going
to get the point of what I'm telling you, even if you spend
the whole of your sad little life poring over my words, you

still won't understand what I'm getting at here, my words will be lost on the wind, no, the best way to understand something is to forget about your ears, your eyes, your arse, it's your heart you need if you want to read what's in my heart, and don't forget, like all things that can't be measured, the heart is not easy to understand, that's what this journey has taught me, the truth is, you can't let your dreams run away with you like some kind of computer virus, what's it called, a Trojan horse, you only need a sprinkling of them to spice up your life, you don't need a torrent, all that does is contaminate the water, like a dose of hemlock in the soup,

TRANQUIL SMASHES HER ROCK AND KICKS UP A STORM

inside the bus, some of the passengers were jabbering non-stop, the seats were arranged in groups, men and women sitting side-by-side or facing one another, some looked worn out and couldn't stop yawning and others were asleep on their feet, but it was ones who couldn't stop talking that really bothered me, I couldn't think straight with all that yammering, everything was all jumbled up in my head, I desperately needed to let my thoughts flow freely, there was nothing I loved more than to spend my time pondering, imagining myself in a world of my own, somewhere quiet and deserted, I was already missing our terrace but I knew had to put it out of my mind, I sat there trying to gather my thoughts but a woman sitting directly across from me kept cutting into my reverie with her piercing voice, going on about how she'd just sold her bananas at the market in Hampanga for next to nothing, who cared if she'd been forced to accept a rubbish price, why did she have to bore us to death with it, what had we done, we'd paid good money to ride in that bus and we were entitled to have a peaceful journey without being subjected to her rant, all she did was complain about the money she'd lost with no mention of the money she had made, no one else could get a word in edgeways, and then another woman started talking over her, she'd obviously decided there was no point in waiting for the banana woman to finish and she wanted to have her say too, and when the banana woman realised someone had interrupted her in mid-flow, she had no choice but to button her lip while the second woman held forth about how awful it was that she hadn't sold her manioc at all, meaning of course that the banana woman should be grateful for the money she'd managed to make instead of feeling sorry for herself, and then a man who'd been listening to all this decided throw in his two cents worth and said *"listen ladies, you're getting yourselves all wound up for no reason, you can't expect to make a fortune from your crops every single day, now why don't you tell us about the good days you've had selling your wares,"* at which some people howled with laughter, and the two women laughed too, although they didn't say anything, and then the man started haranguing them about not being the only ones with problems, take him for example, he'd just had an altercation with one of the town's big businessmen but he wasn't making a fuss about it, the big shots had put pressure on him to sell his bag of cloves at their price, the cloves he'd harvested with the help of his wife and children, God knows what they were going to say when he arrived home, in all the months he'd spent tending his plants by the sweat of his brow he'd never imagined he'd have to sell his cloves for next to nothing, it was a thankless task growing cloves, he had mouths to feed and the price he'd been given was barely enough for a week's food, in the end he'd had no choice but to accept their price, he couldn't go back home to Bambao with his sack of cloves unsold to face his wife and children and their empty stomachs, they'd gape at him in disbelief and hang their heads, he'd be so ashamed, he'd feel a complete failure as a father, he'd have nothing to offer, no money, no explanations, no words of comfort, the sadness would be unbearable, by this time virtually all the passengers in the bus were listening to him, some were visibly moved and couldn't look him in the eye and then one man who'd been having a nap woke up, peered out of the window with a worried look on his face and yelled out to the driver to stop, he wanted to get off, and at this point I took a look at the view outside to see where we were, I didn't recognise any of the towns and villages we'd driven through, I wanted to ask the man sitting next to me where we were but I was scared of looking like a fool, who knows what he'd have said, he might have thought I was being stuck up and made fun of me and given them all an excuse to have a good laugh at my expense, I certainly didn't consider myself any better than any of the other passengers, I didn't harbour any feelings of superiority, why should I, what did I have to feel superior about, but people have the strangest ideas and I knew I had to think before I opened my mouth, by this time, the man who wanted to get off was already on the tarmac and the bus was pulling out and just as I was wondering how to broach the subject of where we were, a woman interrupted my train of thought and started talking to the other passengers about the man who'd just got off the bus *"that poor bloke didn't have a clue where he was, did you see him stumbling around, it took him a while to figure out he was in Bazmine, where on earth did he think he was, he probably thought he was dreaming that he was floating in space somewhere, or maybe he was expecting to find himself in his own bedroom, waking up from his siesta,"* and at that they all burst out laughing, men and women alike, splitting their sides, but I wasn't laughing, I didn't see what was so funny about that poor man, I concentrated on the name the woman had said, Bazmine, it sounded familiar to me, along with all the other places I'd heard mentioned, I'd never been there, the only towns I recognised as we went through them were Mirontsi and Oani, where the airport is, which meant we'd already gone through Patsy and Koki without my realising it, Patsy is where the Coca-Cola plant is and it's also where the most feared prison on the island is located, I decided I'd listen to the other passengers telling the driver when they wanted to get off and that way I'd find out what the other towns were, we went through several more, Mchacojou, Tratringa, Bambao Lamtsanga, which was where the clove man with all the problems got off with his empty sack in his hands, we stopped in Jéjé, then in Jomani, where we deposited the manioc woman with her big sack of unsold manioc, two men helped her haul it down from the roof of the bus, then we went to Shiroroni, where we left the original windbag, the one with the bananas, after which there was peace and quiet in the bus and then at last we arrived at the final stop, Domoni, the old capital, I'd heard the last few passengers mention it, all four of them were from Domoni, two young men who were talking about football and two women, one young and one old, neither of whom were saying anything, the old one looked half-asleep, probably worn out from the trip, we pulled in to the town and the driver stopped in a busy square, where we all emerged from the bus, I watched the young guys head towards a long narrow street while the young woman followed the road straight ahead and the old lady hobbled slowly off towards another street, I decided to follow her, I wanted to ask her a few questions, I'd been reluctant to say anything in the bus for fear of arousing the other passengers' curiosity but here, where we'd been deposited, everyone seemed engrossed in their own business, card games, shopping or what have you, there was clamour and commotion everywhere even though night was falling, I sensed it as soon as I set foot outside the bus and felt a breath of cool evening air on my face, Guarantee had given me some names of places, Papani, Balawi, Mstangombéli but it was in Papani that Guarantee had friends and that was where I needed to go first, so I asked the old lady for directions and she said to follow her, and when we arrived at her house, she gave one of her grandchildren, a kid of about twelve or thirteen, the job of taking me to Papani,

we set off in the direction I'd seen the young woman take and walked for quite a while along a sleeping street where the only signs of life were the occasional passing cars, I was exhausted, disoriented by the rural surroundings and the faint glimmer of dusk lighting our road, now and then I heard the glorious sound of birds twittering in the trees, punctuated with the hooting of an owl, I recognised it as the haunting cry of an eagle owl, an abject voice filled with melancholy that sounded almost like a person sobbing, repeated over and over again, moths flitted about my head as if they were trying to cast a spell on me, one almost went into my right eye and all the while the boy walked ahead of me without saying a word, his silence unnerved me , I needed to hear his voice to be sure he wasn't a ghost, it was the only way to allay my doubts, so I asked him if everything was alright, an idiotic, meaningless question if ever there was one, it's not as if I could have done anything for him if things weren't alright, and he replied *"yeah great,"* I felt somewhat relieved but then I realised that I was ravenous, if I'd been at home I'd have been enjoying my dinner, the kid was marching along taking huge strides and I forced myself to keep up with him even though I was exhausted from the journey, I kept pestering him with questions in an effort to tire him, I asked him if he knew someone by the name of Miraculous, he said he did, so in the same breath I added *"and Survivor,"* to which he replied with the same terse *"yes,"* in fact that was how he answered all my questions, with a blunt one-word response, no more no less, I wondered if it was shyness on his part, I'm always wary of shyness, it's usually just a stone for eels to hide under, rather like silence, something which I of all people should never forget, the timid ones are generally the sort who'll dig their heels in the hardest, there's nothing they won't do to hang on to their eel-shaped life, which is exactly the way I am, if you must know, I've always been shy and reserved but I was digging myself into a deep, watertight hole, and that's as far as I'll go on the subject *"you'll see what comes out of the chicken's arse sooner or later,"* as my father All-Knowing would say,

we got there in the end and at long last I could hear voices

all around me, people chatting right left and centre, I asked
the boy where I could find the people I was looking for and
he led me to a collection of huts, I could see smoke too
a bit further off and I looked around to see where it was
coming from, someone was barbecuing fish kebabs, if you're
wondering how I knew it was fish, I could smell it of course,
I do have a fully functioning sense of smell you know, men
were sitting on benches in the area where the smoke was
coming from, I could see them with my own eyes, seated
round the fire eating and talking, all I could hear was a
hubbub of voices, it was impossible to make out a word
they were saying, and further off still there was the familiar
sound of the waves breaking on the shore from time to time,
a sound I'd heard all my life, and that's another thing you
should know about me, I'm no different from those ocean
waves, I washed up on shore and now I've returned to the
sea where I was born, my ears are attuned to the cries of
my sisters, the waves, it did me good to hear them rolling
in that evening, breaking and turning to foam on a beach I
couldn't see, yes, they were still a ways off but I could hear
them swooshing as they leapt about in wild abandon, they
were playing with me, calling out to me at the tops of their
voices, wondering why I said nothing in reply,

"so we're very close to the beach," I said to myself, I could feel
sand scrunching underfoot, mixed with gravel and bigger
pieces of rock, the kid went over to talk to a man sitting
in the midst of the group, dressed in a straw hat, a cotton
shirt and denim shorts, he stood up and walked over to
me, chewing on a piece of fish and carrying his *brochette*, I

started out by introducing myself, I mentioned Guarantee and he said he knew him well *"he's a good friend of mine, that one,"* he told me and then I explained to him that I wanted to leave that evening for Mayotte *"I'm really sorry, miss, but you'll have to wait till tomorrow, our boat's just left about an hour ago with ninety people on board, my colleague Survivor will be here at sun-up tomorrow and your name will be on the list of people leaving tomorrow, if that's what you want, of course,"* he explained, I was bitterly disappointed, waiting until tomorrow seemed like waiting a year, all I wanted was to get away from the island of my birth without a moment's delay,

Miraculous and Survivor were friends who owned their own *kwassa-kwassa*, Guarantee had stressed that they were known to deliver a reliable service *"you're in good hands with them,"* he'd said several times, the passage to Mayotte was risky and illegal, I say risky because when you climbed aboard one of those boats, as I did, you really did take your life in your own hands but Guarantee said that Miraculous and Survivor had successfully taken a number of people to the neighbouring island and I knew it was only a couple of hours away from me now, I was getting closer, but I hadn't come this far to hang around and wait until the next day, let alone in that strange place with all those people looking like they were getting ready to party all night, I'd rather listen to nature's soundtrack than that racket, nature's song can be unsettling but it gives me a feeling of freedom too, human noise does nothing but set me on edge, but anyway, I let Miraculous show me to his place, it was close at hand, just a few steps away in the middle of a group of huts, we found his wife and children there, his wife was a gentle, comely woman who plied me with cooked bananas, grilled fish and a bowl of rice, but I couldn't eat a thing, I was so desperate to leave I'd lost my appetite, so I lingered outside smoking like a chimney, staring out at the sea in the darkness, those were the best moments of my time there, I felt my heart beating softly in my chest as I gazed out to sea, like a child being rocked contentedly in a cradle, I was in my element, soothed by the crashing of the waves, I imagined myself at home on the terrace, opposite the beach at Mjihari, and gradually, as the chattering of voices mingled with the sound of the waves, I forgot about my cares,

I didn't sleep a wink all night, I lay there in the room I'd been allotted, with my eyes open, wide awake, while swarms of gigantic mosquitoes celebrated my arrival by feasting on me, I began to think the brazen beasts had organised the whole thing in advance, and then there was the room itself, absolutely bare and utterly devoid of any creature comforts, I had nothing to look at throughout that whole interminable night but the flimsily constructed structure of that traditional dwelling,

I went outside early in the morning to gaze at the sea before the sun rose, there was hardly anyone around, a fresh finely-tuned breeze brought a welcome chill to my face as the sea danced placidly beneath my gaze, it's the same wherever you go, the sea in the early morning always has this same calming effect, it's a feeling you can sometimes experience on land too, so long as you don't know what's going on behind all those closed doors, and then all at once, I saw a boat in the distance, lurching towards the shore, it was coming closer, its motor making a deafening racket, then the person at the helm turned off the motor and that was when I heard voices shouting all around me, Survivor, the name was on everyone's lips, it was all you heard, so he's back I thought as the boat slid up onto the beach, Miraculous appeared all of a sudden along with dozens of other people pouring out of the huts to welcome Survivor like a hero returning from the wars, Miraculous walked over to him grinning like God knows what, they both looked pleased as Punch, mission accomplished, I watched them relishing their discussion as they walked slowly towards the huts, glorying in their achievement, laughing and beaming broadly, Survivor turned round to look at me, shot me a rapid glance and carried on talking to Miraculous, and then they were walking towards me and Miraculous came out with *"what did you say your name was, miss,"* I told them and they asked me how much money I had for the journey,

as I went to get my bag, I heard Survivor behind me making fun of my name, honest to God, I heard him muttering *"Eel, what kind of a name is that, Eel, Christ, where on earth did that come from,"* Miraculous told him to keep quiet, no doubt thinking I could hear, I felt myself getting angry, what made him think he could get away with that kind of talk, making fun of people like that, well, I could cut to the quick with my tongue too, I was perfectly capable of coming up with a witty put-down, a real tongue-lashing even, not that he'd understand if I were to tell him the only reason I spared him was because I took pity on him, I had great sympathy for people who'd escaped from the jaws of death, I left them alone, how else could they survive, but what did he think he was doing putting me down like that, what kind of a survivor has no sympathy for his fellow castaways, I'm telling you I didn't think much of this coarse fellow, poking fun wherever he saw fit, some people see nothing wrong with that kind of talk, well if you think it's acceptable to laugh at others' expense, let me tell you, you can laugh all you like, you'll end up with egg on your face soon enough, words don't only harm the person they're aimed at, they can poison the mind of the person uttering them, rather like farting, which can damage a person's health, I think I've already said all this, I probably have, well anyway, I won't say it again, but what gave Survivor the right to make fun of other people's names, what was so wonderful about his name, I'm harping on about it because he really got to me, no, please don't interrupt me, if you're there, that is, hear me out here, where's the glory in being labelled a survivor, God knows, I'd rather be dead than seen as a victim, for in the end that's what survivors are, I don't ever want to be one of them, I'd rather die right here than be rescued and run the risk of being named for that jumped-up wimp, where's the heroism in having to be rescued, anyway, I pretended I hadn't heard what he said but all the same, it left me with a bitter taste in my mouth,

so I handed over to them what was left of my money, all I wanted was to leave, that was the only thing I cared about, I didn't want to stay there one moment longer, I was utterly disgusted with that man Survivor and his personal remarks, I'd had enough, I gave him a scathing look but he was completely oblivious, they were too busy counting and double-checking the money I'd given them, so that was it, I thought to myself, they were only in it for the money, they were nothing but a pair of wheeler-dealers, eventually Miraculous looked up and said *"OK, so you'll leave at seven this evening, we have to wait for more passengers to arrive,"* I wasn't happy with that at all, waiting until seven o'clock in the evening when I was already itching to leave, I bit my tongue and went over to put my bag down in that room where I'd spent a sleepless night and then I went to watch the sun coming up, I sat down under a spindly-looking badamier tree growing at the edge of the waterfront, it wasn't at all like the Mjihari badamier, the tree in our neighbourhood was a venerable giant, it'd seen it all,

from my vantage point I could see all the people arriving and making enquiries of those two rip-off artists, handing over their money and listening carefully to their instructions, there were several women with children or babies, and I began to realise that there was quite a crowd of us there, I lost count of the number of people who I assumed were my fellow travellers, they were dotted around all over the place, there had to be almost a hundred of them, where were the boats that were going to take them all to Mayotte, I wondered, I couldn't see how they were going to pile us all into one boat, like a load of coconuts,

by the time the sun was high overhead it was like a furnace on that beach, children were crying incessantly, their mothers losing patience, some of the women sat huddled in their *shiromani*, a baby at their breast, an old man was listening to a radio at full volume, batting away the flies that were pestering him, I could hear the presenter's voice clearly, the old man gave the impression of being at home there, that he wasn't one of the passengers, and just as I was gazing at all of this, feasting my eyes on the spectacle, I saw a familiar looking figure appearing in the distance, I forced myself to look closely, I couldn't believe what I was seeing, it was none other than Rattler, my sister, in person, heading towards a group of women looking for a bit of shade behind a hut, she hadn't seen me, she was talking to the women rather nervously, asking them something, I supposed she must have been looking for me, so I waved at her, like a person lost in the middle of nowhere trying to attract the attention of a passing vehicle, she still didn't see me but one of the women did, she pointed to where I was and Rattler turned and looked straight at me, it was hard to read the expression on her face but then she broke into a smile and started running towards me, I stood up wondering what she was doing there *"what on earth can she want with me,"* I said to myself, and then, slowing down as she drew closer to me she said *"there you are, thank God,"* she sat down as if she needed to catch her breath and without waiting for me to say anything at all she started telling me *"it was Guarantee who told me where I could find you, I was afraid I'd missed you, I thought you'd have left yesterday,"* and suddenly she fell strangely silent, as if she was waiting for me to say something, yes, she was expecting me to break my silence but I kept my counsel, I wasn't going to give an inch, I was still hiding under my rock, don't ever forget, silence is the best shelter an eel can have, and then as if she'd read my thoughts, Rattler announced weakly *"I'm leaving with you,"* well, of course, I wanted to understand what she meant so I asked her to tell me what had happened at home,

you could have knocked me down with a feather when Rattler appeared suddenly out of the blue like that and announced that she wanted to leave with me, why had she turned her back on All-Knowing and come all this way, what exactly had happened, I peered at her questioningly, examining her every move, she didn't look at me at all as she spoke but gazed sadly and pensively out to sea, she kept breaking off mid-sentence, I couldn't make any sense of what she was saying and before long I was tired of listening and cut in with *"will you stop beating about the bush and tell me what's been going on,"* she wavered again and then started telling me that after I left Guarantee had told Tranquil the whole story, yes, he went all the way to Hombo to Tranquil's house and told her about my altercation with All-Knowing, Tranquil was stunned and went straight to see All-Knowing without a moment's delay and that's when it all came out, All-Knowing and Tranquil were in the courtyard and Rattler parked herself by the door behind the curtain, listening to them for quite some time, both of them were shouting and getting hot under the collar, Tranquil was working herself up into a frenzy, demanding to know why All-Knowing had thrown me out of the house without telling her, and when All-Knowing came out with *"this is my house and they are my daughters, I'll do as I please with them, I don't need to tell anyone else, someone has to impose some discipline here,"* that was too much for Tranquil, she told him he had it all wrong *"what do you mean wrong, are you telling me this isn't my house, they're not my daughters, I think it's you who's got it wrong,"* All-Knowing said, Tranquil was reluctant to say too much at first, she was doing her best not to offend him *"no, what I mean is, you don't have the right to treat these children like that,"* she said, and All-Knowing flew off the handle again and reminded her he wasn't the kind of father to turn a blind eye to delinquent behaviour, he wasn't going to stand for having his name dragged through the mud like that, finding out that I was pregnant had completely thrown him, it hadn't been easy for him either since he'd kicked me out but he wasn't about to let himself become the laughing stock of the town, not after he'd worked so hard to keep us away from just this kind of mess, and when Tranquil reminded him she'd been like a mother to us and insisted that she had a say in our lives too, he turned a deaf ear and carried on trying to convince her that he was cock-of-the-walk in his house and admonished her sternly *"at the end of the day, they're my children, I've said it before and I'll say it again, it's no one's business what I do with them, why don't you go and find her if that's what you want, just leave me in peace,"* once he'd said that he left Tranquil with no choice and she blurted it all out, every last detail of all that she'd kept to herself in silence for seventeen years *"well, you do know they're not even your daughters, don't you, did you know that, huh,"* those were her very words, All-Knowing thought she was just trying to provoke him, to wind him up and he certainly did seem slightly worried *"what did you say, what's that supposed to mean, how dare you come into my house and insult me like this, just who do you think you are,"* he concluded loftily, Tranquil carried on, intoning more and more seriously *"it's true All-Knowing, since when have I been one to tell lies, I know what I'm talking about, they're not your daughters All-Knowing, that's why I didn't want to leave them with you, I did everything I could to avoid having to tell you but you've left me with no choice, so there it is,"* All-Knowing didn't believe what he was hearing, his jaw dropped and he asked *"what do you mean, can you please explain what you're talking about,"* Rattler said that Tranquil's voice suddenly took on a tragic note, yes, she said her voice was breaking painfully, it sounded like she was crying, Rattler could hear her sniffling constantly as she slowly laid it all out, in great detail, she revealed to All-Knowing that our late mother had confessed a shameful secret to her the day we were born, she told her that she was pregnant by another man, that she'd cheated on her husband, she felt terrible about deceiving him but she was madly in love, they used to meet every day when All-Knowing was out at sea, it all happened at our house, in her bedroom or out on the terrace, and then her lover had dropped her, he'd cheated on her with another woman, she never even had a chance to tell him she was pregnant by him and she was sure it was his child and not her husband's, there are some love affairs that are out in the open, celebrated in public, and then there are the lovers no one knows about, the couples who pledge their love with their hearts, in secret, Mum didn't know how to tell All-Knowing, to say to him that she was fond of him but she didn't love him the way she adored the man she held constantly in her heart, so she let her husband choose my name to make him happy, she didn't know she was carrying twins, Tranquil told All-Knowing that Mum used to worry about him, that she was ashamed of what she'd done, for a long time she tried to find a way to tell him but she never did and she suffered it all in silence, All-Knowing had noticed she was out of sorts and losing weight but he thought it was morning sickness, and before long she was sickly and thin as a rail, and that day when she was wracked by labour pains she was convinced she was going to die, All-Knowing had made sure Tranquil was there before he went off in search of medicinal herbs at the market, and while our poor mother was in labour she couldn't keep it to herself any longer, as she faced her final agony she divulged everything but the name of the man she'd given her heart to, the one who'd callously broken her heart, well, that's what they do, those voracious wolves, was it the agonies of childbirth that stopped her from whispering the name of that despicable scoundrel in Tranquil's ear, did she forget to say his name or did she decide she wanted to keep something to herself and not smash her rock completely, just as I kept the name of Voracious to myself,

so our poor mother gave Tranquil the task of being a mother to her child, except that it wasn't one child but two, and not only that but she charged her with seeking forgiveness from her husband *"tell him the truth and then tell him how sorry I am, I know he'll never be able to forget what I did but please tell him that I'll be eternally sorry for it, that he's been a good husband, that he deserved to be loved openly and honestly, that there's no excuse for what I did, I deceived him and behaved despicably,*" Rattler said that Tranquil was shaking the whole time she was telling her this sad story, poor Tranquil couldn't hold back her tears as she told Rattler that Mum's face had been bathed in tears, her eyes red and puffy and her voice full of sorrow as she cried out, Tranquil couldn't tell if it was from the pain of her emotional wounds or the agony of her labour, and then all of a sudden the first baby was born and joined her cries to her mother's, Tranquil didn't know which way to turn, who to attend to first, and then she realised why our mother was still screaming, a second baby was sending her into even greater agonies, Mum was convulsing from head to foot, her body wracked by waves of searing pain and as the second baby came into the world, Mum breathed her last and Tranquil found herself gazing into her sister's wide-open, lifeless eyes, yes, well, what do you expect, Mum had played her part, her soul had departed her body, it wasn't hers to keep in the first place, our soul is like an invisible lamp that's lent to us for a short time while we play our part on this stage, Mum gave hers up when we were born because that's when her time was up, it all happened before Tranquil's very eyes and it fell to her to close Mum's eyes, for once the soul has gone, staring eyes do nothing but inspire fear, they remind you of a darkened stage, a sunless world, so Tranquil was sobbing her heart out, shrieking and giving vent to her pain as she'd never done before and the neighbours and passers-by heard her and came rushing in, and suddenly the house was filled with people, Tranquil said nothing, she stayed silent for a month, people thought it was just the death of her sister weighing on her but there was more to it than that, it never occurred to All-Knowing that his wife had delivered such explosive news to her sister as she lay dying, but it was that incendiary secret that rendered Tranquil mute, yes, she kept it to herself for all those years and just imagine, she didn't even know herself who our real father was, and as for All-Knowing, he did everything in his power to keep us, even crossing swords with Tranquil, who took a step back to reflect on the situation, she didn't want to upset All-Knowing or above all, to tarnish her sister's image, but it wasn't easy for her, the years flew by and Tranquil would always try and avoid poor All-Knowing when she came to see us, for fear of provoking a scandal, she'd always come when he was out at sea and make her exit as soon as the sun started to dip towards the horizon, even refusing to stay for supper, she didn't falter for seventeen years and now they were confronted head on with a scandal of my making, now I understood what all those questions that Tranquil was always asking us were about, she'd often ask us if we were having any problems or if we needed anything and all the time, behind that tranquil exterior, she was concealing something completely unexpected, it was enough to make you wonder who Tranquil really was when you heard all this,

even All-Knowing himself had nothing to say, all his pithy sayings went out the window, he was bereft, left with nothing but a head of white hair, never in all his life had he felt so cruelly betrayed by fate, Tranquil had rendered him speechless, he was dumbfounded, silenced once and for all, Rattler said she heard not a peep out of him, Tranquil's voice was the only sign of life in the courtyard but then she went quiet too, hoping that All-Knowing would break the silence, but he said nothing, the silence went on and on, weighing more and more heavily, until finally Rattler heard the slow creaking of the door followed by the staccato sound as it slammed shut and she realised it was All-Knowing leaving without a word, so stunned that he needed to be alone, or maybe he just didn't know what to say to Tranquil, although that doesn't seem very likely to me, I mean, I never knew him to be lost for words,

Tranquil called Rattler and told her despairingly that she'd have to come with her, she couldn't stay there with a man who wasn't her father *"I don't know how he's going to look on you now he knows the truth, I can't leave you here, get your things together,"* she said, All-Knowing would have to talk to her so they could at least come up with a solution together but he'd gone off without saying anything, Rattler was knocked sideways by all of this, fate seemed to have treated her cruelly and she too was lost for words, and then she told Tranquil she wanted to know where I was first *"I need her, we've always been together, I want us to live together again like before,"* she said, Tranquil told her I was leaving the island for Mayotte and she didn't know where I was at that point, and then the door creaked again, and in came Guarantee, he'd just seen All-Knowing and he gave Rattler all the information he could so she could come and join me but he made it clear he didn't think she'd have much chance of finding me in Domoni, it was already getting dark and she wouldn't be able to leave until the following morning, so Rattler spent the night at Tranquil's house, and Tranquil made sure she had everything she'd need for the journey to

Mayotte with me *"if you run into any trouble, I'll always be here for you, I'll be waiting to hear how you're getting on,"* she said to Rattler several times before she let her go,

Rattler was coming to the end of her story when I saw a great commotion in the distance, passengers were milling about and scrambling towards the shore, I saw the figure of Miraculous in front of them, it was time to leave, it had to be, the rabble seemed to be preparing to take the plunge, so I told Rattler it was time to go, I'd already let her know the time the boat was supposed to be leaving so she could make up her mind whether or not to come, she said she wanted to go and pay for her passage, so I took her money and strode towards Miraculous, I had to make a determined grab for him with that mob shoving and pushing all around us, I managed to talk to him about my sister as I traipsed along-side him, huffing and puffing to keep pace with his giant strides, stumbling over the pebbles and rocks underfoot, he talked to me without slackening his stride one bit, smooth operator that he was, he snatched Rattler's money from me without a moment's hesitation, there was no discussion, no haggling, no umming and ahhing, for him it was just another business deal not to be missed, I'm quite sure that if any more newcomers had arrived he'd have been happy to take them on board too, so long as there was money to be made from them, although there was already quite a crowd of us to cram into that minuscule boat and as he was pocketing the money, stuffing it like a thief into his trousers, he was telling me that we'd be on our way in just a few minutes, I wanted to call Rattler and tell her to follow the crowd, when I realised I didn't have my bag, I'd left it in the room where I'd spent the night, so I had to run back to fetch it, I found the door to the room left ajar, I yanked it open and hurled myself into the room, flinging myself through that door with great gusto, and there, Heaven help me, you won't believe it but I swear I saw it with my very own eyes, honest to goodness, a scene of such brazen effrontery, I cannot tell a lie, it was beyond belief, do you know what I saw there, I saw two pairs of lips, like suckers, pulling themselves apart at the shock of the sight of me appearing like that, lips as red as beetroots from sucking so hard for so long, of course they were none other than a man and woman's lips, well, what else would they have been, huh, what did you expect, two men kissing, lesbianism, no way, neither one of those, although either one would have been an improvement on what I saw there, as I said, it was a man and a woman but here's the thing, this couple looked much more familiar to me, much more eel-like, than you might expect, it was Survivor and Miraculous's wife, yes, his friend's wife, the very same woman I'd found to be so gentle and calm, she was just another cheater, you see now what goes on underneath the rocks, nothing but perfidy, oh, what is this world we live in, or rather what is this show we're in, why is there so much treachery, so much outright deceit, everywhere I turn, staring me in the face, what a curse, well I've had it up to here, listen, none of this is my doing, I'm just telling you exactly what I've witnessed with my very own eyes, down to the last detail, if you want to know what I think of all this vile behaviour, and that's what exactly what it is, vile, well I've always been appalled by it and I still am, grand passion, fling, whatever, you have to know what you want in life, don't misunderstand me here, I'm quite happy to listen to my heart resonating in my chest, asking me for the gift of this plaything or that, I don't deny it, but this heart of mine has never told me to love two men at the same time, I don't get it, what's to be gained from fooling around, every heart is made for one other heart and one heart alone, it's what gives nobility to the realm of our existence, our poor little lives that ask only to be lit by a single lamp, a lamp that loses its glow once a second flame is added to it, that's what makes it so extraordinary and that's what those hotheads don't want to understand,

when I surprised those two hearts celebrating their union under a rock that day, I pretended I hadn't seen anything, which is probably how they wanted it, don't you think, and Survivor and Miraculous's wife froze, facing one another at arm's length, heads bowed like naughty children caught in the act, they didn't make a sound as I walked between them to fetch my bag from the mattress, I wondered why I hadn't come upon them on that mattress, moaning as they enjoyed their forbidden fruit like Voracious and I used to or like the cats I used to catch in the act on the terrace, but they were standing back from the mattress, almost as if they were afraid of it, shit, that would have been quite a show and what I did see was quite enough, but that really would have been the cherry on the cake if I'd found Survivor on top of Miraculous's wife *"carry on then, go on, you villain, don't mind me,"* I'd have said, you think I'm joking but that's exactly what I'd have told him, but I'll tell you what I actually did say to him before I left, I was planning to leave without speaking to them but something made me stop in the doorway, I knew I had to give Survivor what he had coming to him, why should I smile sweetly at him, he deserved to hear me tell it like it was, he prided himself on his name but he probably didn't know what it really took to be a survivor, he was too knuckleheaded for that, as I saw it this was my chance to teach him a quick lesson, so I looked him straight in the eye and said *"so that's what being a survivor is all about is it, betraying your friend's trust by cheating on him with his wife, the heroic survivor who sneaks around like a snake in the grass and manages to escape the jaws of death, I see, well, so much for that, you just carry on being whatever it is you think you are,"* and with that I turned to Miraculous's wife, I had nothing against her and I wanted to reassure her, so I said *"don't worry, Madame, I always turn a blind eye to things that don't concern me, they don't call me Eel for nothing, I'm just trying to survive here,"* and without further ado, I walked out of that dump, that eel tank or whatever it was, although as far as I was concerned it was nothing but a dump,

I hurried over to where I'd left Rattler, she was still there in the same spot but as soon as I set eyes on her I stopped in my tracks, she was sobbing her heart out like a little kid who'd lost her mummy, I asked her what the matter was now but she couldn't string two words together and kept pointing towards the old man with the radio *"what about him, poor old bloke, he's just sitting there listening to his contraption, does he scare you, have you never seen an old guy sitting in the sun listening to a radio before,"* I said off-handedly, thinking it was just Rattler being a cry-baby as usual but she still couldn't say anything and pointed at the old guy again "*listen*" was the only thing she managed to say, so I listened to the voice on the radio making what seemed like an important announcement, I couldn't follow what it was saying with Rattler sniffing all the time but I did pick up the name All-Knowing, the announcer kept coming back to it, repeating it over and over again, oh God, I felt like my brains were being bashed in, I moved closer to the old man to hear better but the announcement was already finished and they were playing a piece of music that pulled strangely at the heartstrings, it was a doleful tune, a lament, the kind of tune I can't stand, but I needed to ask the old man what they were saying about this All-Knowing, the radio was making such a racket he couldn't hear me, he had to turn it down so I could make myself heard, and after he'd listened to what I had to say, he took pleasure in informing me, like a teacher delivering a lesson to a slow pupil "*it's about a fisherman from Mutsamudu, a seventy-year old called All-Knowing, or something weird like that, they're saying he went out in his boat last night without his fishing tackle, he must have been in a state, the people who saw him leave said he went without saying a word to anyone and then no one saw him come back, his friends found his empty boat this morning, out at sea, just drifting, if you ask me there was something wrong with him, he wasn't right in the head, going out like that at that age, poor sod and what makes it all worse is that his daughters have gone missing, sounds like that family was destined to disappear, the fish are probably feasting on the old bloke by now,*" the old man gabbled, entertaining himself saying whatever came into his head, while I was thinking about All-Knowing, in the end I had to move away to where I couldn't hear him, I was starting to lose my cool, I hadn't asked him for his views on the subject, why do people have to go out of their way to answer questions they haven't been asked,

I was plunged into a sudden reverie by this news, so All-Knowing had died at sea, he wanted to die rather than accept the role of husband in a sham household, to live with the image he'd been forced into without his knowledge for all these years, poor All-Knowing, he'd worked so hard since the death of his wife to remain untouched by painful wounds and now two more blows were being inflicted on him, one after the other, each as lethal as the other, and those two blows had sent him to his death under the sea, after he'd equipped himself with everything possible to avoid such disasters, after all the warnings, all the advice he'd given, after he'd preached at children, adults, old men and women, people of every generation, he'd considered himself a rich man because he was satisfied with what little he had, to the point where he poked fun at people who always wanted more and now there he was, with an arrow in his chest and then a second one straight into his heart, destroyed by a fatal blow, he must have pitched himself into those fathomless depths knowing he wouldn't come back up, he didn't want his body to be found, he did his best to vanish for ever, to escape not just the image of being a victim of a marital misfortune but to escape all the acrimonious remarks, for there were certainly plenty of malicious tongues ready to wag, just as there were always too many pairs of eyes whenever misfortune befell another person,

what people need to know is that it's not enough just to issue warnings, to give advice or preach, you have to know yourself, you have to know where you are, when to open your mouth and when to keep quiet, before the rooster opens his mouth to crow he has to make sure he's not standing next to a troublemaker ready to cut him off at any moment, I'll say it again, just because the cock crows like a prince, it doesn't mean he knows what's going on under his own roof, there are always traps to be wary of, there are traps everywhere and once you start to play too many parts, you fall right into the worst of them, yes, we're all actors and we do have multiple roles to play but sometimes we switch roles without paying attention and that's when misfortune strikes, as and when it chooses, it shows up out of the blue just as it pleases, like death, so my advice is to keep your masks on, even if the stage directions are telling you to take them off, you'll understand eventually what it really means to be an actor on the stage,

LOVE ME OR LEAVE ME

as I was hurrying over to join Rattler I noticed that all the passengers had already climbed aboard, Miraculous was standing waist-deep in the water attending to the motor, Survivor emerged from his tryst with that woman he was sharing with Miraculous on the sly and stopped at some distance from the shore to observe the boat and its cargo before walking over to join Miraculous, I watched the two of them bending over the motor like doctors conferring over an ailing patient, meanwhile Rattler was still blubbing and I told her there was nothing to be gained from wallowing in misery, it was time for her to decide, was she coming with me or not, I reminded her that she was old enough to know her own mind, All-Knowing was dead and there was nothing we could do about it, his number was up but ours wasn't, it was time to face reality, I was determined to get on that *kwassa-kwassa* and go to Mayotte, but what about her, what did she intend to do, she said nothing but the ferociously questioning look she gave me made it quite clear she didn't like what I'd just said, as far as she was concerned I was nothing but a cold fish, callous, heard-hearted, unfeeling and I don't know what else, to hell with all that, I say, what's the good of worrying about what other people think of me, the world is full of folk who are only too quick to judge, people who think they've found all the answers but I ask you, for all their so-called intelligence, what do they know about what goes on in the depths of the ocean, all they do is look at the surface of things and claim they've understood them and then off they go, holding forth on this that and the other, right, left and centre, no, I'd had enough, I mean what did my cry-baby sister think, that I'd sit down next to her and start crying too, like two little kids who've lost their mummy, did she think I'd go all girlie, no way, not me, not this eel,

as I was gazing unmoved at Rattler I head a voice shouting in the distance, from somewhere out on the water, it was Miraculous calling to us *"come on young ladies, hurry up, we're waiting for you,"* they'd finished checking the motor, so I shot one last look at Rattler, I didn't need to say anything, and she spoke up and said *"you go ahead, I'm staying, I'm going back to Mutsamudu, someone has to be there to grieve for our father, after all, let's face it, he was our dad, so that's it, I've made up my mind, you do what you want,"* I wasn't at all surprised to hear this, I was expecting her to say something of the sort, Rattler was always changing her mind, one minute she wanted one thing and the next minute it was something else, when I wasn't there she set her sights on leaving with me and now all she could think about was putting on some dumb show of grieving, as if all the floods of tears she'd just shed weren't enough to mourn his passing, no, she had to put on a public display of weeping, so people would say how much she loved her daddy, poor little girl *"oh, poor child, what an angelic daughter All-Knowing had,"* no thanks, I thought to myself, the sooner she leaves and takes her tears with her the better, I mean how does it help to cry when the person's already dead and gone, eh, tell me that, I know you're there, even if you can't actually hear me, you're all the same, you performers, none of you ever want to bow out, even if you're messing up your part, boring the audience to death, you'll do anything to stay in the spotlight, doesn't it occur to you that the audience might end up wishing they hadn't wasted so much time on your little performance, so I gave Rattler a kiss, yes, a peck on the top of her head *"best of luck"* was all I said, and with that I ran towards the sea, my beloved ocean, I could hear Survivor on the shore yelling frantically at Miraculous *"she's coming, wait,"* Miraculous had just cast off, he was already in the *kwassa-kwassa*, I stumbled through the water as fast as I could, soaked from head to foot, two men stood up in the boat to help me in, stretching out their hands to haul me up out of the water like a big fat fish they'd just caught with their bare hands,

inside the boat, I was stunned by what I saw, in the midst of that rabble was a goat lying on its back, its feet tied together with a thick piece of rope, the creature was as still and quiet as the grave, not even flinching with displeasure at the flies landing on it, this wasn't at all what I'd imagined, I sat down on a fuel container right next to Miraculous, just to his left, it's probably the one I'm hanging on to now, clinging on to it so I don't drown and get swallowed up by those furious, raging, boundless depths,

we were piled up in that boat like sardines in a tin, I need hardly say I felt uncomfortable amongst all that rabble, to my right I was jammed up against a chunky woman with a baby, with another lady who seemed a bit younger in front of me, there were more than eighty people aboard that doughty little skiff if you counted the children and of course the goat, they'd loaded the wretched creature on board while I was getting my bag or else while I was preoccupied with the news of All-Knowing's disappearance, I was gazing pityingly at the goat when I realised someone was talking to me, it gradually dawned on me that Miraculous was asking me a question *"what about your sister, changed her mind, did she,"* I turned round and saw that he was looking at me so I quickly said yes and then I noticed that all the other passengers were staring at me, all with the same look of displeasure, it was quite intimidating, and then a woman spoke up, a hefty woman with two children, a babe in arms and a kid leaning against her, gawping at me, maybe she realised I was uncomfortable with them all staring at me and giving me hostile looks, so she came right out with it and said what was probably on all their minds *"young lady, an undertaking like this needs determination and courage, especially since it's a group effort, and you made us all wait, the two of you, do you realise that there are eighty-four of us, all of us being forced to wait for you two,"* another woman sitting by her frowned and said *"drop it, it's over and done with now,"* I realised I needed to say something by way of apology to them, so I made my excuses and explained that it was my sister who'd held things up, someone asked me why she'd changed her mind *"we just found out that our father died,"* I said, at which they all looked dismayed, in fact they hung their heads to avoid causing me offence with their stares, and without looking up they told me how sorry they were, they should have been more patient, they didn't realise, they felt my pain at this cruel loss, and like a gang of drunks realising they've done something wrong as a group, they took turns to apologise and then one woman spoke up with a question *"and you mustered up the courage to leave anyway,"* and another one retaliated with *"but her sister went back, there's no reason for both of them to go back, I mean, just because one man dies, it doesn't mean other people can't get on with their lives,"* and then they started squabbling, one woman saying one thing and the other contradicting her, until one of the men told them to calm down *"out of respect for the memory of the young lady's father,"* he added, I looked around and mentally counted the number of men in that boat, eleven in total, including Miraculous, there was a moment's silence, all you could hear was the noise of the engine, which was pretty loud, people had to shout to make themselves heard over it,

by now I could see the town of Domoni far away in the distance behind us, although I couldn't make out the beach we'd left from, it was all a bit of a blur, I fixed my gaze on the receding landscape and the more I looked, the more I wanted to go on feasting my eyes on that vista, I felt an unfulfilled longing come over me in waves, intensified by the ravishing spectacle of the sunset, it was as good as a wedding night, you know that tingling sensation you get when you find yourself alone with the person who sets your heart aflutter, that was what I felt coursing through my veins, a pulse stronger than my very lifeblood, what greater nourishment could the heart crave than a declaration of love beneath a setting sun, you see how easy it is to become bloated with love, people are taken completely unaware, I gave my heart to a man who let me down, who broke my heart and threw it back in my face like dross, but what on earth was I doing, thinking about love, I don't know what got into me, let's get back to business, enough of this gimcrack nonsense, but it's true, my thoughts did turn to love when my gaze fell on that mysterious ball, the sun can be a bewitching creature at times, and when I realised it was dragging me back to the very place I'd sworn to leave for ever, I snapped myself out of it and turned round to face the open water and saw the foaming path that rackety boat was carving out, that rust-bucket, carrying us like a cargo of rotten tomatoes, was slicing through the water, showing no mercy to the waves, trampling on them and flattening them as if they were specks of dust,

while I was gazing at the froth churned up by the *kwassa-kwassa* as it cut through the waves I became vaguely aware of a man's voice, recounting his achievements in Mayotte, I turned round to see who this person was but I couldn't really see his face because of his position in the middle of the crowd, all I could tell was that he was wearing a white baseball cap and a black cotton tee-shirt, he'd apparently been living in Mayotte for a long time, he openly admitted that he wasn't legal, in fact he was shouting it out loud for all to hear, he'd been arrested climbing out of a dinghy he'd taken to get from Grande Terre to Petite Terre for work, he was a painter, a house painter and he and a friend were in the dinghy together, the friend had spotted the police and run off as soon as he came ashore and just managed to get away, so this painter who'd been thrown out just the day before kept saying that he was going back home *"Mayotte is my home, I'm never leaving it,"* he said, ranting on about how he was going to go straight back to work, he intended to carry on with the job he'd just started as if he'd never been arrested or thrown out, he was going to carry on making his living in his profession as a painter, he wasn't going to stop looking for new clients, he was planning to have a family, nothing was going to stop him from setting up home there and nothing anyone could say or do would make him change his tune,

another man, sitting across from the painter, was talking about what a good time he was going to have when he arrived, he was a carpenter who'd done well for himself in Mayotte, he said he was looking forward to eating the dinner he'd cooked himself before he was arrested, he'd made chicken in sauce and he was sure it wouldn't have gone off, he'd been thrown out the day before too, and not for the first time but every time he was thrown out he went back the next day, he was quite relaxed about it, he'd eat what he'd prepared the day before and carry on with his work as if nothing had happened, as if he'd merely been for a walk *"I make the most of all this free travel, once a year at least I go and see my family, the only difference is that I'm handcuffed like a common thief before I'm put on the ship, but otherwise I'm like a prince with his retinue, it's all just a bit of fun, isn't it, you've got to have a laugh, even if the cops are involved, life's too short,"* he crowed, people were cracking up and one woman who I couldn't see very well, although I could just about hear her, asked him how he'd got himself arrested, so he launched into his story, it seems he was involved in a fight with an old friend, well maybe he was more of a client, you can't really call someone a friend if you've had business dealings with them, not when your reputation is at stake, it's more about keeping your word, doing the right thing, saving face and we all know full well that when it comes to money, it doesn't take much to muddy the waters, you can't be sure of anything until you've been paid, cash on the nail, so this client, a big shot official, mind you, was trying to get away with making him work without paying him the fee they'd agreed on, he'd commissioned the carpenter to make him some furniture, that was after coming to see him every day for several months and marvelling at all the furniture he'd made for other clients, they'd become friends in the end and the carpenter trusted him, and then the day came when the official ordered some furniture for himself, the carpenter got to work and made the furniture without dilly-dallying, expecting to be paid the tidy sum his friend had promised him but when the commission was ready, the official only paid him half the money, swearing he'd give him the rest within the next few days, the carpenter took him at his word and let the official take the furniture then and there, well, that was when the big shot went back on his word, he helped himself to that furniture and didn't give another thought to the money he owed and that was the last the carpenter heard of him, several months went by, then a year, then another six months and all this time the official went out of his way to stay well away from the carpenter's place, even though it was on his way home, he took to going home by a different route to avoid bumping into him, and the carpenter didn't know exactly where the official lived, but then one day they ran into each other at the supermarket, the official was just about to get into his car when he realised the carpenter had spotted him and was striding resolutely towards him, the scoundrel tried to make out like he'd been meaning to contact the carpenter but it had completely slipped his mind and then he went all smarmy and started making all sorts of fake excuses, which really riled the carpenter, that cheap-skate claimed he'd completely forgotten about the money he owed him, so the carpenter told him he wasn't going anywhere until the official coughed up the money, he'd waited a year and a half and he wasn't waiting one second longer, he wanted his money right there and then, no excuses, he was ready to fight if he had to, to hell with their so-called friendship, and when the official tried to ignore him and make a break for it, the carpenter grabbed him by the collar and by this time there was quite a crowd forming, people thought it was an altercation between a thief and a cop, and in fact, the police showed up just as the two men were about to come to blows, the cops dispersed the crowd and the carpenter started to explain but the official kept interrupting him *"don't listen to him, he's a thief, this is how he operates, this is how he tries to swindle people out of their money and I can tell you, I'm not the first he's tried it on with,"* he said, sounding like he knew what he was talking about, the carpenter offered to show the police his workshop and swore blind the official was lying through his teeth, but then the official said to the cops *"he's an illegal, he doesn't have any papers, ask him for his ID if you don't believe me, he's always avoiding the law,"* which stopped the carpenter in his tracks, he couldn't deny it, he'd never made any secret of where he came from or of his status in Mayotte, so the police, who made a habit of questioning anyone who fell into their clutches, asked them both for their ID, the official went to get his out of the car, while the carpenter said he didn't have any papers but he wanted his money all the same, then they arrested him and cuffed his hands behind his back, he tried to resist at first and went on demanding his money *"I'm not going with you unless he pays me what he owes me, right now,"* he said, the police weren't even listening, in the end they pushed him roughly into their vehicle and the poor prisoner could see the official smirking at him as he got into his car, you can imagine how humiliating it was and he yelled at him from the police car *"I'll show you who the crook is here, you low-life, cheating dog,"* they took him to the police station and then an hour later to the port, along with all the other illegals, including the house painter, apparently the police had carried out several raids that day in various places, they loaded them all into a boat to send them back to Anjouan like unwanted packages or bringers of bad luck, a kind of toxic rabble, but the carpenter, and the housepainter for that matter, saw these expulsions in a different light, as far as they were concerned they were entitled to live in Mayotte, they were full of encouragement for the other passengers *"don't take any notice of all that guff, just think of it as we do, they're giving us a free trip home to see our families, can't complain about that, it gives them something to do, otherwise they'd be feasting on chicken and drawing big fat salaries for doing nothing, no, they're doing us a favour, Mayotte is our home, brothers and sisters, don't fall for any of that tricolour flag stuff, all those idiots calling themselves French, all puffed-up with pride, it's pie in the sky, I'm telling you they're living in cloud-cuckoo land,"* you'd think he was a teacher and we were his pupils, he had the floor to himself for quite some time, he was getting seriously carried away like a preacher addressing his flock, his voice battling against the booming of the engine, they were locked in combat for more than an hour, vocal chords pitted against machine, spit against petrol, narrative against racket, history against bottomless, resounding emptiness and then the carpenter was saying that whenever he was deported he always met up with people he knew in the boat, for example, just the day before he'd run into other friends working in Mayotte as farmers, fishermen, electricians, and tailors too, and housepainters like the one on the boat with us, they'd been together since the day before, it occurred to me that the carpenter was something of a painter himself, painting for us with words the ridicule they had to endure when they landed in the port of Mutsamudu in Anjouan, he said they'd hear people shouting at them from all over the place *"there they are, today's pweré catch, a good haul today,"* pweré is what we call tuna and these pwerés were caught by the Mayotte police, but that was really the only time they ever felt any shame or embarrassment, most of them seemed completely unperturbed, in fact they were full of enthusiasm about setting off again *"we're heading back there today, the pwerés will be back where they came from in less than twenty-four hours,"* and somehow the fact that they went along with the joke and called themselves tuna fish made them seem not so much stubborn as courageous, tuna fish they may have been but they weren't like any tuna found in the sea *"what kind of pweré can take itself back into the sea after it's been fished out, eh, must be a pretty smart fish,"* they'd say and even the most incorrigible of name-callers had no answer to that,

the whole time the carpenter was telling us all this, I could hear a baby screaming at the top of its lungs, non-stop, blotting out the carpenter's voice, at some point I realised it was dark, I hadn't noticed the last glimmers of dusk or the sun slipping behind the horizon, I'd been doubled over to stop myself throwing up but it was too late, my head was spinning, maybe it was because I'd been working so hard to keep my eyes on that streak of froth I'd been so fascinated by, I tried to resist the invisible weight pressing down on my eyes as they gradually succumbed, my eyelids felt heavy, then my head and finally my whole body, it was too strong for me and then I started to heave sickeningly, I was shaking violently, gagging and retching uncontrollably, I had to be sick but all that came up was liquid, the first time it happened I watched it land on the back of the neck of the woman in front of me, I could see it running all the way down her neck onto her back and gradually soaking her dark blue dress, it was nothing but yellowish liquid, I'd been so intent on getting away I hadn't eaten a thing that day and all my insides could produce was this burning acid, I had a good look at it before the woman turned round to give me a look of disgust mingled with pity, it was a while before she turned round, I don't know why, maybe she thought she was being doused by the water thrown up from time to time by the wind, sorry, lady, you were wrong there, I sullied you, I spat fire and acid at you inadvertently, I etched my suffering onto the back of your neck, your back just happened to be my copper plate, you were a victim of sorts, I suppose, I felt so ashamed of myself when she gave me that dubious look, I couldn't really tell what to make of it, all I noticed were her chubby cheeks, I wondered why she felt sorry for me, maybe I looked like a real wreck to her, she had no reason to pick a quarrel with a half-dead creature like me, I began to think there might be something seriously wrong with me, or maybe it was obvious that I was pregnant and now the passengers would all know about it and start bombarding me with questions, trying to outdo each other, I wouldn't be able to take that, why should I be given a grilling, eh, but in the end, what was it to me, so what if they guessed something, but I really did feel bad about that woman, there was nothing I could do about it, it just came up like a volcano erupting and can you stop a volcano erupting, no way, I did just manage to keep half of it back in my mouth and I turned towards the water to spit it out, which wasn't easy in the midst of that scrum, people were jammed up against each other, their heads banging together all the time, slamming up against each other like wine bottles, which reminds me of my favourite tipple, as I was trying to say, I had to take care not to cause offence to any of the others in the boat, so I had my head down between my legs, which dulled the sound of the engine a bit and like that I was able to focus on the carpenter's tale, every once in a while I felt the soothing touch of a wave rising from the depths, raining down droplets of salt water and wetting my hair, hands and back, I tasted it to make sure it was sea water and not from the heavens, yup, it was too salty for rainwater and then I heard the baby crying again, a really piercing wail much louder than the engine noise, I looked up and thought maybe the kid's really scared, how was he to know where he was being taken, although it wasn't too dark at that point but the worst was still to come, no one had any inkling of what lay in store for us at that point, although things didn't bode well, my father All-Knowing had a baleful saying he liked to use when he wanted to speak of the harm that might come to someone he couldn't stand *"when you see the tether, you can be sure the cow's not far behind,"* and before long the squawking kid had infected the other children with his fear, they'd maintained a resentful silence until that moment and all of a sudden almost all of them started to cry at the same time, a great crescendo of cater-wauling, a tangle of competing voices, it was like being in the middle of a choir where everyone was out of tune,

by now, the mothers of all these whining, blubbering little rebels were getting worked up too, they knew it was up to them to stop the racket their kids were making but the fren-zied lament just went on and on, the very opposite of music to my ears, and eventually our choirmaster Miraculous couldn't take it any more, he started yelling at the women to calm their children down *"I'm warning you, we can't take this kwassa anywhere near Mayotte with that racket going on,"* he shouted threateningly, and while all this was going on I began to wonder if we were actually anywhere near Mayotte, I realised the sky was filling with clouds, becoming black and heavy and all of a sudden we were engulfed in nightmarish darkness, we could feel it in our bones, weighing down on us, everything was plunged into deep gloom, I felt myself in the grip of a leaden fatigue, as if I, and not the engine, had been carving out our path through the waves, one by one the children quietened down but the baby who'd started it all wouldn't be comforted, people were taking him in their arms to rock him and sing to him, talking and babbling at him, trying to distract him with anything they could lay their hands on, plastic bottles, bits of bread, water, gurning and making all sorts of faces, they tried everything from sweet smiles and furious, crazy looks, to fake demented laughter but nothing would stop that baby's assault on our ear-drums, and then came the gigantic rollers to drench our clothes, our bodies and our spirits, I heard the sounds of women and children vomiting like poisoned cats, then I heard men droning on saying things that sounded really scary, about a dim light in the distance that could have been the Mayotte police on patrol, those jumped-up bastards who liked to take clandestine boats by surprise, everyone seemed seized with fear, not of the raging seas but of that obscure glimmer they all thought was a police signal, and then the wind picked up, I heard a sound like a snake hissing as if an unseen creature was coiling itself around my ears, I felt the wind stroking me relentlessly but I paid no attention to it, huge waves were pounding us, soaking us continuously, hammering down on our bodies like a rain of bullets, gunfire, that's what it was, unleashed on us by the Earth's wayward sister, Earth's irascible, recalcitrant twin sister, the one that harbours her envy and resentment beneath a pall of hostile silence, Earth's sister, the sea, with a dazzling diversity of creatures in her belly, they're both pregnant with untold riches but the Earth has always considered herself superior because she can count human beings among the creatures she's given birth to, she thinks that humans, with their gift of reason, can shape her, render her beautiful or hideous, make her life-sustaining or uninhabitable and when they've done with her, they can take control of the sea and colonise her in turn, to pollute her and turn her to land once they've finished pillaging her treasures, so the battle rages on in silence between these two little-understood women, people don't know too much about it, because, as I said, they're women of mystery but it doesn't stop them delivering surprises and there is one battle they let people get a glimpse of, a battle that's far from silent, one that pits them both against a common enemy, I'm talking about human cruelty here, the one thing those two sisters can never forget, the cruelty of people who've behaved like preposterous, unruly kids ever since the curtain rose on this stage, braggarts who've shown what thugs they are in the ways they've chosen to decorate their stage, they've treated it as a plaything instead of the rich, eternally harmonious work of art it is, the saviour of the human spirit, our environment, our salvation, oh, how we love to blow our own trumpet, we humans, but all that boasting is toxic for the human soul, people get drunk on it, they don't know what they're doing, it's poison,

so the sea was taking its revenge that day, yes, waves came crashing down on our heads one after another, like rollers breaking against the rocks, saturating us with salt water, we were no more than rotten sponge, the children's cries only served to intensify the mists and blasting wind, gone was the gentle breeze of sunset, this was a wind that whipped us in the face without warning, all eyes were still fixed on the unearthly glimmer in the distance, almost everyone was mouthing prayers of some kind or other, mantras or verses from the Quran, some were praying aloud, their hands clasped in supplication, the constant muttering sounded like flies buzzing around the boat and then all of a sudden the throbbing of the engine stopped, I turned round to see why, it was our leader who'd shut it off intentionally, he said he had to, it was what they always did when they came close to the coast of Mayotte, they had to make as little noise as possible to make sure the police didn't hear anything coming, and so the boat had to float through those furious waves and surging tides like an insect creeping over a mad woman's dress as she thrashed and flung herself about, a mad woman with no benign smile on her face,

the waves were coming thicker and faster, the kid was still bawling, and now Miraculous seemed really rattled, he pulled out two oars to speed the boat through the water and someone took hold of one of them to help him row, it looked exhausting, then a voice said there was lots of water in the boat and the goat was in distress, our skipper announced that we'd have to throw the goat overboard to speed things up and stop the boat from sinking, the owner of the goat was taken by surprise, he'd paid a lot of money to bring his goat to Mayotte, he said, but he had no choice, he had to agree if he wanted to get out of this mess alive and at that moment, nothing else mattered, the poor goat had swallowed too much salt water and seemed half-dead already, so we chucked the wretched beast into those raging depths and I thought perhaps the sea might calm down a little now we'd fed it a large hunk of meat but no, that wasn't enough, it went on doing its best to make us capsize, rowing was impossible against the violent churning of those monstrous waves, the two men struggled but in the end the man helping Miraculous lost his oar, the monsters simply tore it from his grip and swallowed it up, the poor man almost fell into those raging jaws too but he managed to steady himself, and then I saw Miraculous looking deflated, his face set in a grim expression, then suddenly his eyes darkened, he gazed around as if he was searching for something to calm the waves but they were at the peak of their fury, firing torrents of water at us, I realised with alarm that I could no longer hear the children crying, the only sounds were the mumbled prayers, the buzzing of lips, the crashing of the waves and the relentless roar of the water and then I began to wonder what or who had calmed that squawking baby, an eerie, leaden silence reigned for several minutes and then all of a sudden, God's honest truth, I heard a woman cry out *"no, my baby, no, oh God, what have I done, I've killed him, with my own hands, God have mercy,"* people were stunned, the praying stopped and all eyes turned hurriedly towards the weeping woman, what on earth happened, you ask, well, the woman had covered the infant's mouth and held his arms and legs still to stop him crying and struggling and at some point, she must have blocked her baby's nose with her hand, she'd been so intent on quietening the child, she'd squeezed and squeezed as hard as she could, with all her strength, she couldn't take any more of the accusing looks that said she was a terrible mother for letting her child cry like that for so long, driving everyone up the wall, she'd acted without thinking of the harm she might do to that innocent little creature, she hadn't even looked at him, she forgot for that moment that children are little angels who are noisy by their very nature, that a child is a hard-won treasure that never gives the mind a moment of peace, even when you hold it in your hands, and now she'd lost her treasure and all because she wanted to stop him from being a killjoy, the little one had struggled but in vain, in the end he'd succumbed, he'd gone limp, his eyes wide open and when the woman saw what had happened, it was too late, the bird had taken wing and was off on that long journey, far from this theatre of tragedy, heading backstage, behind the curtain, to wait for his mother there, for she too had only a few minutes left of her tragic life before going to join her child, like so many other mothers and children silently devoured by the sea that separates Anjouan from Mayotte, if you were to count up the number of women and children swallowed by that one stretch of water in the time it's taken for the author of this play to compose the text of the spectacle unfolding before our eyes, you'd understand how wretched and heartsick the principal players are, which doesn't stop the play from going on, no, and it doesn't stop people from embarking on the journey as an illegal migrant and perishing in that death-trap, none of it makes any difference, what matters is that the show must go on, that's all,

the mother was wailing at the top of her lungs, clutching the body of her child to her breast, other women were sobbing too, beseeching God in the most pitiful fashion, and then all the children starting howling, as that wretched craft pitched and reeled, swaying like a drunkard, yes, like that old soak Voilà, we were tossed this way and that, jerked and jolted by the waves that went on and on flinging us about like trash in a can, jostling us around until we were all mixed up together, piled one on top of the other, turned upside down, women's thighs and men's chests stripped bare, children suffocating, trapped at the bottom of that ghastly heap, cries would suddenly ring out, followed by agonised lamentations, sobbing and sighing, people tried to stand up and regain their seat only to be thrashed again by another wave, and so it went on, I was exhausted, all the other women were too, none of us moved an inch but the men kept trying to stand up and shout loudly for help, cowards that they were, it's not enough just to be equipped with that apparatus between your legs, a real man doesn't scream like a lunatic when faced with death, pathetic, dumb-arse cries, what is it about death that scares you feeble-minded fools so much, have you forgotten that your time on this stage is limited, that you're not here for all eternity, people had given up on all their praying, so no God after all, no, the aim of all that yelling was to be spotted to by the police, so they could laugh at us, heap scorn on us and spit in our faces as they rounded us up to be handcuffed and sent back to where we came from, I was disgusted, that's no way to act, all that grandstanding, you have to play your part seriously, like an eel, as I think I've said before, I never for one moment expected to be rescued by the authorities, not like that coward Survivor being rescued off the coast of Mozambique, and after all that he still had the nerve to mess around with his friend's wife,

I didn't want to hear about those police patrols, away with those thoughts, I kept my mouth closed, locked and bolted, I had no intention of joining in those despicable outbursts, I couldn't stand listening to it, not that I was impervious to fear, in fact my heart was going a mile a minute, but I looked with disdain on those men yelling and hollering and with pity on the women and children sobbing, I wondered if they were in fact the same people who'd been so full of vim and vigour only a few hours earlier, how strange they seemed now they were suddenly as miserable as sin, I was ready to accept my eel destiny but they were hoping they'd be rescued, thinking they could escape death, well, there's a sucker born every minute, and not just that, they were so desperate to be rescued they were ready to be handcuffed and hounded out like pariahs, you see what I'm saying, why bother leaving if it means you're going to end up being treated like dogs, rounded up like common criminals, tell me that, why stick your neck out at all, well they didn't get what they wanted, they were barking up the wrong tree, no one heard us, there was no one there, believe me, no one came to our rescue, the whole thing was a pathetic farce, they all perished and as for me, well, I'm still here, I've been granted a bit of time to let off steam like this, you see how this show's been playing out, I'm still alive for a while, all thanks to the fuel container I'm hanging on to, the rest of them are already fish fodder, easy prey for the feeblest of fish but no fish is going to get me,

oh God listen to me, what am I saying, are you out of your mind Eel, anyone would think you'd been hitting the bottle, what's up with you, have you lost track of where you are, my dear Eel, you're screwed, you reap what you sew, you're getting what you asked for, to die like a proper eel, like one of your sisters, to die and be swallowed up by a real predator, a voracious shark or a sperm whale for example, you're an eel after all, forget all this humbug, or you can keep jabbering like a pig-headed fool if you like, you'll see what's going to happen soon enough, you're down to your last few seconds here, you empty-headed sap, and all you can do is brag about still being alive, the cheek of it, life is nothing as you well know, for God's sake be yourself and die properly, good heavens, it's true, I'm as good as dead here so I might as well hurry up and get it over with,

it's bitterly cold, so let's wind up this episode with the *kwassa-kwassa*, okay, so I'll come back to the mortal peril that befell us earlier this evening, I don't know if it really is evening, there's no one around to tell me one way or the other but there's not much I can do about that, I'll just carry on talking to you, as if you were there in front of me, listening to what I have to say, whether you can hear me or not,

so we were given one last shake, once and for all, wham, and then silence and at that point I remember a lull and seeing myself floating for a moment up in the sky like a bird and then, whoosh, into the drink, I'd gone under, everything went black, all I could hear was water gurgling and glugging and then I came back up again to this ghostly surface where I am now, poking up like an iceberg, the wind whipping around me, I'd surfaced right next to the fuel tank I'm hanging onto now, thank God, I don't even know how to swim, do you use your head or your backside to swim, I haven't got the first idea, why don't you say something, I was brave though, I paddled around madly, I wouldn't call it swimming, it was more like a duck flapping around in a storm-tossed lake, I was puffing and panting pathetically, but I managed to grab hold of this tank pretty quickly, I'd already swallowed plenty of water by then, I'd drunk so much seawater, I had a bellyful of it but I battled on, I wasn't going to give up, come hell or high water, I've been given a reprieve and I have to put my back into it and make the most of the time I've been allotted to take stock of my life, because my life is worth taking stock of, I am an entire world, every organ in my body is a continent and every moment of my life an ocean, I've told you I want to explore all four corners of my mind, if I can just have some more time,

so the question I'm asking myself is this, am I still alive for the moment or am I already dead, well, I'll stick my neck out here and guess that I'm being rewarded for the courage I've shown, I couldn't have done any of this without a good measure of courage, its why I'm still here, and thanks to this fuel tank, I lucked out with that, so I'll keep going until my light is snatched away from me and I go to sleep *ad vitam aeternam,*

if you're worried about this fuel can I'm hanging on to, don't, I'm holding it tight against my chest, with my arms around it, like a lover, a real lover, my true love, that's what this tank is, your true love is the one who saves your life, even if it's only for a few seconds, a few minutes, a few hours, it doesn't matter, your true love stays by your side until you send him packing, I can't give him the push now, how ungrateful would that be, I'm telling you, this lover of mine may be a deaf mute but at least he is faithful,

battered and beaten as I was by gigantic raging waves, and despite the deafening thunder of those monstrous surges, I could vaguely hear the sorrowful wailing of people crying for help, I could barely distinguish the men's voices from the women's and maybe there were children's and babies' voices in there somewhere too, I couldn't say, my throat felt dry even though I'd swallowed a belly-full of water, I couldn't see a thing, I had no idea where those nightmarish voices were coming from, nor the blows raining down on my flesh and then a few seconds later, everything began to fade, sounds and sensations all abated, God's own truth, it was like a dream, sounds were dwindling, as if they were drifting off into the distance and sinking into the depths, fading and sinking, the shouting and yelling were no more than feeble moans ebbing farther and farther into the distance, I don't remember what happened next, I'm sorry, I think I must have passed out, yes, that's what it was,

and now that I'm awake again, I can't see, can't hear, can't feel anything at all but as I think I've already said, none of it matters one bit, it doesn't help to keep singing the same tune, it doesn't change anything, why bother, it's all futile, enough is enough, why keep hammering on about the same old topics, going over and over things, braying like a donkey, until they lose all meaning, all you do is end up polluting the environment, and your mind, and everything else around you, but there is one more question I want to ask you, it might be the last one, I don't know, what on earth has happened to that rabble, why is there no sign of any of them, no inkling of a trace, a dead body for example, a head, a foot, an eye at least, or even a lock of hair, nothing, okay, no sign of the boat either, it's all been flushed away, as if someone's tried to hush it all up, and left me here for a reason, to make me give in to some kind of blackmail, to cloud my thinking and let me sink into despair, in short, to make me sorry and force me to ask forgiveness of the people I've let down, the people I've hurt, starting with All-Knowing, that's right, well, no way, I'm not in the least afraid of dying, the Grim Reaper doesn't scare me, I'm not worried about anything and I don't regret a thing, who's ever seen an eel move in reverse, you don't have to be an expert on eels to know that you'll never see an eel snaking back on itself, that would be

cowardly, an eel moves forward, straight ahead, I'm telling
you the truth, remember this, devil take me if I'm lying,
an eel has no regrets, never and when she heads off into
the mists nothing can stop her, even the most determined
enemies of freedom, I've made my choices in life, I've done
as I wished, I chose my path and the speed I took it at, this
is where I have to stop, where I give up the ghost and expire,
while I'm still in full flow, living my eel's life, I deliver myself
up, throwing myself in with a fearless heart,

hey, what the hell do you want from me, where does it come
from, this black bitterness invading my once carefree spirit,
like the murky depths seeping into my inert, unfeeling body,
oh God, let me remember again, just one more time, I'm
forgetting it all, everything I used to remember is melting
like snow in the sun, images are vanishing, oh, for the love
of an eel, where are my fleeting visions, who scared them
away, who are you, where am I now, is this hell or am I in
heaven, I dare say there are some cowardly types out there
who might have the effrontery to answer that question, as
if they really knew the difference between heaven and hell,
they'd probably even have the nerve to say they know where
they're going after they die, well I don't give a toss about
where I'm being sent now, I don't care two hoots, the same
sun shines on all of us, am I already in the spirit world or am
I still in the land of the living, it makes no difference to me,
none of it does, I'm ready for anything, I don't give a damn,
whatever, I was a *houri* on earth, an angel, a star, a goddess,
everything you can imagine in your dreams, yes, you're the
ones I'm talking to, you womanisers, with your hearts of

stone, with your dreams of fantasy women, oh my good-ness, what stupidity, what foolishness, what nonsense, you're swine, all of you, voracious skirt-chasers, like Epicurus and his pigs, that's what you are, all you think about is seducing women, nothing else, you live under a dark star, where even a rose's perfume is noxious, where birdsong insults the ears, because quite simply your souls are all dried up and I'm not talking about leaves that wither before they fall,

oh, my God, where am I, what is this, okay, so it must be time for me to slip away offstage, it's my turn isn't it, I know it's all over, don't worry, you don't need to spell it out, it's over, Eel, you big dummy, there's no two ways about it, this is it, time's up, this is how an eel meets her maker, Mutsamudu my love, and you, my beloved medina, I bow humbly to you as I leave the stage, here amid the wreckage of all my hopes and fears I bid farewell to earth and all its delights, the raging seas have claimed me, I'm dying, with the black heavens thundering down on me and now that I'm, phew!

About the Author

Born in Anjouan in the Comoros in 1987, Ali Zamir now resides in France. He is the author of three novels. First published to wide acclaim as *Anguille sous roche* by Le Tripode in 2016, *A Girl Called Eel* was awarded the Prix Senghor and is Ali Zamir's first novel.

About the Translator

Aneesa Abbas Higgins became a literary translator after a long career as a teacher. Among the authors she has translated are François Garde, Vénus Khoury-Ghata, and Elisa Shua Dusapin.